LATE CITY
SUMMER

Visit us at www.boldstrokesbooks.com

LATE CITY SUMMER

by
Jeanette Bears

2021

ISBN 13: 978-1-63555-968-2

This Trade Paperback Original Is Published By
Bold Strokes Books, Inc.
P.O. Box 249
Valley Falls, NY 12185

First Edition: September 2021

Credits
Editor: Shelley Thrasher
Production Design: Stacia Seaman
Cover Design by Tammy Seidick

Acknowledgments

I have always been a student of history. Storytelling is inherently historical, whether set in the past or looking to an imagined future that is based on the things we've learned. So when this story took root in my imagination, I couldn't wait to bring a piece of the past, particularly the place where I live and love, to a pair of characters.

I hope that Emily and Kate, and their love story, help us all reflect on our collective queer history and the real lives that were so often lived in secret. That we can remember those who fought to be their authentic selves, think of those still forced to do so, and remember that we still have so much work to do to bring justice to those who are marginalized.

Black Lives Matter, Trans Lives Matter, and love always, always, always wins.

CHAPTER ONE

Boston, 1946

"Emily, you have a call in the lobby," said a fellow classmate from the open door of Emily Stanton's dormitory room. The room was lit by a single lamp shining over her crowded desk of textbooks, notebooks, and sketches. Emily looked up from the text she was buried in, put down her pencil, and leaned back in her chair. She noticed the time, rubbing her eyes; only one person would call at such an hour. She was relieved to have the distraction but dreaded the coming phone conversation.

"Thanks, Annabelle. I'll be down in a minute."

She reluctantly stood, flipped up the needle on the record player in the corner, and headed for the door, only to quickly turn and grab her notebook and pencil. She took her time walking downstairs to the lobby, where a distinctly unhappy middle-aged receptionist sat with a book of her own. Without looking up, probably immersed in some new romance novel, the receptionist sat the rotary handset on the counter and continued reading.

"Hello, Mother," Emily droned as she picked up the heavy phone receiver.

"Now, however did you know who it was, dear?" Amelia Stanton asked from the other end.

"Perhaps because this is the fourth night this week you've called." Emily dragged the rest of the phone across the counter.

She opened her notebook and, without thinking, began to sketch.

"I just wanted to make sure you had the appointment scheduled with the florist and—"

"Yes, Mother. I have their number, and I'll plan to finish the rough seating chart by this weekend."

Emily sketched as her mother continued on a long list of tasks she had previously reviewed during three separate phone calls. As her mother went on, Emily looked up from the counter to the doorway to see a young man standing just outside the entrance of the dormitory building. She waved him in.

From the other line, her mother screeched. "Emily! Did you even hear my question? How can you possibly be so distracted? Is any of this important…"

Looking up at Tommy, expecting to find some sympathy, Emily only found a look of, what was it—amusement?—on her fiancé's face. "No. Tommy has a meeting with his father before he gets set up with the firm and—no, we weren't planning on it. We've been engaged for nearly a year now."

Tommy gestured for Emily to hand him the phone. She gladly complied, gave him a kiss on the cheek, and took up her sketching once again.

"Well, you might as well have the photographer take engagement photos once you get there," her mother said.

"I'm sure we'll find someone, Mrs. Stanton. We need to document every moment possible, yes?" Tommy asked, smiling at Emily.

"Tommy! How are you?" Amelia Stanton's enthusiasm was audible to Emily through the headset.

"I'm just wonderful, ma'am, and don't you worry about things. We have it all taken care of," he replied with a wink to Emily. She looked up at him with a grateful smile. He really was charming in such a classic way. No wonder her mother adored him.

Emily looked back down to find an elaborately detailed sketch of a city skyline etched onto the page of her notebook below the last set of notes for her final exam. It was the Manhattan skyline and had often been in her thoughts of late, for obvious reasons. But still, she wanted quite badly to drive any memory of it from her mind until the wedding itself. Memories of the place always seemed to come slipping into her mind when she wasn't expecting them. She was getting married there, after all, and was excited for her wedding; she just had to tell herself she was excited for the *wedding,* not the city.

Tommy handed her the phone. "Really, Mother. I need to be going. I have my last exam in the morning."

"You study too much. You already know you're graduating. Why worry so much?"

"I actually enjoy what I study, as unbelievable as that may be," she replied.

"Go spend some time with that handsome man of yours, and I'll see you next week."

"Good night, Mother." Emily returned the phone to its front desk owner as hastily as possible. She took a deep breath and turned to Tommy, relaxing at his calm demeanor. "What are you doing here so late?"

"I just wanted to come see you. Thought I would wish you luck on your exam tomorrow."

"Thank you, but I still have a few chapters to cover upstairs. I wish I could stay and be with you for a bit." She curled into his open arms.

Tommy bent to kiss her forehead, "I wasn't planning on staying too long, I just—"

"Young man, it is nearly ten o'clock. You should be getting back to your dormitory," the old receptionist stated, not looking up from her reading.

Tommy laughed quietly. "Thank you, Helen. I'll be leaving in a moment."

Helen looked up briefly from her book, obviously exasperated, shook her head, and returned to it without another word. The two of them walked away from the desk toward the stairs to Emily's room. "You'd think she'd know your name, by now. I really do need to finish up though. I'm sorry, love."

"Of course. I'll see you tomorrow then? Pick you up at seven?"

Emily returned the question, confused.

"You must be stressed to forget dinner with Allie."

"No. I didn't forget. I'll see you then." She gave Tommy a chaste peck on the lips, and they turned their separate ways. Emily started up the stairs as Tommy stopped at the door.

"Until tomorrow, my love," he called. As she rounded the corner on the stairs, she gave him a small wave, hurrying back to her studies.

❖

Tommy and Emily walked down the crowded Friday-night street, taking in the bustling, lively area. Nearly everyone from the nearby campus was out for a break from the hectic exam week. Restaurants and bars were packed to the brim, couples arm in arm walking down the sidewalk, and the local theater marquee lit up the night, the latest showing of *Mrs. Miniver* having let out just as they rounded the corner.

"Em!" shouted Allie, Emily's cousin. Just behind her cousin was Art, Allie's husband. It was such a joy to see Allie, especially now, when things were changing so much. Allie was always there for Emily, even though they lived hundreds of miles apart. They rarely saw each other, and Allie was so grateful that they had come up to see her for graduation.

"Art, you look fantastic! I can't believe I haven't seen you in, what, three years?" Emily smiled genuinely and gave them both a tight hug.

"Of course I do. What else would you expect?" Art said with a smile of his own. "It's great to finally be home for good."

"Not just for you," Allie commented, wrapping her arms around him. Tommy and Emily looked at them, admiring them as an example of what they could be as a couple. She was reminded again how lucky she was that Tommy hadn't just finished a tour in the military during the Second World War, one that no one thought would ever happen again.

"Shall we?" Tommy broke into her thoughts and gestured toward the restaurant.

❖

The two couples sat around the patio table at the small, crowded restaurant, talking over their dessert plates. They never had enough time to catch up on everything. It felt so good to see Allie.

"So you're home for good now, right?" Emily asked Art.

"Yes, ma'am. Did my time and lived to tell about it," he replied, only to be hit in the arm by Allie. It was a playful blow but also expressed the seriousness of being overseas in the war for so long.

"I can't say I envy you, Art," Tommy added.

"Education is an important thing, and you did what was right for you."

Emily noted the shift in Tommy's demeanor. She squeezed his hand under the table, a small offering of comfort.

"Sounds like you have a big opportunity coming out of school in a few weeks, no?" Allie asked Tommy.

"Hopefully. I have a meeting with my father's firm next week to set things up." His mood immediately brightened.

"That means you're all set too then. Right, Emily?" Art asked her.

She picked away at the remains of her dessert. "If by set, you mean soon to be a housewife, I suppose so."

She meant to tease but realized she had bitterness in her voice.

"You know I wouldn't force that. You're setting yourself up just fine. You've worked hard," Tommy said.

"Of course. It's all just moving quite fast." she said, failing to completely hide the undertones behind the reassurance. Tommy, oblivious, replied, "Although I still don't know what you want to do with a degree in art *history*."

Just as she looked up to begin a rebuttal and share some of her own news, she looked over Tommy's shoulder, and across the street was...no, it couldn't be. The woman was tall and dark haired. But she didn't have the confident, sometimes rebellious gait that Emily vaguely realized she was looking for. Even from across the street, the attitude was different. It did look like her though, and not a lot of women dared to wear trousers.

For a moment, her memories pulled her back to a time when seeing her *not* in trousers. She remembered all too well the amusement that had come with seeing her discomfort of being forced into a dress, but how beautiful she'd looked too…Emily pushed the thought away.

She realized she was staring, as Allie was halfway through a rant about how Emily "wouldn't stop painting on her own, even if she wasn't studying someone else's work."

"What is it?" Tommy asked, surprising Emily when she noticed his annoyance. She looked back at her dessert. "Nothing."

"How is the wedding prep coming along?" asked Allie.

"Everything's fine. My mother's asking that question every night she decides to call. Which has been every night this week." She realized she'd snapped and blushed a bit. It wasn't their fault her mother was mercilessly hounding her.

Art looked around at the table, "We should probably be going and not make you rehash it all. Parents, right? Big day tomorrow!"

"Indeed. We'll see you both at the ceremony," Tommy added.

"Congratulations again, both of you," said Art.

"I've already had my day. This is Emily's," Tommy replied, one arm around Emily. He winked at her again, and she smiled back.

❖

The couple walked back through the small campus town toward the dormitories. Tommy took Emily's hand as they walked.

"I really am proud of you."

For some reason his remark felt patronizing, but Emily brushed it off. "Thank you."

"It will be nice to have all this behind us and be able to settle in finally."

Emily stopped and stared at him. "Settle in? It's our chance to actually do something exciting instead of school."

"Something like what?"

"Like anything! Travel, or—"

"Travel?" Tommy laughed. "Don't worry. Once we get settled in, we'll have all the time in the world to do that. It isn't as though you aren't well traveled already."

She was getting frustrated but tried to remain calm. "I've been meaning to tell you. One of my professors offered me a position—"

"You know something? You are perhaps the most..." he paused, "ambitious woman I've ever met."

"You say that like it's a bad thing." Emily continued to walk.

"Not at all. Lucky catch for me, right?"

She didn't respond.

❖

The gymnasium was still overflowing with students and proud loved ones after the ceremony; all collected into individual packs huddled around ecstatic graduates. With a graduating class of just over a hundred, Emily was part of one of the still-small groups of women given the opportunity to receive such a quality education. She was humbled by the thought and wanted to take full advantage of her opportunity. Today was the day to celebrate the opportunities that lay ahead and be thankful for those that had already come to pass.

She was quickly surrounded by her parents, Allie, Art, and Tommy, who slid his arm around her, beaming as proudly as possible. Congratulations flowed from the group, Emily answering each one individually. This truly was one of the most important days of her life so far, and nearly all the people she cared about surrounded her.

Who else would be there? And there they were again. Why in the world did they come into her thoughts so often lately? It was as though she were longing for sarcastic remarks about "wasting time sitting in a classroom when you could be out experiencing the world." Well, that was just what she was planning to do. A small surge of anger followed, about how they themself wouldn't step out and do the hard thing, the risky thing. But they'd helped her even unintentionally, hadn't they? She shook it off and focused on the moment.

Her mother pointed out, "I was just telling Allie how now that this is all over, you can finalize the wedding preparations," much to Emily's exasperation. Why must the world revolve around one day?

"I told you, everything is fine, Mother."

"Congratulations, Miss Stanton," said Susanna Clarke, Emily's advisor and occasional professor. She had recently offered Emily a position in the art history department, one that Emily would be a fool to pass up if she wanted something permanent and advanced for a young woman of her age. The position even afforded her the opportunity to travel, lecture, and continue doing her own work. It was the perfect combination of opportunity, flexibility, and advancement. The proposition truly excited her, yet she hadn't been able to actually tell anyone about it. "Have you thought about the position we discussed?"

"Yes. I—"

"Position?" Tommy asked. "You never mentioned—"

"I haven't had much time to discuss it with you, with the wedding preparations and graduation." *Not as though I have tried, multiple times.*

"That's right! Congratulations again, and I completely understand. It is still available in the fall, however. Just so you're aware," her professor added.

"Thank you. I will definitely be in contact after the wedding is over."

Her professor smiled. "Enjoy the rest of your day." She made her way through the crowd, congratulating other graduates.

As if on cue, her mother spoke up. "You never mentioned an assistant opportunity, Emily."

"Like I said, I've been busy, and I didn't want to add something else for you to worry about, Mother."

"Well, you won't really need it, I don't think," Tommy interjected.

"Well, perhaps I want it, Tommy." Emily replied with more edge than she intended.

"I think it's a great opportunity, if you take it, sweetheart." Emily's father piped up. He always seemed to take her side on the rare occasion he added his opinion. For that, she was grateful.

"Thank you, Daddy."

As always, Allie seemed to calm the mood, or at least end the tension by changing the subject. "All right. Well, we'll see the both of you in New York next week?"

"Nowhere else, right, Em?" Tommy asked with a smile.

Oh, how he thinks it's our *special place.* "Nowhere else…"

CHAPTER TWO

It was a nearly five-hour drive from Boston to New York. Emily sat next to Tommy and took in the scenery, the changing landscape. Emily was grateful for the silence in the car as Tommy drove, and she recalled the last time she was in the thriving metropolis of New York City. She was excited to be back in the place where she had spent only a short time, but one that had made a lasting impression on her.

She was also nervous.

Irrationally, she assured herself. It was a city of millions, and there was no chance of dealing with anything from the past that she didn't want to. That was the beauty of being away from a city constantly changing for so long. She had a purpose for being here this time. She was different and could handle whatever obstacle might get in the way of what was supposed to be the happiest day of her life. She wasn't the same young, restless, oblivious-to-the-world child she had been before.

Then why did she secretly hope that something...*wrong* might happen? Because it would make things interesting, she knew. Emily didn't want something to go wrong. She wanted to enjoy her time there, but she desperately longed for something unexpected. She wanted to experience a rush. And just think of her mother's face! She smiled as she looked out the window.

"I'm glad to finally see you smile," Tommy said as she realized he'd been watching her. "With all the stress, it hasn't happened all that often lately."

"Just excited for our big day." She returned her gaze to the window.

Four years earlier, 1942

Emily sat looking out another window, on a train bound for the city, watching the landscape. Vast open meadows, cornfields, and the occasional homestead raced by. The fields seemed to shrink as the train rushed on, the homes getting closer, growing together. Factories rose as the train sped toward the city she was so looking forward to experiencing. Finally it bounded right through the tightly packed suburbs, and she tried to imagine the traffic people experienced living so close to the system, dealing with it to live closer to the urban hive.

Months earlier, she had been able to convince her mother that it would be an exciting opportunity to spend the summer with her cousin Allie, her aunt, and her uncle in New York City. Her mother had reluctantly agreed that Allie was a good influence on her and that their Upper West Side apartment in Manhattan would be a hub of culture in the overpopulated madness of the tiny island borough.

Her steady, Tommy, had just finished his first year at Harvard Law School that summer and was beginning a small job with his father's law firm for experience, so he was unable to join her. That made Emily both nervous and excited, which seemed to be true of all her feelings on the summer trip. This was an opportunity to step away from expectations and have an adventure. Tommy always had an easy way of interacting with others and taking the lead, and she was excited to stand on her own and make something uniquely hers.

The train continued toward the city, at least Emily suspected. All that surrounded her were crowded town houses, tightly packed streets, and large factory buildings. As the stops increased, the train grew more and more crowded, and Emily was grateful to have a seat near the window.

"125th Street, Harlem. The next and last stop is Grand Central

Terminal," the train porter announced, walking down the crowded aisle. Emily kept her gaze out the window. Harlem. She certainly wasn't getting off there, from what she'd heard about it. Her mother's, or Tommy's reaction, would have been priceless to see if she told them she'd wandered around by herself. But that was impractical. She would just have to find someone who had street smarts in the area. The artists in Harlem couldn't be passed up. Her summer checklist began.

The train finally made its approach underground with every seat filled. Even this underground network of transportation already had Emily's mind racing. The train sped through the dark tunnel and, a short time later, pulled into the station. Emily's anticipation momentarily faltered when the daily commuters surrounding her pushed their way into the aisle to exit the train. She looked out the window, wondering what all the grandeur of Grand Central was about when she saw another train just across the dimly lit, crowded platform.

Instead of pushing into the aisle, she waited for it to clear before taking her bags from the overhead compartment and fighting her way to the door. She followed the flow of people, making it to the small staircase that became the bottleneck for the increasingly frustrated morning commuters. With all her bags, she received more than one less-than-gentle push while getting onto the staircase. She tried to remember why she'd packed so much, and how she'd ever thought she was packing light.

At the top of the stairs, the corridor opened, and signs pointed toward the exits. Though nicer than the platform, it still wasn't the Grand Central Terminal she was expecting. She turned with her bags and followed the signs toward the main terminal, almost sweating in her travel clothes. The already increasing June heat didn't help the situation. If she could just find the infernal clock in the main terminal where Allie had told her they would meet, she would be past her first challenge. *Why are there so many signs?*

She rounded a corner and there it was! She smiled at her small victory and rushed forward. Then she stopped just at the entrance of the main hall and looked around. All the sounds and people brushing past faded away as she looked around the massive hall, the beauty of it taking her—

Suddenly she was on the floor and realized someone had just knocked her over. Her assailant was up and about to take off before Emily realized what had happened. Emily started to pick herself up in disbelief.

"You have to be—this cannot happen today!" Her assailant had stopped and was kneeling to help collect the contents of the suitcase that came open in the collision.

"What in the—" Emily finally composed herself, looking at the spilled items, and started helping. She glanced briefly at the frazzled young woman and realized she was irritated. *Why is everyone in such a rush?* For that matter, why was this woman dressed to do construction or head off to a factory? But with the war, such clothes weren't all that uncommon. She stared while the noticeably tall, dark-haired woman scrounged through her things as quickly as possible.

"Sorry," the woman mumbled as she shoved the last of Emily's things back into place. She seemed resigned to miss whatever train she was headed for, but without waiting for a response, she was running once again. Emily looked on in shock as the figure bolted around the corner toward an outbound train. *Welcome to New York.*

After collecting herself, Emily looked up. All the people hurrying past her in every direction and the sounds of train announcements and conversations rushed back as she swerved through the crowd, this time determined in her mission. She couldn't miss the clock, the center of it all, as she weaved in and out of people. How did every single one of the people manage to be going in a different direction? She was here, in New York City.

"Hey there!" She turned to spot Allie waving her down. Her relief was noticeable, Allie rushed over with Art, who quickly took her bags. Allie threw her arms around her. "You made it!"

"Barely! I basically got run over less than a minute ago by one of these speeding crazies."

"You'll learn to navigate," Art piped in.

"Oh, goodness. I almost forgot!" Allie exclaimed, grabbing Art by the forearm. "This is my boyfriend, Arthur. Art, this is my cousin Emily."

Putting down one of Emily's bags, he held out his hand. "It's a pleasure. Allie has been talking about you for weeks. Literally." Allie gave him a playful shove. "We should head out though, or I'm going to have to feed the meter."

"Blessed sweet Jesus, you have a car!"

Allie gaped at Emily. "It couldn't have been *that* bad. You'll figure out the madness. A pro in a week, guaranteed!" She led the way through the crowd, Emily behind, and Art bringing up the rear with the baggage.

"I hope Kate made her train," Art murmured to Allie as they passed the passageway out of the building that led to the local subway platform.

"She's the one who had us running late," Allie replied. "Waited in the car for her for fifteen minutes. She should have to hustle a bit if you want a ride halfway to work, and then decide to take the train when traffic's bad."

Emily was busy taking in her surroundings with each step.

Once they were outside, the crowds weren't smaller, but less condensed, and traveled in two directions on the sidewalks as opposed to every direction known to mankind. Emily looked directly ahead and sidestepped those in their own worlds as they crossed 42nd Street. She refused to get pummeled again. Once for the day was quite enough.

They rounded the corner and loaded the car. Once they were squarely inside, Art maneuvered out of the tight-knit parking spot and into the madness of traffic with a confidence that terrified Emily. Allie apparently thought nothing of it and left Art to the task.

"So how was your trip here?" she inquired.

"Long, but quite beautiful. It's amazing, the landscape you see before the city comes out of nowhere. I guess for such a small space it makes sense."

"We'll make sure to get you familiar with it. There's always somewhere new to discover, I promise."

Despite Emily's earlier run-in and the initial chaos, the hustle excited her. She wanted to catch on to the workings of the island. She sat back as Art swerved through taxis, delivery trucks, cyclists, and the not-so-occasional rogue pedestrian who took advantage of their right-of-way. She found herself jumping at what she thought were close calls but still managed to take in her surroundings. She was here! The center of it all. Maybe her perceptions of the glamour and fame of Manhattan would change, but the personality of the place was striking. She could see that already.

"You should go through Times Square," Allie told Art. He gave a look of desperation, clearly not wanting to drive through the hub of the area, but smiled nonetheless and switched lanes, eliciting a honk from the taxi directly behind them.

Emily kept her face up against the glass, taking in the sights. If Grand Central was crowded, this was true madness. Pedestrians trudged in packs going two directions down the paths that would be sidewalks if they could be seen, and more than occasionally they broke off from the crowd to cross the street.

"So is that where the New Year's Eve madness happens?" Emily asked, not looking away from the billboards that lined the streets, promoting everything from shows to stores to a giant Planters peanuts billboard. She could barely reach the tops of the buildings with her gaze as they made their way uptown. *I suppose if you can't build out, build up.* They continued uptown, along the west side of Central Park.

"I never realized how large the park is. We've been driving for thirty blocks already." Emily was amazed. A park that large in the middle of the urban hive? Definitely not a single-day walk in the park. She added another item to her mental checklist.

They finally turned off on a street, and an avenue later Art stopped in front of one of the brownstones that stood in long lines from end to end. It was a quiet street, as opposed to the bustle they'd just driven through, trees lining the sidewalks. A child ran ahead of their parents with the family dog. It amazed Emily once again that one turn down a street and a compact suburbia began and ended between stop signs.

"Let's get you upstairs and unpacked. We can go to the diner around the corner for lunch," Allie said. Art took her baggage from the trunk, and the three of them ascended the steps to the brownstone building that Allie called home with her parents, Emily's aunt and uncle. Allie still lived at home, as she was taking classes at New York University, and Art helped run his family hardware store in Brooklyn.

"I don't want you to be exhausted right off the bat, but do you want to go out tonight?" Allie asked, opening the door.

"I'd love to. The train ride wasn't bad." Emily wanted to get out and see the town. "Where are your parents?" she asked, following Allie up the stairs of the small, homey apartment.

"They should be in from the store—"

"Allie!?" Allie's mother, Jane, called from down the stairs.

"Any minute," Allie said under her breath, preparing herself. "Up here. Just showing Emily to her room."

Hurried footsteps grew louder up the narrow staircase and around the corner. All of them gathered together, with not nearly enough space.

"Afternoon, Mrs. Miller," said Art, attempting to remove himself from her path.

"Hello, Art," Jane said distractedly, pushing through. "Emily! So good to see you, sweetheart!" She attacked Emily with a fierce hug. Allie smiled apologetically over her mother's shoulder. "I'm so happy to have you here!"

"I'm very excited to be here, Aunt Jane," Emily said, barely able to breathe.

"We were planning on getting back before you got in. I hope everything's set up the way you want it," Jane said as she scurried about the room. She adjusted the sheets on the immaculately made bed, moved the bedside lamp to a slightly different position, and homed in on Emily's luggage. Lifting it onto the bed, she had begun unzipping the bag when Allie interrupted her.

"Mother, I'm sure she can unpack her things herself," she exclaimed, obviously embarrassed.

"Of course. Sorry, dear. I'll let you go ahead and settle in." Jane let herself have one last fidget, resisting reaching back into the bag for more.

"It's great to have you here, Emily," called a voice from down the stairs.

"Thank you for having me here, Uncle Carl!" Emily said.

"Dinner should be ready in about an hour, once you're settled in."

"We were planning on taking Emily out tonight!" Allie complained to her mother.

"You can still go out, but you're staying for supper. Art, I assume you'll be here?" She directed her gaze at him as he stood quietly in the hallway, attempting to keep out of the way.

"I suppose so, ma'am." He responded shyly.

"Honestly, Art. Ma'am?" Jane asked.

He blushed profusely.

"Fine…" Allie mumbled, crossing her arms. Rolling her eyes, she left the room, grabbing Art along the way. Jane paused in the doorway.

"I do hope you enjoy your stay here this summer, Emily." She smiled and turned to leave.

Emily approached her already opened suitcase and started unpacking. Among other things, she took out a sketchpad and pencils. The afternoon light poured in through the window and caught her attention. As she stepped close, she took a moment to admire the view.

She didn't know what she'd expected. Perhaps a bird's-eye view of the entire park? The contentment she found in looking out the window onto a simple street surprised her. If she put her forehead to the glass, she could see the park, but just looking around put everything into perspective. The world truly was smaller than it seemed. Maybe this one piece of the metropolis could be hers. Although she might not know every part of this place, she could make the most of getting to know her part in it.

CHAPTER THREE

"Can we even get in?" Emily asked as the three of them exited the subway platform and turned to see the dance hall in the East Village.

"We're early. There's plenty of room." Allie pulled her and Art ahead.

"Try to keep up," he mumbled to Emily as Allie hastily escorted them through the throng of teenagers and young men in uniform gathered outside. Emily couldn't begin to imagine how all the people outside could have room in the small building built right into the street corner, let alone everyone she suspected was inside.

After weaving through the crowd, they managed to make it to the bar and huddle together while Emily finally took in her surroundings. Despite its outside appearance, the dance hall seemed big enough to fit every young person in the city. Couples stood chatting in their own worlds, and soldiers flirted with young girls who ogled over polished uniforms. The dance floor was crowded and lively.

Emily looked through the haze of smoke to a band playing music that easily overcame the chatter from every person in the room. It was bustling with life and youth.

"Can I get you ladies something to drink?" Art yelled over the commotion.

"Such the gentleman." Allie gave him a kiss on the cheek, and he blushed once again.

"Whiskey!" Emily replied immediately. She suddenly was

more alive and excited than any time she could remember. She felt herself moving to the music as she waited for Art to struggle through to the bar and return. The crowd was constantly shifting around her, and in a second a young dark-haired soldier inadvertently backed into her.

"So sorry, miss," he yelled, turning around.

"Not a problem. You can make it up to me with a dance." Emily took his hand. She stopped abruptly upon seeing Art, grabbed the shot from his hand, and downed it, much to the surprise of everyone watching. Allie looked on in obvious shock as Emily gave her a glowing smile.

"She's fitting in just fine, I'd say," she heard Art say as she reached for the boy's arm.

"She seems to have forgotten that she has her own boy at home!" Allie replied and took her drink from Art. Emily dragged the boy toward the dance floor.

After at least five songs, Emily hustled back through the crowd to the bar, where Allie and Art seemed enamored by their own conversation. Sweating and out of breath, she was smiling harder than she had in such a long time.

"This is fantastic!" she said, turning toward the bar for a glass of water.

"And just what would Tommy think about that?" Allie asked, somewhat seriously, but still grinning.

"It won't hurt anything, Al," she replied, chugging the water and then ordering another shot of whiskey. "He's back home, and I plan to have a good time. It isn't like we're married…"

"Well, I'm sure that won't be the case for long."

Emily paused, looking at Allie, a nervous jolt running through her.

"We've only been dating for—"

"Kate! You made it!" said Allie, looking over Emily's shoulder. Emily turned to find a young woman, just a bit taller than herself, approaching the group. Allie flew by her to wrap the stranger in a fierce hug. *Why does it seem like I know her?*

"You were right. I missed the damn express this morning and

got into work late. I stayed late to make up time." Kate separated herself from Allie.

"You should have just taken the train from the start. Or driven yourself, in *your* car," Allie said.

Kate turned to the bar and ordered a drink. Emily continued to stare at the young woman, who was surprisingly dressed in slacks. Despite her classic beauty, her look was natural. She wore a plain, white, button-down shirt, her dark hair stylish but not overdone. As she caught herself staring, it dawned on her.

"You!"

"Me?" Kate turned back to her, seeming confused but somewhat amused.

"You ran into me at the station!"

"Oh." She sipped her beer. "I thought you looked familiar."

Emily stared, this time in growing frustration as Kate merely smiled at her as though it were a non-issue. "Familiar? A minute off the train and I get run over, and all you have to say is I look familiar?"

"That's the city for you—"

"The city!?" Emily was almost yelling at this point.

"Emily, this is my friend from school, Kate Alessi," Allie said.

Kate held out her hand for Emily without a trace of remorse for their earlier interaction. Emily hesitantly offered own, still angry. "Emily."

"Well, it is nice to meet you. Allie told me her country-bumpkin cousin would be in for the summer."

"I said no such thing and you know it!" Allie pushed Kate's arm playfully.

As if she weren't there, Kate leaned across Emily to the bar and ordered another drink, which she handed Emily, replacing her empty glass.

"Country bumpkin!?" Emily asked, not letting the subject drop.

"Art, help me out here," Allie pleaded.

"I wasn't even there when you told her..." He feigned innocence. Art and Kate smiled as Allie hit Art on the chest.

"You can take me to the dance floor for that!" said Allie,

grabbing Art's arm. The two scampered off into the crowd, leaving Emily and Kate at the bar. Emily took another long drink from the whiskey Kate ordered for her, which seemed to surprise Kate, and once again she laughed.

"Better slow down there a bit. Wouldn't want to have to carry you home later."

"I'll be fine, thank you very much." Emily glared at the other woman. She wondered even in her admittedly tipsy state why Kate was staring at her with only a smirk.

"It's obviously your first time in the city. So, first impressions?" Kate asked.

"Why is it obvious I've never been here? You're the one who can't catch a train," she replied, proud of her point. Kate kept watching her and seemed to want to keep her riled up.

"I could have if someone had been moving and not gazing around all starry-eyed at the fancy station."

Emily searched for a response as Kate grinned in clear satisfaction. Emily took another drink. *Even her voice is annoying. Deep and smooth and—* Emily shook her head.

"Aside from a few interesting individuals," she looked Kate over, "I happen to like what I've seen."

Kate nodded, apparently enjoying the sparring, "Incoming at four o'clock."

"What?"

Another young soldier approached Emily as Kate took another drink.

"Hey, sugar. I'm Ralph. How 'bout a dance?" he asked with a false sense of bravado. He was clearly nervous. Emily looked at Kate, who merely smiled and then turned back with a contemptuous smile of her own.

"Why of course," she answered, earning a genuine smile from the young man. The two of them headed off for the dance floor, passing Allie and Art just as they returned.

She heard Art laugh and say, "Another one!? She better slow down, or she'll have every man in this place following her." She couldn't help but imagine what the three of them must be saying about her. Their probable conversation played out in her mind as she danced.

"Better be all but one man," replied Allie, giving Art a kiss.
"Well, at least she took Ralph off my hands for a few minutes," Kate said. "He'll talk her ear off out there."
"I'm telling you she has her own back home already," Allie complained pointlessly.
"Let her have the summer," Kate said, watching Emily as she danced carefree, laughing all the while.
"Ooh! I love this song! Come on!" Allie once again took Art onto the floor, leaving Kate alone, leaning against the bar.

Emily noticed their expressions and actions from the dance floor, but Ralph was rambling on and on about himself. "I ship out at the end of this month, which should be really exciting. You seeing anyone? I bet you are, all the pretty ones are taken. Kate over there never will gimme a dance though—"

"Really now..." His last sentence caught her attention. She waited until the end of the song, listening to Ralph continue about his deployment, his excitement to go to war, the honor of the military, and on and on. When it ended, she pulled Ralph back over to the bar to meet Kate.

"Ralph here says you never give him a dance! Now that's just impolite, even for you city folk!"

"Well, I don't dance, so I usually don't make an exception for Ralph there," Kate replied, seeming nervous. Emily had caught her in her own trap.

"Well, now you do." Emily pushed Kate at Ralph. Then she gave Kate a determined, smug look, waiting for Kate to refuse. Kate scowled back but let Ralph lead her into the crowd, shaking her head as if she had no idea how that had just happened.

Art and Allie returned at the same time, Allie staring in disbelief as Kate and Ralph passed them.

"How in the world did you manage that!?" she asked Emily. "She never gives in to that poor boy."

"Us country bumpkins aren't completely socially handicapped."
Emily ordered yet another drink from the bartender.

❖

Late into the night, the four of them stumbled out onto the
street. All were in good spirits as they walked away from the dance
hall, which was still bustling, crowded, and noisy. The evening had
cooled the town, and most of the bars in the area had closed up shop.
They wandered away from the hall, Art holding Allie, Kate keeping
her distance in the back, and Emily leading the way. All but Art
were clearly drunk, and luckily he knew where they were going. If
and when Emily made a wrong turn, they wouldn't be wandering in
New York City all night long.

Kate watched from the back as Emily continued boldly, though
she swayed slightly as she walked.

"I knew she was going too fast. I couldn't have handled half of
what she drank," Allie complained.

"You did have half. At least." Art lovingly put her in her place.

"That's what happens when you let country bumpkins find
out what a real party is like," Kate yelled over them to Emily, who
immediately stopped and turned as if to dispute her remark. Emily
let Art and Allie wander ahead and drifted back to join her.

"Yeah? Well, you should have seen the look on your face
when—" She tripped on the sidewalk and stopped to take off her
shoes.

Kate instantly wanted to help her, but stopped herself. "Yeah.
I know. When you pushed me into the endlessly rambling Ralph."
Emily stopped and bent over in laughter. Kate looked on with a
smile, then took Emily by the arm and guided her forward. "Come
on. I don't want to be out here all night."

"Always in a bad mood." Emily scrunched up her face
mockingly and giggled.

"Me? You got all huffy about the station. Not me," replied Kate.

"Well, you fancy city people think you're hot sh—"

"Emily!" Allie stopped her. Emily giggled.

Kate caught Emily looking over at her more often than necessary, but she blamed it on the alcohol and her apparent need to pick a fight. She hadn't let go of Emily's arm though, fearing the other woman would trip again. She felt Emily loop her arm through hers and lean into her. Kate caught herself having to hide a satisfied look as a warmth spread through her, caused by having Emily so close.

She convinced herself she was resisting making a sarcastic remark, but then she realized she just didn't have one for once. She was simply enjoying the moment. Maybe they could be friends, despite the constant harassment. She seemed fun, and she was Allie's cousin, after all, so that meant a lot.

They turned the corner onto Allie's street and stopped in front of the apartment. "Well, at least I didn't have to carry you like I thought I would," Kate said in a joking way.

"We're just full of surprises, us country people," Emily replied. "Like you could, anyway."

"I'm sure…well, I'm heading home."

"I'll walk with you, Kate," Art said.

"Wouldn't want her to have to try to catch a train all by herself, now would we?" Emily said.

"No. Some other clueless pretty girl might be waiting to get in my way again," Kate retorted.

Emily glared at her but didn't reply. She resigned herself to the steps, not waiting for Allie. Kate smiled in victory. "Nice to meet you, Emily."

Emily didn't stop but waved her hand as she opened the door. Kate watched as it closed and said her good-byes to Allie. As she and Art headed off, she thought it was probably the best night she'd had in a long time, and she looked forward to seeing Allie's cousin again soon.

CHAPTER FOUR

Four years later, 1946

Emily entered the grand hotel room first, followed by the bellboy, who set down the multiple bags he had hefted as professionally as possible. Tommy ignored his presence and immediately opened his briefcase at the desk, pulling out paperwork and settling in. Resisting the urge to gawk at the vast space, Emily turned to the boy and pulled out a bill to tip him. He smiled graciously and left.

She took a breath and allowed herself to take in her surroundings. Tommy's parents had insisted they stay in a suite at the Plaza Hotel for the week, a small gift for the newlyweds. They had, however, assured two separate rooms within the suite, to uphold a sense of propriety until the day of the wedding. Emily would have gladly stayed with Allie in her and Art's home in Brooklyn, but it was impossible to argue when a stay at the Plaza was being offered.

The room granted a stunning view facing north. The intricate carpet designs and contours of the chandeliers hanging from the expansive ceiling added to the air of sophistication, but they left Emily with a sense of sterility. This would not be something she would get used to. As she admired the paintings that adorned the walls, it was difficult not to critique the choices of the hotel decorators.

She was surprised. These paintings, at a glance, seemed to match each other, but her years of studying gave her the knowledge that each was its own style, time period, and quality level, along with strikingly different content, a few of which were blatant imitations of known works. She mused that much of her environment seemed to function in this way. On the surface, so many people in her life displayed themselves with pomp and arrogance, as though they were the most valuable and unique creations to be admired, but if you took a moment to look…Imitators all around.

"There's a wonderful view of the park," Tommy said, not looking up from his paperwork. Emily made her way to the vast windows at the end of the sitting area and smiled to herself. She didn't have to strain her neck this time to gaze upon the vastness of Central Park. It never ceased to amaze her—the existence of an endless natural haven, directly in the center of the concrete hive that was Manhattan. Just across the street was a gateway between the urban bustle and the natural serenity, even as polished as the park might be.

She remembered discovering all the city, truly being part of it, knowing so much more of it than what the tourists saw. Sitting perched above it all, she felt stuffed in, only an onlooker. Emily stifled a jump when Tommy wrapped his arms around her from behind.

"You really do love it here, don't you?" He spoke softly into her ear.

"Yes." She felt reluctant to allow him to experience her nostalgia. She attempted to relax in his embrace, and she could. She knew him, she loved him. He was her norm. But this was her place, and his question felt somehow like an intrusion.

"Why? I mean you spent only a few months here." Emily could sense his genuine curiosity, and it surprised her. Of all Tommy's attributes, perhaps she admired most his inquisitive nature. He always scoped out the entirety of the story, and even though he judged quickly, he questioned in fresh ways. This attribute would prove useful for a lawyer, the career he wanted to pursue. Having pressure from his father was likely encouraging.

Emily took a moment to contemplate his comment. "Pieces of

a place stay with you sometimes. They're like memories of a person, and when you're there it feels right, like seeing an old friend again."

Emily felt Tommy unexpectedly tense, as though something was wrong. He held his silence for a moment, then turned Emily in his arms and smiled a smile that failed to fully fill his eyes. "I hope this week will stay with us."

Emily turned and gave him a quick kiss before gently dislodging herself from his embrace. He turned away and began unpacking the rest of his materials. Emily stopped him just as he sat down at his layout.

"We have to meet Ann, Mother's wedding planner, in twenty minutes," she said, arranging her own belongings so she could quickly freshen up from the trip.

"I really don't see why you need me to come along," he replied, this time stopping what he was doing to look at Emily with a hint of desperation.

"We're getting everything for the reception locally, and she wants to show us around to make sure we're pleased with the arrangements."

"You know I trust you." He put on his most charming smile.

Although she returned the smile, his attempt to weasel out of the meeting didn't faze her. "Well, that's just fine, but we should get it all taken care of so we can enjoy the rest of the week."

Looking back down at his work, he replied, "I still don't see how that requires my presence but—" He met Emily's gaze, instantly silenced and resigned. "Is she meeting us here? I need to meet Philip from my father's firm at three, remember?"

"I'm sure we can be done by then. Wouldn't want you to miss that," she added a bit sarcastically.

"Well, first impressions make a difference." He was now fully engaged.

"You've known Philip your entire life." Emily stood powdering her nose at the mirror. She tried but failed not to show that his lack of cooperation bothered her, let alone the thoughts that poured through her mind at his exaggeration about the meeting.

"Not professionally, Em. This is important for *us* too."

"Vital," she mumbled to herself.

Tommy had not once truly had to work for anything thus far in his life. And for *us?* She dared not bring up that argument, because, as she thought bitterly, the husband knows best...She stopped herself. When had she herself truly been in want of anything in her own life? Perhaps a bit of her own unrest lay in that fact.

Tommy stepped over to Emily and placed a kiss on her cheek apologetically, although she suspected he didn't know what he was apologetic for. She stopped herself abruptly. When had she become so cynical? She was back in an incredible city and resolved at that moment to make the most of it.

Amelia had not only insisted that the couple hire a coordinator for the wedding preparations. She had hand-picked one and thrust the woman upon them. Emily was actually grateful for her mother's overbearing gesture, in that she had someone to present her with choices and had to do much less research to find the venue, the reception meal, and, at her mother's insistence, the photographer. Emily was nearly numb to all these decisions, because every time she offered input, her mother, or now the coordinator, had an opinion.

Emily had discovered through her mother that it was a growing fashion to hire a photographer for the day of the wedding to catalogue all the stages of the ceremony, along with family photographs and formal shots of the newlyweds. Emily immediately thought so many pictures obnoxious and unnecessary, but having a document of her friends and family, here in this place, intrigued her. Even if she didn't get much say in the decisions surrounding the event, at least the photographer's work would make it memorable.

Emily and Tommy followed Ann, their personal wedding coordinator, through bustling midtown. After nearly two hours of traveling around by bus and subway, they had tasted their wedding cake, met their florist, and observed the ballroom at the hotel where they would have their reception. Although it had all been prearranged, Emily felt a satisfaction in ensuring that it all had come together. She was also satisfied that Tommy was making a genuine effort to remain engaged in the conversations.

Crowded sidewalks lined the towering buildings of Fifth Avenue, pedestrians spilling into the street to relieve the combustion. Ann glided smoothly through the throng of busy residents, Emily and Tommy struggling to keep up and avoid being trampled by a disgruntled young businessman late for work or a seasoned old lady who could move with surprising speed. They were out of practice.

While Ann traveled on, she pointed out a number of historical landmarks, revealing an impressive repertoire of knowledge about their history. She also noted details about new shops and entertainment from block to block.

"...and last year, the day the war ended," Ann commented, "I've never seen the streets as crowded. Major parades in the city are held here down Fifth, and New Yorkers seem to find reasons to celebrate just about anything. Almost two million people were out and about that night."

Emily recognized the area, memories flooding her as she took in each site. Seeing each place seemed to unlock memories of her time there last, but only as she saw them. People, buildings, the sights and smells all around her. Already, the city seemed to be bringing her back. She turned and took Tommy by the hand, pulling him along, smiling, as they tried to keep up. She was glad to be there with him.

They weaved through the last of the pedestrians, trash cans, delivery trucks, and occasional dog on a leash, until they caught up to Ann just as she stopped abruptly in front of a grand, ancient cathedral. Laughing now at how they'd almost lost Ann completely, Emily took Tommy's face in her hands and kissed him softly. As she turned toward the steps to the church, however, she froze.

The shadowy corner just outside the towering oak doors of the structure transfixed her. The building's stone archway stretched over the doors, providing shelter just outside. Instead of the details of the architecture, the memory of a sudden summer rain, an argument, and the shelter of that very corner assaulted her.

"This is St. Patrick's?" she asked, pulling her gaze away.

"Of course it is. Your mother showed you the photos of it, no?" Tommy responded, walking up the steps. He held the door open for her, a gesture to hurry her disguised as courtesy. Her eyes stayed riveted on the spot, however, the shadowed corner, and her heart grew tight. She clung, involuntarily, to the distant memory but caught herself before Tommy noticed her distraction.

Inside, they surveyed the vacant cathedral as Ann pointed out the seating arrangements for the day of the ceremony, provided details outlining the decoration arrangements, and recounted the vast history of the historic building.

"It really is a lovely church, and photographers love it for the lighting," she said to Emily. Tommy had fallen behind, obviously having little interest in the conversation, and even less in the magnificent artistry that adorned the cathedral.

"My mother has insisted on finding a local photographer to take engagement photographs of the two of us. I know it's extremely late notice."

"Not to worry! The photographer has long been booked, as you know."

Nope. Emily nodded in blind agreement.

"Your mother actually just let me know yesterday afternoon that she's spoken with your day-of photographer, and you'll have an appointment tomorrow morning, I believe?" She combed through her notebook. "Yes. I'll give you the details when we're through here. Also, I must say it's the perfect person if you want someone who really captures the city in their work. You did quite the good job choosing them." Ann added a note to her quickly filling notebook. Emily hadn't the slightest idea what other things she was penciling in.

"I've actually worked with this particular photographer on several occasions, and they typically avoid indoor studio work. It's a wonderful opportunity to explore the city and capture yourselves in it."

"It's only mildly ridiculous that it is six days before the wedding…" Tommy added, joining the conversation.

"If I recall it was you who guaranteed my mother documentation of every event within the next week."

"I suppose…" he responded, already giving in to the argument.

"Are we squared away? I really do need to be going."

"Go ahead. I'll meet you back at the hotel," Emily suggested. She didn't feel like keeping him occupied any longer or having to hear about the grand importance of a meeting with the man who was practically Tommy's uncle. It was easier to just let him go.

"Thanks, darling," Tommy responded, suddenly jovial. With a quick peck on the cheek, he turned and rushed out of the church, leaving Emily staring after him.

After reviewing a few more details, Emily thanked Ann and left the church as well. Walking as briskly as possible down the stairs of the church without glancing again at the corner, she wandered alone down the street, once again taking in her surroundings before turning back to the subway entrance.

CHAPTER FIVE

Four years earlier, 1942

The two young women rushed down the stairs, taking out any exiting subway passengers standing in their paths. They bolted for the turnstiles, refusing to miss the open doors of the train. After only a few weeks, Emily had become a sleek professional at catching the oncoming behemoths before the doors closed and left her stranded. Tokens placed, they were admitted and flew into the doors, both pulling their purses in as the doors shut.

Emily smiled with satisfaction at Allie, who, like her, was breathless from the sprint. Allie caught her breath as the train jolted forward. "So I thought this weekend would be great to go to Coney Island since you've never been."

"That would be great!" Emily exclaimed, nearly falling as the train took a sharp turn. She was still working on her ability to balance in the crowded cars and not end up in a commuter's lap.

"It sure will be. I invited Kate and—"

Emily gave an exasperated sigh. "Oh, good..."

"What? What's wrong with Kate?"

"She's presumptuous and rude, and—"

"She's anything but rude!"

Emily scrunched her face and spoke in a childlike, sarcastic voice that sounded nothing like Kate, "Oh, that's what happens when country bumpkins find out what a real party is like..."

Allie laughed hysterically, drawing glances from commuters who previously hid their faces in newspapers or paperbacks. "Kate can be tough on people she likes."

"She didn't even apologize for practically running me over." Emily threw her free hand into the air, about to launch into a tirade.

"She really was in a hurry, Em." Allie's tone grew somber. "She has to transfer there to get to the shop. We gave her a ride there, but with traffic I'm not sure it would have gotten her to work any faster. She works so much. She barely sleeps. She must be tired all the time…"

"You said yourself she has a car." Emily refused to take pity.

"Yes, and she's driving this weekend, so complain to her yourself."

"So she can drive to the beach when she isn't in a hurry, but not to work so she doesn't run over innocent bystanders?"

"I've been telling her that since she finished the thing." Allie sighed.

"Finished? Her car?"

"Yes, her and her father—"

Emily saw an elderly couple sitting on a bench a short way down the train car. They sat close together, the woman resting her head casually on the shoulder of the man. The closeness wasn't just physical. They had a familiarity beyond that, which anyone could see. Their hands rested together, and they sat in silence, waiting for their stop. Emily caught herself staring.

Weaving her way awkwardly through passengers, she walked over to the couple and asked them a question. At that precise moment the car stopped, and nearly everyone exited the train. Emily sat across from them as Allie commandeered the seat next to her before it was taken. Emily was already rifling through her bag.

"I won't take long, I promise," she mumbled, ignoring Allie's questioning stare.

Emily produced a small blank pad of paper and pencil from her purse. Allie looked down as the form of the couple began on the page, the seemingly random lines connecting as Emily continued.

"Em, that's incredible," she said as Emily added the finishing touches.

Emily took the sketch and gave it to the couple. The gentleman reached for his wallet, but she stopped him. The train doors opened once again, Emily exited smoothly at their intended stop, with Allie nearly left behind staring at the couple. They turned to wave at Emily though the grime-covered windows.

"And why exactly do you want to just study art history?" Allie asked, following Emily as she briskly walked toward the street level. "You should be attending some European art school, or studying with a famous artist-protégé program or whatnot."

"I don't need to study technique," she replied calmly. She had thought of this subject before. "I love learning what others did and applying it to my work. Or, it's more practical to get married. That's what I'm supposed to say, right?"

Allie looked directly at her. "Don't waste what you have. Your talent is incredible."

Emily stopped as well, the crowded street sounds dissipating as she assured her friend, "I won't."

❖

Emily had never seen so many people or anything like it on a seemingly normal Saturday afternoon. Allie, Art, Kate, and she stood before the sea of humans that crowded near the body of water that only resembled the ocean well out to the horizon, as it was littered with swimmers from end to end. They couldn't find an open patch of sand on Coney Island beach and ended up making camp among the crowd hugging the boardwalk.

Thousands of families—children, teenagers, and adults alike—were enjoying the water and sand. Kate immediately took full advantage of the crowd, incessantly snapping photos with what Emily noticed was an elegant and expensive, but well-used camera. Emily was immediately amused and intrigued.

They set up their supplies on a tiny strip of unoccupied sand.

"The draft board is getting longer every month," Art stated in response to the now usual conversation about the war overseas. He seemed lost in his own thoughts.

"I see new girls at the shop every week," Kate added. "Doesn't seem like it's letting up anytime soon."

"Means more people to take a few shifts off your hands, eh?" Allie asked.

"Not with production upping right along with the number of new workers. Plus it's not like I have much else to be getting into."

They all laughed at that. "Now that I don't believe." Emily chimed in. "You just want to work all the time."

"I want to do my part. Both for the war effort and..."

Emily wondered what had gotten to her, but she didn't pry.

"Enjoy the beach while you've got it, folks." Art crossed his arms behind his head and leaned back into the warm sun. Allie scooted closer to him.

After a bit of silence, taking in the sunshine, Kate turned to Allie and Art and snapped the shutter multiple times as they sat talking with each other.

"How can you possibly want to take more pictures of us?" Art asked in exasperation.

"I never tire of your disgusting sweetness with each other," Kate answered dryly, and with a grin. "Now lean over so I can get the park in the shot."

Emily rolled her eyes at the remark as a young boy building a majestic architectural sculpture from the sand in front of her caught her eye.

"You should do family photography, Kate," Allie stated, clearly as an attempt to distract Kate from further photo taking.

"No. I can't stand studios, too formal..." She shivered as though the idea were a hideous disease. "Plus, it's not something you make a career of."

"What is it with you people and not doing something you're amazing at?!" Allie exclaimed, startling everyone except Emily, who appeared to be immersed in a sketch of the same young boy.

"What?" asked Kate.

Allie flippantly pointed at Emily, who still seemed oblivious to the conversation. Kate waved a hand in front of Emily.

"What." It was a statement, not a question, as she continued to sketch.

"How is whatever world you just drifted off to treating you?"

"Huh?" she said, finally looking up. Kate grinned at her and gestured to her work, leaning over to get a glance.

"Whatever..." Emily scoffed and returned to the drawing.

Kate pulled it out of her hand.

"Hey!" Emily immediately attempted to snatch it back.

"Not bad. Although I've taken ten shots in the time it took you to do that," said Kate, handing the notebook back.

"Because the camera does all the work!" she responded, suddenly feisty. *How in the world does this woman get my temper up so quickly?*

"I'm about ready to stop looking at the water and try it out," Art suggested. He stood and pulled Allie along with him. Emily looked over at Kate, who seemed about to make a rebuttal to her comment. But before that could happen, Emily smiled, stood, and walked away toward the water after the other two. Kate followed as well.

Kate caught up to Emily at the edge of the water, where Art and Allie were frolicking farther out, oblivious to anything in the world but each other. She stopped and shook her head. Not looking away from the water Kate said, "The sketch really was good."

The simple compliment startled Emily. She looked at Kate to read her expression and decided against caution. She wanted the banter. "Instant results. And one of a kind, I might add."

"So are photos!" said Kate, taking the bait.

"All ten that you took in five minutes?"

"Every single one," Kate stated with confidence, crossing her arms and bucking up her chin.

"At least I'm not a complete sap for romance," said Emily. She was now the one who turned away, staring at the water.

Emily once again imitated Kate in the worst possible way. "Lean over so I can get the park in the shot. You too are soooo sweet. Aww..."

Kate huffed, "Sap, huh?"

"Yeah—"

Kate grabbed Emily around the waist and launched them both into the cold Atlantic water. Emily quickly recovered, out of breath from both the sudden attack and the frigid temperatures. Flicking her now-drenched hair out of her eyes, she found Kate casually swimming out farther into the water with a satisfied smile.

"You're dead!" Her voice was deadly, but she knew her face betrayed her fierceness. She threw herself on Kate and pulled her underwater, drawing no one's attention in the crowded waves. Everyone was just as crazed around them.

Kate immediately recovered, grabbing Emily from behind and pulling her in over her head and splashing them both back under the surface. Emily refused to stand for it but had no method of attack, so she ended up with her arms around Kate's shoulders, desperately attempting to leverage her weight to pull Kate under. Unsuccessfully.

She stopped immediately when she realized Kate's arms were around her waist and found herself staring into dark eyes a color just short of black. Her thoughts started racing all at once, catching her off guard. Droplets of water glistened on Kate's neck. Kate was holding her up off the surface. She struggled to look away only to find her gaze wandering down to Kate's lips. Heat leapt up and spread throughout her. *What the hell?*

Kate quickly ducked down and out of her grasp, and Emily let her. Heat rose in her cheeks, despite the cold water surrounding her. Whatever the hell that was mercifully ended faster than it started. *Don't be awkward.* She followed Kate a ways behind to shore, and found she had to catch her breath. While she didn't know why, she thought it might not be from treading water.

❖

The day continued as the ladies and Art strolled the boardwalk and took in the attractions of the nearby amusement park of Coney Island. Emily couldn't remember a time even in childhood that she was spun around in as many directions and mindlessly entertained on different roller coasters and amusements as she had been in those few short hours. They all were exhausted and completely ignoring their fatigue, even as the sun quickly descended far in the distance.

The throngs of people had grown even denser throughout the afternoon. Now, the crowd was finally abating as children and families were escorted home, preparing for the week ahead.

"Are you sure you don't mind, Kate? I know you have to be at the shop early tomorrow," Allie asked. "Em's got to have the whole experience."

"Of course. It isn't everyday a countr—" She stopped herself when Emily glared in her direction. "Someone not from the city... can rarely get a view like this." A grin almost made it to her eyes. When Emily noticed, she seemed to stop herself and looked down at her feet, finding something of great interest there. Did her reservation stem from earlier?

Kate had been almost cordial throughout the day, even when Emily attempted to start something, which disappointed her each time. She was increasingly fascinated with the woman as she engaged Art and Allie in conversation about the city, her thoughts about its culture, and her surprising knowledge of actual life in this place.

As they approached the giant steel wheel now lit in the fading twilight, a group of young boys came flying at them, and the last and smallest, in his attempt to swerve through the line, ran right into Kate. He immediately looked terrified.

"Sorry, ma'am," he said, looking past her as if thinking of how he was possibly going to catch up with the group. He waited only a second before bolting, only to have Kate grab his arm.

"Help us out," she said to him, unslinging her camera from her shoulder. Emily observed as she pulled the camera to her eye, expertly and quickly set the exposure settings, and handed it to the boy. Briefly and efficiently, Kate instructed him what to do, both on the camera as well as pointing at the sign behind the four of them. The ten-year-old appeared immediately fascinated, as was Emily. Kate clearly loved to teach, and her passion for the art was deep.

The boy stepped back, lined up his shot, and the group posed in front of the chipped, paint-covered Wonder Wheel sign. Kate hurried over and stood next to Emily, who pulled her in with her arm around Kate's waist. Kate relaxed when she saw Emily's gentle smile and threw an arm around her shoulder, the mysterious awkwardness of earlier suddenly vanishing.

"Thank you, sir." Kate took back her camera and reached for a few bills. "Here, have fun." She handed him the money, and his face lit up instantly.

"Gee, thanks!" He held it up, then turned and bolted away after the group that was likely long gone.

"What?" Kate asked.

Emily was doing it again, staring at her as though studying her.

"Shall we?" Art called to the group.

Kate watched as Emily looked up again at the enormous steel structure before them. The hand-painted sign at the entrance declared, "Twenty-two years and zero accidents."

Above them each individual car was loaded as the wheel spun. But the uniqueness of the attraction was that certain cars hung from railings in the center of the wheel and flung themselves from the inside supports along the rail out to the edge. Swinging cars?

"Nope. No possible way!" Emily shook her head.

"Oh, come on," Kate said. "Didn't you read the sign? It's perfectly safe."

Emily looked directly at her. "No."

Kate could barely contain a grin at the stubbornness that had just come from Emily.

Fifteen minutes later, after much discussion, Emily and Kate ended up in a fully stable Ferris-wheel buggy, while Art and Allie entered a swinging one that Emily kept claiming was sure to be a deathtrap.

Kate had inadvertently chosen to completely ignore a very nervous Emily and was taking photographs incessantly while the cars were loading. Emily hadn't moved a muscle, including those in her white-knuckled hand that gripped the frail metal bar holding them in. Kate stopped momentarily to look over and, without saying anything, pointed to their right.

As if made of stone, Emily managed to move only her eyes, not even tilting her head in the direction she was shown. But that was the key that unlocked the rest of her. She instantly relaxed. "It's incredible!"

"It's an even better view than from the buildings downtown, in my opinion."

It was as if the view put her totally at ease. "We should have gone on one of the swinging ones with Allie and Art."

Kate flung her head around. "We just spent the better part of ten minutes convincing you to get on this thing at all!" She shook her head. "Besides, they're probably busy with each other, and I wouldn't want to watch."

Emily's sudden laughter startled Kate, and she immediately loved the sound of it. She couldn't help but snap the shutter as she turned to look at Emily.

"You never stop, do you?!" Emily exclaimed in faux annoyance when she heard the shutter snap.

"The best moments are when you don't expect them, so I take as many as I can and hope for the good ones." Although Kate truly believed that the best moments were those unplanned, the ones that blindsided you and imprinted themselves in your memory, she had to add the quantity argument just to stir up debate. It worked.

"Where's the art in that?" asked Emily. "With paper and a pencil you get to capture the world the way you want. Make something unique out of how you see life."

"But that's altering it. A photo makes something ordinary into something unique just by framing it. Like a moment captured in time." She explained, truly getting into the debate. "Think of a memory, one you would give anything to relive. That's a photograph. Our minds fill in the recesses of memories, but on the surface, they're just fleeting images. Whatever you see you can capture in an instant, and you will always have the photo to remember that moment. It's fascinating."

She looked down at her camera and away from Emily. She even felt a bit embarrassed, as though she had revealed some part of herself to this person without even knowing it. It excited her that she was able to express what she was thinking though, and have someone who seemed genuinely interested in her thoughts. She never did that, even when teaching—let herself be that passionate.

They both sat back and looked out across Brooklyn as lights turned on in the twilight, as though stars were lighting up the landscape. Past the train stations leading to the beach, the perfectly lined homes spread toward the horizon with a surprising amount of space between them. It was a sight she'd often seen but never tired of.

"Really?!" Emily exclaimed when Kate snapped the shutter again in the fading light.

Kate smiled and turned the camera in her hand, so the lens pointed toward the two of them. "Here—" She held the camera at arm's length and leaned toward Emily. Emily smiled into the lens, and Kate took the photo.

"So how did photography come about?" Emily asked after a moment of silence. The wheel began its first full loop, having been fully loaded.

"Well, these fellas back in the eighteen fifties…"

Emily cut her off with a light slap on the arm. "The sarcasm never ceases."

"All right, all right." Kate conceded. "My father got me this camera for a high school graduation present. He made me think about all the rubbish I just told you about capturing memories, and I've loved it ever since. He wasn't a photographer, but I've always appreciated the way he saw things."

"Just as a hobby though?"

"Well, working at the shop pays for the hobby, so for now, yes, but hopefully not always. Don't know right now…"

Kate brought her camera back up to her eye and took a few more shots. The silence, although not uncomfortable, was too long for her taste, and knowing it would stir her up, she turned the camera and once again snapped yet another of Emily. She was surprised, however, when Emily snatched the camera from her hand. She turned it with no idea what she was doing, found the shutter release button, and attempted to take a photo unsuccessfully.

"You have to advance the film," Kate said, laughing.

"What? How—" Emily looked at the thing as though it were a strange alien object.

Kate gently took the camera back and set the exposure. "There are a bunch of different controls you need to adjust, but *obviously* the camera does all the work." Her face lit a bit with her sarcasm. Emily rolled her eyes and took back the camera.

"So where is the Statue of Liberty?" she asked, looking into the viewfinder and flailing the camera around toward the water and into the distance.

Kate laughed. "You definitely can't see it from here." She reached to take the camera, just as Emily turned and snapped a photo right in Kate's face. Kate sighed, but knew she was getting a taste of her own medicine.

"Well I still haven't been and Allie is planning on taking me around—"

"The last thing you need is to let Allie take you on a tour of the city."

"Why not?" Emily asked.

"You'll miss out on the good stuff," Kate replied, taking the opportunity to snatch back the camera. Emily glared.

"The good stuff?"

"Yes," she replied with confidence, "we'll just have to give the country bumpkin a real tour of the city soon—"

Emily hit Kate again on the arm and shook her head. Kate was never going to let that joke go. She watched Emily smile, turning away while rolling her eyes, and hoped she didn't take it too seriously. Country bumpkin or not, however, Emily was here to enjoy the summer, and Kate hoped she could be the perfect person to do it with.

CHAPTER SIX

Summer had settled on the streets, and the heat sat stagnant and heavy between the sky-scraping buildings across the city. Emily sauntered down amongst what she was told was the East Village after dropping off Allie at school for her summer job. She had mentioned that there were interesting shops around, including new artist galleries and fashion outside of what Emily was normally surrounded by, and Emily was excited to explore. She had the day free and insisted she have the day to herself. Kate was, she assumed, working as always, so she didn't ask.

Trying not to get lost, she realized that the streets in the area maintained a crisp grid until she ventured south of Houston Street, where the madness of the lower portion of the island began. It was the remnant of a time before someone had thought to organize. She came to one such street, with a massive, beautiful Episcopal Church standing guard to her right. The building sat at an angle, not facing any street, but straight out at the corner, evidence of how the landscape had changed while the building stood strong. What was its history, and that of so many other places around her? Despite how things so quickly changed, she was living amongst the past as well.

She came across a park eventually and found a bench as children played around her. This place seemed to become just another neighborhood wherever she traveled within it. The hundreds of streets and cross-streets, inhabited by millions, all melded into a life-sized world with approachable people. The hub of the world could become your backyard.

She tilted her head into the sunlight and closed her eyes as a gentle breeze mercifully drifted across the park through the trees. When she looked down, a teenager sat on a bench across from Emily. Her knees were bent up on the bench, supporting a pad of paper as she intensely sketched, looking up from the page occasionally to observe her subjects, the other children running around merrily in the park. Emily knew that feeling of being in the world that you are creating, if even just for a moment.

After a bit she resumed her explorations, seeing a row of shops lining the far edge of the park. As she strolled along the sidewalk, she looked in at the assortment of businesses, from a fish market to the children's toy store next door. One of the last stops before the corner caught her eye. It had no sign in front, no indication of its business type. But, through the large front window scattered and crowded with a random assortment of items, she saw a few paintings and a shelf that held all manner of art supplies. Even though it seemed strange from the outside, Emily could use some supplies since she'd limited what she brought with her.

Once inside, she fully took in her surroundings but didn't see anyone working or shopping. The shop itself looked small, much like every other one within miles, but the rows of items inside were nearly impossible to traverse. Products covered shelves from the floor right up to the ceiling, varied in their use. Although she was immediately attracted to what she now realized was an entire aisle of art supplies, she looked through the row of kitchen utensils and an aisle of canned and dry foods, along with an entire section of children's toys.

After browsing she noted that the shop wasn't as small as she imagined. Through a large service door off to the side of the shop was an open space that she recognized as a studio of sorts. Interesting.

In the far back corner she found what she assumed was the cash register. A tall counter was surrounded by papers, items overflowing from the rest of the store, and a small open space where someone could perch on the stool sitting there. She was instantly distracted, however, by a massive collage on the wall behind. The wall itself was invisible behind masses of strips and pieces of paper, and even a photograph or two posted onto it. It was covered with hundreds of small pieces, each page its own piece of art. There were sketches, paintings, writings…While some were beyond recognition, each one conveyed a message, and Emily needed to know what their purpose was.

She looked around for anyone to explain the mystery, or the store in general for that matter, and was startled when an old man emerged from an office hidden behind a small door surrounded by all the randomness.

"Afternoon, miss. Can I help you?" he mumbled as he shuffled papers along the counter. Emily took in his appearance as he gazed at her through small spectacles, clearly waiting for a response. His gray hair was awry on his balding head, and his back had a bit of a hunch. As intimidating as his initial appearance might have been, his eyes were warm and welcoming. Emily felt immediately at ease with him.

"Oh." She stumbled for a response, looking back to the wall. "These are wonderful. Who is the artist?"

The man shuffled about at the counter, as though it were a common question. "Everyone who comes in. You're next." He pulled a similar sheet of paper from a stack on the counter and gestured for her to take it.

"Excuse me?" she asked, confused.

"Yes, ma'am. Here you go."

"Oh, no. I couldn't. I was just looking around." Nervous, she regretted asking.

"Use whatever you'd like." He gestured back to the art supplies behind her and the bucket sitting on the counter. When she didn't move, he laid in front of her an ordinary stationery pencil. He was so matter-of-fact, Emily thought him more than a bit strange, but she skeptically picked up the pencil, since it seemed as though she could not avoid this strange ritual.

The man returned to shuffling things around and sitting on the stool hidden amidst the clutter, already ignoring her. She shook her head and thought of what to draw. Her hand made its way onto the page, lead to the paper. Just as the young girl she had seen in the park, the image in her mind started to appear on the scrap of paper, her hand the vessel.

"How did you find your way down here?" the man inquired. Emily remained focused on the work forming in front of her.

"Oh...um...just exploring."

"Not from around here?" He ignored the fact that she was ignoring him in return.

"No. I wish," she mumbled. "I'm visiting for a few months."

He waited patiently until Emily added the finishing touches. She looked over her work, only to be stunned at what she had drawn, though she hadn't really been thinking about it as she worked. She'd created a silhouette of a woman looking out onto a vast landscape. Beyond the woman stretched a field, hills rolling into the far distance. Just at the edge of the horizon was an outline of...New York? *What in the world?* This was completely uncharacteristic of anything Emily produced on a regular basis, and far too abstract for her liking. She scrunched her eyebrows together.

Not wanting to think more about it, she slid the completed sketch back across the counter, looking at it as though it were not something of her own creation, and awaited the old man's response. Instead, he merely looked down at it, nodded, and pinned it onto the far side of the wall. He turned to come back just as a young girl bolted through the door. Emily recognized her as the same girl she had seen immersed in her work in the park. She carried the large pad she was sketching on, as well as a satchel full of other supplies on her shoulder.

"Hey, Gramps!"

The old man immediately lit up. "Mia! What do we have today, young lady?"

She enthusiastically handed him the pad. He studied it for a moment, and Mia turned to Emily.

"Which one is yours?" she asked.

Emily pointed to her sketch at the far end of the wall. Mia looked over at the drawings and started pointing, but not at Emily's.

"No, the one under that one," Emily said.

She leaned in close and her eyes widened, "Wow! That's amazing!

Emily smiled in spite of herself. "Thank you. And I should say the same thing to you!" she added, looking down at the sketch the old man had set on the counter. She had created an elaborate scene of the park from her viewpoint on the bench. Emily noticed issues with perspective throughout but could immediately tell the girl had talent.

A thought struck Emily as she looked back up at the girl. *Why does this kid look familiar?* It wasn't just from seeing her sketching a bit earlier. She looked like someone…

She added the book to her bag and slung it over her shoulder. "Can I use the studio for a little while?"

"Don't make a mess in there," he mumbled, but with a smile. "I'll be in to help you with some perspective work on that when your sister gets here."

She bolted across the room, maneuvering the mountains of items with ease, clearly familiar with the space.

"You come by this weekend, I have some people you should meet. I'm sure they would be quite interested in your work," the old man said, startling Emily again.

"My work?" she asked. *This is the strangest person I've ever met.*

"Unless that was a fluke," he said, pointing over at her sketch. "You should let people see it."

"Really, it's not worth taking anyone's time—"

"I'll see you Saturday then, Miss…?"

"Um." She couldn't imagine what her face must have looked like. "Emily."

"Alfonzo." He pointed to himself and then held out his hand. "Well, Miss Emily. I will see you next Saturday afternoon?"

Definitely not. "Sure." She quickly made her way to the door.

❖

As Emily continued down the street, she was still in a daze from what had just occurred. She supposed she would run into at least one eccentric in this town, so she brushed the incident off with little more thought. She decided to head back to Allie's, hoping that it would be acceptable for her to return by this time. She still hadn't broken the habit of looking around to observe every element of the surroundings she possibly could and almost ran into Art as he exited what she noticed was a jewelry store.

"Well, well, well!" she said. He looked panicked, and she suspected she knew why but thought of playing with him. "What were you doing in a place like that?"

"Emily!" He attempted a greeting without acknowledging the question.

"Art." Emily crossed her arms.

After much hesitation and Emily blocking his way, he pulled out a small box from his pocket and opened it for her to see.

Emily covered her mouth in shock and excitement. His face relaxed and he smiled.

"Art! Of course I will!" Emily squealed in mock excitement, covering her mouth with one hand and holding out the other.

Art looked immediately horrified at the miscommunication and confused at the reaction. "Wha—"

Emily laughed then, letting him off the hook. "Art, she's going to love it," she told him sincerely.

"You think?" He hesitated, but his eyes glinted with excitement.

"It's from you, so of course," she assured him with a pat on the arm. "When are you going to propose?"

"I haven't exactly worked it all out…"

"Oh, good! We'll figure everything out and it will be absolutely perfect and—"

"Emily, I don't think anything big would be necess—" They were talking over each other, Emily growing more excited, while Art shuffled his feet awkwardly.

"Of course it is!"

"We've been talking, and I'm planning on—" He attempted to get a word in.

Emily started planning in her head, from where he should do it, to when, and what to tell Allie. "It obviously has to be a surprise—"

"I'm enlisting next week."

They stopped and stared at each other. He looked her in the eye and shrugged. He had apparently already made the decision and was resolved to do it.

"I suppose it's surprising you managed to avoid the draft board this long."

"It's really a matter of time. We thought that after I get back from basic training would be the best time, and we've talked about it all, but I…I don't think I want to wait." Emily detected happiness beneath it all and was once again in awe of the two of them. They knew each other as though they had lived a lifetime together already, and she hoped they would be together that long.

"That makes the surprise even better."

CHAPTER SEVEN

The room was pitch-black despite the sun just beginning to pierce the horizon. Emily thought she heard a faint knocking on the door but reasoned it away in her dreams, since it couldn't be nearly time to wake yet. Hearing her name whispered was just part of the dream as well. She flipped her head away from the blinding light of the hallway that spilled into the room when someone opened her bedroom door.

"Em," Allie whispered. "Em! Kate is outside."

Emily looked up to see Allie silhouetted in the doorway, barely awake with an unhappy look on her face.

"Kate?…What?…"

"She said you said you were meeting her and you…you're late?" Allie mumbled in desperation to go back to sleep. "I don't know. Just go deal with her."

"Tell her to go away—" She pulled the covers up and turned back into the comfort of the darkness.

Kate appeared in the doorway and passed Allie on the way into the room, startling both Allie and her. She charged to the window and threw open the curtains as if to let in the glorious sunlight. The dramatic gesture merely opened the curtains to the still nearly dark outdoors.

"Nope. Let's go." She spun around to Emily, who was now glaring at her. "You said you wanted a tour, so up up."

"I never said I wanted a tour!" Emily nearly yelled, breaking the silence of the house at this hour.

"Well, I'm up already, so no use wasting daylight or my time," Kate said with a conspiratorial smile.

"Your time?!" Emily exclaimed. "That's the least of my worries."

Allie had retreated from the room with a roll of her eyes. Kate, when Emily stubbornly stuffed her head in a pillow, pulled the sheets off her. She jolted straight up and shot daggers at Kate, who now retracted the grin she'd worn moments before.

Kate refused to question why she was determined to rouse Emily at this hour. She truly did want to experience the city she knew with Emily, and this was the time to do it, but the added flourish of being obnoxious was, she admitted, a bit unnecessary. Yet in the end, Emily would enjoy the experience, and Kate liked that a bit of torment brought that determined look on Emily's face. That look was forming right then, even in her sleepy state—a resolve to fight back and spar with her. Kate had to grin at the adorable scowl Emily wore.

"You are absolutely infuriating," Emily mumbled to herself as she rose from the bed. She didn't know if she was angrier at the abrupt wake-up call or the fact that she couldn't truly say no to the woman. "I'll be downstairs in five minutes."

Kate said over her shoulder leaving the room, "You've got three."

Emily resisted the urge to throw her pillow at the retreating back.

Four minutes later she locked the door and joined a still-smiling Kate on the front steps. Kate took off down the tree-lined sidewalk, leaving Emily behind.

Emily huffed along, still attempting to wake up, "Why are you walking so fast?!"

"If we plan to make it on time, you should try to keep up."

"Make it where?" she asked, exasperated, "Nothing is open this early!"

Kate stopped abruptly, causing Emily to nearly run into her, and Emily saw her once again stifling a *goddamned* grin. She turned to her car parked right next to where she stopped and earned another glare from Emily.

"Do you try to be annoying, or does it just come naturally?"

Kate slammed the door she had just opened and almost put her keys in her pocket. "I suppose if you'd rather actually walk, we could—"

Emily climbed into the car without a second glance.

"Maybe we should go to the station and actually be on time for a train," Emily suggested. They sat in what Emily noticed was Kate's extremely well-maintained car interior, no litter or dust on a single surface. Kate smoothly navigated the Manhattan streets. Even at the early hour, there was congestion at some points. Emily noticed they were headed downtown but had no idea of the destination.

Kate responded after a moment of silence. "Is my inability to utilize public transportation the only point you can continue to come up with? Besides, we are taking the trains and walking once we get there. I just need my car later this evening."

"Where? Seriously, where are you taking me?"

At the lack of response Emily stared out the window. The sky continued to collect light, but the sun had yet to show itself through the slits between buildings. However, the colors painting the sky and reflecting off all the various surfaces that Emily could see down each street were magnificent. Early morning workers made their way down into the underworld of subways as homeless folks lay asleep with their collections on corners and under overhangs of buildings. Even at this hour, the city remained awake and moving.

She looked away from the scene and back into the car. She noticed the polished wood dashboard, personalized gear shift, the leather-upholstered seat she sat on. Each detail seemed carefully chosen, and she could tell a lot of hard work had gone into the machine.

"So how in the world did you come about a car like this?"

She noticed Kate's camera sitting between the seats and picked it up. She brought it to her eye and began observing the outside once again, but through the lens.

"It's more complicated than just point and shoot, you know."

"I can see that. But the camera's still doing the work." She kept looking about and could tell Kate was deflecting. She pointed at her through the lens. "Story."

Kate sighed, Emily not letting her get out of an explanation. "My father and I built it together."

Emily stopped and put the camera down. "Built it!?"

"Mostly him. I was twelve when he got it in rough shape. It took us almost six years to fix it back up."

"You seem close with him."

"We were." Kate's face lit with a genuine soft smile. "I mostly slowed him down. He showed me everything he was doing as he worked, and I got to hand him tools like a nurse."

Emily didn't press.

"He passed two years ago."

Emily nodded.

"Before you ask, my mother took off when I was a kid. She needed to get away, I suppose, or at least my father claimed. Must have taken a lot of courage to up and walk away."

"So just you now?" Emily asked.

"What makes you think that?" Kate said at the assumption. Emily wasn't being touchy or pitying her.

"I bet you were such a tomboy." Kate raised an eyebrow. "It doesn't seem like anyone's tried to change that. Plus, I don't know who could put up with your constant berating."

"I don't know. I think I'd make a fine sibling." Kate didn't answer the question. "Only child, I assume?" she asked back.

Emily blushed. "I hope I don't act like it…"

Kate laughed. "That would just be the *worst*, now wouldn't it?" Emily shoved Kate and shook her head, and both of them smiled in spite of themselves.

❖

Weaving down the island almost to the bottom, Kate turned a corner and pointed out the window across a huge construction site out to the water. "They're building a tunnel across the water to Brooklyn. This is the Battery."

Past it all was the faint outline of a statue, one Kate saw often on her trips such as the one they were taking. She watched Emily try to look over the harbor that the lady on her pedestal guarded, a beacon that had led so many there. Kate saw Emily's excitement grow seeing the signs, realizing she wanted their first stop to be the iconic New York landmark. But Kate had other plans and took a turn leading to the Brooklyn Bridge.

"Bridge? Why are we going to a bridge!? Tour of *Manhattan*! Where are we going!?" Emily turned in her seat.

"So cranky in the morning." Kate sarcastically scrunched her face, "All the time, come to think of it..."

"Wanting to know I'm not being kidnapped is reason to be cranky at five a.m.!" Kate didn't respond, and Emily sat back with her arms crossed like a petulant five-year-old.

"Brooklyn Heights? Where in the world are we?" She once again was rewarded nothing. "It's nearly impossible to see anything surrounding the bridge, and who takes someone on an iconic structure before they've even had the chance to look at it?"

Kate pulled the car into what seemed to be a vacant backlot of a warehouse right along the water, which Emily was blind to in her aggravation. Kate grabbed her camera and got out of the car. Emily threw up her hands and flung open the door.

Kate pointed up and away toward the river. "Look."

Emily's mouth dropped open at the sight. It turned into a smile as she stood a silent statue. Kate looked on, but not at the landscape. She brought her camera up and captured Emily in her own world before she caught herself. Emily heard the sound of the shutter and turned. Kate expected a glare, but her smile remained. She returned it, more satisfied than she expected that Emily was already appreciating it.

"It's New York," Kate almost whispered, and then she turned to look for herself.

The sun had just appeared over the horizon as the two of them gazed west. The city was bathed in the brilliance of the morning colors but stood proudly against the harbor and river that surrounded it. The most magnificent part, however, might have been the iconic stone structure at the right of the panorama. The Brooklyn Bridge jutted across the water toward them where they stood at its eastern base, its arches allowing the morning sun to stream through onto the neighboring borough. It was the clearest view of the bottom edge of the urban hive Kate knew.

"It's beautiful," Emily said. Kate turned her head toward the other woman and, for the briefest of moments, found she agreed, until she realized she wasn't looking at the landscape. She shook her head and brushed off the odd thought.

She suddenly remembered her plan then and ducked into the car. She produced a blank sketch pad and set of pencils and handed them to Emily. "I'm going to prove my point today."

Emily's eyes narrowed, but the playfulness remained. "We'll see about that." Kate seemed content as she took another photo.

Kate watched as Emily immersed herself in a sketch, the lines that made up each building and transferred and took shape on the page.

Kate turned her back and headed toward the bridge. "Come on now. We don't have all day."

Emily snapped back, "Oh, calm down already." She took a few extra moments of sketching. Kate kept walking until Emily bolted after her, catching up at the pedestrian bridge entrance around the corner.

Even at the early hour, a few stragglers were making their way in both directions. Most were on foot, an occasional bicyclist, and none looked the part of tourist. They were commuters, those that started the days before the sun had an opportunity to rise and worked each day in order to live and thrive for what was considered the American dream.

"Where now?" Emily asked. "You're leaving the car there?"

Kate chuckled. "I'm not driving downtown during rush hour.

Feel free to, if you'd like to give it a try." She smiled at Emily. "We'll pick it up later today."

"Wait, wait, wait." She halted suddenly, just at the base of the first of two stone pillars that gave the bridge its renowned shape, and pulled out the pad and pencil once again. Flipping the page, she started anew. Kate took the opportunity to line up another shot of not only the bridge itself, but of Emily once again in her own magical, creative world.

"All right, I'm done. Come on."

"All right, all right. I get it! Let me finish this one." Emily was pleading. "Anyone can push a button on a camera," she mumbled.

The sun continued its ascent into the morning sky, and Emily was already sweating. In her limited experience, although the subways seemed more convenient, they were actually a system of tunnels that sprang straight from the depths of hell. *Or at least it felt as though they were.* She needed not worry, however, because they passed three stations on their way on foot through lower Manhattan. Kate was also walking at an infuriatingly fast pace, which she must have realized eventually. She slowed, which allowed Emily to look around.

As they moved away from the bridge and wandered deeper into the hive of streets and buildings that comprised the bustling area, Emily grew more cautious. She wondered at the confidence Kate exuded as she navigated block after block. Already at the early hour, these streets were alive, and unlike any of the places Emily had seen thus far, this was a place Kate apparently wanted Emily to experience. Emily, however, hesitated at the rough conditions of the area and the rumors and cautions she had been told about as they walked.

"This is a place you won't see in an Allie-hosted tour," Kate stated. She didn't look at Emily but surveyed what was before her. Emily did the same.

The brick and stone buildings, all seemingly identical in structure, stood cramped together closer than seemingly possible. Their colors were hidden by the gated railings of fire-escape staircases and black painted windowsills, all of which provided space to dry the clothing of those who resided within. Trash littered the gutters along the streets, run-down bicycles left discarded lay on sidewalks, and nearly every storefront built into the bottom of each building contained at least one missing letter on its often hand-painted sign.

"This is the real New York City," Kate stated with almost a sense of awe. "The real American dream."

Emily realized they were staring on the heart of one of the most deprived but resilient collections of individuals, all of whom experienced the indescribable hardships of surviving in this sea of madness, all to make a life for themselves. She had of course heard of the tenement housing and poor conditions of immigrants to this fine country through news and stories of those passionate to help, but to see it firsthand erased all her preconceived notions.

"Amazing, no?" Kate asked, looking at Emily for the first time. She didn't seem judgmental in her question, but Emily was confused as to its intent.

"How so?" she asked. Kate had already surveyed her surroundings and was capturing it on film. She took a moment and then pointed ahead of them.

An old man sat on the stoop of an unremarkable building while a few roughly clothed children played around him. A woman, clearly their mother, yelled from above on the balcony as she strung clothes on a line hanging across the street. Kneeling, Kate engrained the scene on film.

"Not a day in my life have I been without a meal, without a place to sleep, or had to work for less than what I could imagine to survive on. They have." A small smile touched her face. "But look around. The resilience and love for life is so visible in everyone here." Emily looked from Kate to the scene in front of them and pulled out her paper once again.

As Emily looked around, she tried to think of the appropriate reaction. She attempted to muster pity for the unfortunate, the lowest side of the spectrum that divided the populous, but looking at the genuine smiles of the raggedy children, the calmness of the elder worn down from a life of labor, she found none. Walking past them was a man carrying his lunch pail, covered in grease. He lifted his hat, wiped his brow, and wandered toward the children.

"Papa!" they exclaimed, throwing themselves into his arms. The woman from the balcony reemerged to repeat her threat but also stopped at the sight. The children followed their father into the building, and Emily realized that in the midst of whatever seeming hardship was on the surface, happiness was possible.

Kate allowed her the time for this one, and Emily appreciated it. Kate was giving her the opportunity to realize the scope of diversity in this place that Kate called home. She knew it wasn't for the amusement of seeing her reaction or an attempt to invoke pity for these individuals, but so Emily could share with her the appreciation of those who built the city. They were the life force of New York City, and always would be. When Emily looked over, she hoped Kate counted herself among them and lived a life that exemplified living to the fullest in spite of circumstances and enjoying every moment of it.

❖

"So where to now?" Kate heard Emily ask from behind her. They headed south again, the way from which they came, only a few street names recognizable even for a seasoned New Yorker. They made no logical sense in their structure, and she much preferred to be higher on the island, where the streets were numbered into a user-friendly grid. Here, she was at the mercy of Kate's directional skills.

"South" was Kate's only reply. Emily sighed, much to Kate's amusement.

They had reached the bottom of the island, the water of the harbor in front of them, when Kate stopped and looked around. Although it was only for a second, Emily cleared her throat to grab Kate's attention and expectantly crossed her arms.

"Aha!" Kate pointed in satisfaction. She bolted to the left toward the sign reading *Staten Island Ferry.*

"Staten Island?" Emily asked. "Why do we keep going out of Manhattan on this *tour of Manhattan?*"

"Easiest and best view of the Statue of Liberty," she answered with confidence, but then mumbled, "or so I've been told."

"You've never been to Staten Island?" Emily asked.

"Why would I need to?"

"You've lived in New York City your entire life. Why not?"

"It's just never come up. I've never had a reason to go." Kate brushed it off.

"So this tour is an excuse?"

"You could say that." Kate found the aperture dial on her camera suddenly interesting, and warmth crept up her neck. Finding something new in the city seemed so difficult sometimes, and she was excited for the opportunity to do this. Yes, it was perhaps an excuse, but she made it a point to never get bogged down in the routine of life. This "tour" was a pleasant change to the grind, and if she could add excitement for herself in it as well, she was going to. So far, seeing that Emily truly understood the magic of this place had reminded her how enchanting it was. These were the times when she wanted to look up at the buildings all around her as she did as a child, when she was as much in awe of the beauty of it all as someone seeing it for the first time. She envied Emily in that way.

How well traveled was Emily? Hopefully this small gesture was worth something to her, compared to the trips to Europe she was nearly sure Emily had experienced. She'd have to ask sometime.

Together they boarded the ferry, fighting amongst the daily commuters for a position outside. On a stifling summer day, those coming and going from the neighboring island borough sought a seat outside, allowing the wind and saltwater air to cool them, as opposed to the stuffy, crowded cabin of the ferry. It would be worse on the return trip, with so many coming into the city for work at that hour. As they were traveling at a non-rush hour, they found room at the railing to secure a spectacular view of their departure and surroundings.

The ferry pulled away from the dock with expert maneuverability and progressed slowly forward. The buildings looming over from the island condensed and shortened as they traveled farther out into the harbor. The skyline, this time from its southernmost point, began to take shape. The harbor was as alive as the city itself. Boats, ferries, barges weaved in and out, toward and away from each other, in a meticulous ebb and flow between machines. Sailboats floated amongst the massive supply barges heading for various ports. Seacraft of all sizes dotted the waters as far as Kate could see, each as diverse as the individuals that inhabited the island.

"It's nice to have someone native to explore with," Emily said, nearly shouting over the roar of the ferry engine and the swoosh of the water below them as she stared back at the skyline. Kate looked over at her.

"It's nice to revisit places once in a while," she said after a moment. "When you get caught up in life you forget the things that make this place beautiful. It's wonderful to share them with someone who's seeing them for the first time. It brings back the magic of it all."

"Do you want to live here always?" Emily asked abruptly.

Kate hesitated. She had considered the question but never had to answer it to someone other than herself. She didn't really know. "Why would I need to go somewhere else?"

"Well, not *need*, but don't you want to explore? See places just as enchanting but different in their own way?"

"Sure. I'd love to see other places, but travel is a luxury. I have a life here, one that I can't afford to skip out on. Unlike some people, I don't have the means to—" She stopped herself. Emily had never mentioned her ability to travel as she pleased through her family's generosity, and Kate didn't want to draw attention to it. She wanted to ask her about her experiences, not judge her. Emily blushed slightly. "I just mean that I have so much to do here, and it's the best place on Earth, in my opinion. Why would I want or need to do something else? I don't see how I could even if I wanted to."

"There's so much out there to experience," Emily replied. When she looked up she stared silently at the statue, wide-eyed. It was now so close to them.

Kate chuckled at her starry-eyed expression, only to look up and stop herself. The Statue of Liberty stood proudly on her pedestal. Kate thought of the thousands before her who first viewed it as so much more than just an attraction or amusement. For so many it signaled a new life, the hope of reconnecting with family who had journeyed before them, and the prospect of becoming part of something great. The world offered so many new experiences, and this was one of many she wanted Emily to take advantage of.

She'd seen the statue many times before from a distance, but while thinking of the previous question and contemplating the history of what she was observing, she questioned herself. *What if I am missing out?* Even in her favorite place in the world, she could discover this new perspective and find adventure. She thrilled at the prospect of seeing something new and exciting each day and capturing it, just like this moment. She lifted her camera and preserved it not only in her memory.

"Excuse me. Would you please?" Kate asked a commuter to take their photograph, to which the commuter agreed after pulling his face out of the newspaper he was engrossed in. She put her arm around Emily and moved so that she hoped Lady Liberty would be visible. Emily turned back and continued the sketch she had started, then looked up briefly.

"Thank you," she said.

"I'm happy to drag you out of bed before sunrise anytime you'd like," Kate responded. She smiled and pulled her camera to her eye once again. "You're welcome."

When the ferry pulled into the Manhattan dock, Emily wondered if one place existed here that wasn't constantly a blur of people traveling in every possible direction. The sun reached its noon-time peak in the sky, and Kate and she exited back into the madness of those on their lunch breaks from the office buildings that surrounded them. Wasn't any place not a constant blur of people traveling in every possible direction? So far, she had yet to find one.

"Now I can say I've been to Staten Island," Kate said.

"You stepped off the ferry and got back on five minutes later, only because they made everyone clear off."

"And?"

Emily shook her head. "Where to now?"

"Subway" was Kate's only response. The one-word answers got no less annoying as they continued, but Kate hadn't steered her wrong yet, so she followed her.

Emily beamed when she found the correct track uptown just before Kate pointed to it. She was starting to understand the system but couldn't imagine yet being left alone to find her way. She was confident she'd get it soon, but the unbearable heat of the platform squelched any other thought. The hordes of people fanning themselves while waiting on the next car didn't have the logic that a cool underground could provide. At the end of the tunnel Emily saw the train approaching. The blast of hot air that preceded the train approaching from the end of the tunnel was in some demonic fashion even hotter than the platform itself, as was the car they entered.

Kate was silent through the entire process, but beads of sweat ran down her neck. Her long dark hair was pulled back loosely in a style that was classy but casual, much like Kate herself. Past her attempts to be sarcastic, she was an intelligent, *elegant* woman.

When Kate motioned that they had arrived at the desired stop far too many stops later, they shoved off the train and out of the station.

Above ground Emily realized they were at Columbus Circle, the southwest corner of Central Park. That station was one of the busiest in Manhattan, as it connected the residential Upper West Side and beyond with the bustle of Midtown and below. As Kate looked around for something, Emily gazed down the street that lined the park. To the left was the lush overgrowth of green springing from the park, while just on the other side stood an endless line of stone buildings.

She had little time to gawk before someone thrust a piping hot but altogether strange food item under her nose. She looked up at Kate, who shoved her own item into her mouth without explanation while waiting for Emily to take hers.

"Have you never had a frank before?" she garbled through her stuffed mouth.

"It came from there?" Emily pointed to the short, round old man digging into a compartment of the cart from which the sausages appeared. He was one of many, she realized, all competing for service with odd items for sale. Carts marked with items from "ice cold sodas" to "roasted corn ears" dotted the circle and lined the park edge to lure in tourists and commuters as they made their way in and out.

Kate nodded. "With mustard. What do you want to drink?" She gestured to the options that lined a shelf on the cart. Emily silently took a soda and stepped back as Kate paid. Well, she was eating it, so it couldn't be completely horrid, right? She sniffed it skeptically.

"It's not the best thing you've ever had, but it's edible," Kate answered without being prompted, taking yet another bite and smiling around it. She walked toward the park.

They followed one of the endless winding paths deeper into the lush greenery of the park. Emily was still distracted and hesitant at the meal but stopped just as she was about to take a bite. The sounds of rushing cars, honking horns, and the hum of conversations all had faded away as if the two of them were suddenly in the serenity of a secluded oasis. Children ran to and fro as parents looked on from benches. Mothers talked with each other and held babies on their laps. Dogs explored every patch of field with their owners, and lovers strolled arm in arm along the paths. Kate led her to a bench looking out at a boathouse provided for the pond in front of them.

A mother duck guided her chicks on an outing across the water. Farther out, couples rowed boats across the pond, engaged in silent conversation. The world seemed so at peace compared to what Emily had experienced during the last two weeks.

"It's amazing that in the middle of all of the chaos of this city, there's this." She tilted her head up to gaze into the trees that swayed in the warm summer breeze. Kate only nodded as they continued their walk in silence. Unlike the endless back and forth of their travels thus far, something about the park calmed even their interactions. Both of them seemed content to walk in silence, taking in this side of the city. This section, which was just as alive and moving, was a peaceful sliver of nature and earth placed directly in the center of the concrete jungle.

Emily nearly forgot the frank she held in her hand. Attempting to erase the image of the cart-man pulling the steaming sausage out of a vat of murky water, she tried it. Expecting some New York hidden delicacy, she was almost disappointed when the food was in fact...average. She found a sort of amusement in that fact.

"Like I said, edible, right?" asked Kate, breaking the silence. Emily nodded and continued eating. "We can sit right over here." She pointed down an enormous set of stairs right off the main pathway.

Emily recognized it immediately. The fountain stood in the center of a pavilion looking out onto the lake near the boathouse. The sun glinted off the water as it reached overhead in the early afternoon. Families gathered around the pool of the fount, and children ran and played. Music drifted across the space, the light, calming notes from a saxophonist accompanying the low chatter and occasional peals of laughter of the children.

"Did you know a woman sculpted this fountain?" Kate nodded. "The only structure planned in the construction of the park."

"Emma Stebbins," Emily replied. "I studied modern sculpture in a class last semester. The cherubs below the angel...they're health, purity, peace, and temperance."

"Well then, I see you know more than me about my hometown." Kate smiled, clearly impressed.

"She lived in Rome for years, had a lover there." Emily hesitated. "Very bohemian lifestyle. When her lover died, she never produced another sculpture."

She didn't add that her lover was a woman.

The contagious laughter of a young boy and girl running in front of them drew Emily's attention away from the story. She pulled her sketch pad out and began anew.

"Allie tells me you're planning to do graduate studies after you finish your degree?" Kate broke the silence. "That's quite an accomplishment."

Kate's last remark brought Emily out of her work. She met Kate's eyes and studied them. For one of only a few times, she felt respected, not as though it were an amazing and unbelievable fact that she as a woman would choose to continue an education that seemed absurd to many in her life. "Thank you."

"What are you studying?" Kate asked.

"Art history, but I haven't quite decided on my specialization or even thought of a thesis yet."

Before she realized it, Emily was whisked away into her passion, speaking of artists that inspired her, those that stepped out of convention to make something new, and the way some art captures the past.

After a pause, Kate asked, "But why do *you* make art?"

Emily stopped. She'd never been asked the question. She knew why the work was fascinating, but it had always just been a part of her. She thought for a moment, knowing the reoccurring wrinkle between her eyes whenever she was finding her words was showing. Kate was waiting for her to answer.

"It's a release. Perhaps it's the only time in life when I feel as though I have the ability to create and control how life is portrayed. The only time I have a voice in the world around me." She added, as though to herself, "Perhaps it's all for selfish reasons."

"I don't find that selfish," Kate said. "How we see the world and what we do with it is how we find ourselves. Going along with the majority and seeing the world through someone else's eyes strips us of our uniqueness, I think."

"Very philosophical." Emily laughed, but Kate pressed her on in gentle silence.

"It's where I'm happy."

"I know exactly how you feel. It's my world. It's the one time in life when I'm content, and creative, and everything I want to be. Behind the lens I can determine what I want the world to see. Shaping light and surroundings…There's nothing like it."

Emily smiled at the genuine response from Kate, enjoying getting a look into her mind. Emily realized that this day had been one of the most peaceful yet exciting days she could remember. She was so happy to know just a bit about the person she sat with, and to share something of herself in return. But it would end, which saddened her.

"We can walk from here back to Allie's place." Kate pointed westward.

Emily's shoulders dropped slightly, unable to hide the disappointment she felt.

"But the park is beautiful. We could take the scenic route for a bit?" Kate asked. "You know, if you think Central Park's beautiful, we need to get you to Brooklyn. Prospect Park. In my opinion, it's even more so. There's so much more to the city than just Manhattan."

"I'd love a tour sometime then," Emily said, and they fell into companionable silence again.

After another stroll around the park, weaving around pedestrian paths and across grassy slopes, they came to the edge of the park, walked down the appropriate street, and arrived at the apartment. They had reached the stoop when Emily stopped and turned to Kate.

"Thank you." She couldn't say for what, but she knew they had shared something truly special that day. Emily also realized just how much of herself she had shared inadvertently, and was surprised that she was okay with it. Although she had felt part of this place from the beginning, now she thought maybe she knew a bit more about it, as well as the person who allowed her the experience.

Kate nodded, accepting the thanks and holding Emily's eyes for a moment longer than Emily expected. She finally looked away to the apartment door.

Emily wondered if Allie would question how they'd filled their time since early morning. As Emily unlocked the door, she heard animated conversation and laughter from inside. After looking into the dining room, Emily stopped abruptly, causing Kate to bump into her from behind. Both of them stared at the new addition to the residence.

"Tommy."

Chapter Eight

"What are you doing here?" Emily asked, an unintended edge to her tone. Tommy stood with a smile as though oblivious to that edge, wrapping her in his arms.

"I thought I'd surprise you! Your father arranged for me to help out at Ed's office the rest of the summer. I'm staying with my uncle while I'm here, all set up already." He smiled genuinely and placed a kiss on Emily's rapidly heating cheek. She in turn forced a smile onto her face. She hated that she knew Tommy really was excited to be there and that she wanted to send him right back home. It seemed like an invasion. That this was her place, her time. She felt already protective of this place, in just her short time there. Not just of the place, but of—she turned quickly away from Tommy.

"Tommy, darling, this is Kate." She gestured toward Kate, who had gone rigid and remained silent. "She's a friend of Al—a friend." She willed Kate to meet her eyes if only for a moment. Kate relaxed imperceptibly but quickly looked away. "She's a true New York expert," Emily added with a smile. Kate's sudden and uncharacteristic shyness mildly confused her, but she felt obligated to entertain everyone in the room.

"Very nice to meet you," Kate replied, extending a formal handshake. "I apologize. I need to be heading out." She turned before even finishing her sentence, and Emily rushed after her to the door.

"You don't need to leave!" She caught Kate by the arm and turned her around. The intensity in the gaze she fell into stunned her.

"I hope you enjoyed today. I'm sure I'll be seeing you all soon." And she was out the door, leaving Emily beyond flustered as she returned to the dining room. Her aunt and uncle, Allie and Art, and Tommy all sat around, once again in conversation. Allie looked over at Emily with a small smile, as though she empathized in some way with whatever predicament Emily found herself in.

She had shared one of the most wonderful days she could remember with Kate, but now she was already gone. And now, she had to entertain Tommy for the remainder of her trip. This was supposed to be her chance to escape all that. She ignored the nagging question of why she was attempting to escape in the first place.

When she returned to the dining room, the only available seat was next to Tommy. Yet all she wanted to do was run after Kate to find out what had turned her away.

With every step, Kate attempted to squelch the barrage of emotions running through her. She failed to clear her thoughts as she walked onto the subway platform and paced while awaiting the oncoming train. What had she been thinking? The sight of the man in the apartment had illuminated every thought of Emily in a completely new light. The sting of embarrassment replaced the smile that Emily would have provoked just a few moments earlier.

Of course Emily would have someone waiting for her at home, someone who found a way to be with her and give her some familiarity in a strange new place. He was exactly the type of person she would expect Emily to be with. *Was he, though?* He was obviously confident and sure to be successful. But in her short time with Emily she had sensed a bold, adventurous woman who seemed trapped in a world that stifled any of that, and she clearly didn't know an alternative. Didn't know a world outside of the shelter she'd been forced under her whole life. But that day Kate saw someone different, someone not under the pressure of their everyday expectations. But she did know that she barely knew

Emily and shouldn't make assumptions. She had chosen him, and he must suit her well.

After the day they had shared, Kate realized then that she *liked* Emily. She very much liked her. The day had been a chance to get to know more about the woman and to reveal herself and the place that she loved, but in the end she had come to realize just how remarkable she was. She found herself hoping for more adventures and experiences that she somehow realized would be enriched by her presence. Perhaps for the first time, she had found true friendship.

Those eyes though, she thought to herself, for some reason angry at the times she'd caught herself staring. What fascinated her so? They seemed to hold her captive...They were hazel, just short of brown, with flecks of green scattered throughout, visible in just the right light. She seemed to have them burned into her memory now.

Her thoughts snapped back to the apartment. She recalled the man's presumptuous stance as he placed his arm around Emily, as though she were his. He wasn't aware of the action. *But why should she care?* Emily was an intelligent woman and could choose whom she surrounded herself with...but she just couldn't imagine Emily truly being content with someone like that. *You don't even know the guy! You saw him for thirty seconds, for God's sake.*

Why then did she not only scold herself for what she now saw were inappropriate thoughts, but remain unable to quench her surge of anger? She fought the insistent urge to compare herself to Tommy. She wanted to be the one to put her arm— She stopped herself once again. *What in the world?* It was the protective instinct of a friend. As she stepped onto the Brooklyn-bound train, she swallowed the ball of heat rising through her and slowly recognized it as jealousy.

Four years later, 1946

"We're meeting the photographer at the Brooklyn entrance to the bridge," Emily said to Tommy as she put her earrings on in the hotel room. "I didn't catch their name, but I'm assuming it will be the only person with a camera waiting around for someone."

She held off the thoughts of the last time she was at that location. Perhaps she and Tommy would have a chance to explore a bit in the afternoon. She was sure things would have changed during the last four years, especially with the end of the war. As she stared into the mirror, she thought of how she'd changed. She pushed the thought away, not contemplating how she maybe did not like what she saw.

"What exactly does your mother intend for these photographs again, darling?" Tommy asked, walking over to the mirror. He wrapped his arms around her, looking at her reflection as they spoke. Emily took him in, her gaze wandering across his form-fitting shirt, freshly pressed and starched trousers, polished shoes. His hair was combed back, not a single strand loose. His appearance was so like his personality—confident, clean-cut, and manicured, exactly the type of man she had been cultured to desire. She saw no surprises, no new discoveries in his eyes—eyes that she realized were waiting not so patiently for a response.

She hesitated because she herself didn't truly know why the pictures were necessary. "Mother has been fascinated with every possible new trend in weddings these days. She has planned a display of our photographs for the reception and apparently has a photographer scheduled to follow us around the entire day." Tommy's utterly bemused and somewhat nervous look made her smile. For once they could agree on the ridiculousness of the situation. Who needed that many photographs? Their wedding wasn't a *New York Times* piece. This was one trend she was sure would never catch on.

She let herself laugh with him at the ridiculousness, leaning back into his arms. So he did have some genuine emotions lying around, even if he took a back seat to the planning of this grand affair.

❖

Emily and Tommy exited the subway station in Brooklyn and strolled hand in hand toward the water until around the bend the full view onto the island appeared. The Brooklyn Bridge stood as solid as Emily remembered, memories of the first time she saw it flooding back. It stood proudly before the mass of buildings, and new structures stood where others had on her last viewing. The picture was just as majestic, but it had indeed changed. Just like when she had looked out at the park the previous day from her hotel window, she hoped that she could meld into this place once again, change herself. Perhaps this time it could be with Tommy.

She was proud of her memory for guiding her in the correct direction. She let her excitement grow, at last allowing herself to enjoy these moments with her future husband. He had never been across the bridge, and Emily found much happiness in being the one to show him something new, something about the city. Doing so brought her heart closer to this place. She remembered the time Kate had explained that feeling to her. *No.* She refused to think of the past. This was now, and she wanted to live it.

She leaned into Tommy and relaxed as they reached the bridge walkway.

"Are we supposed to wait for them here, or farther up?" Tommy asked. They both surveyed their surroundings, looking for anyone clearly not a commuter but also not a tourist.

"All Mother told me was that they agreed for us to meet at the base of the Brooklyn side of the bridge." Emily hated that her mother had scheduled everything so thoroughly that she hadn't actually spoken to anyone but her mother. Tommy didn't need to know that.

Ten minutes later, they were still waiting. Emily leaned on the railing with a small sketch pad. She drew the sight before her line by line, at this point nearly from memory, inevitably thinking of the first time she sketched it. And in place of the frustration she normally found thinking of it, she smiled. Regardless of anything that had happened the last time she visited this place, that day was one of the best she could recall.

"Perhaps I should check the stairs?" Tommy suggested.

Emily looked at her watch, then back at the completed sketch, "Why don't you let me? Enjoy the view." She kissed him on the cheek and wandered back toward the entrance stairs. She couldn't help but glance at her work once more, distracted by it. How many times had she drawn—*SLAM!* Emily's work lay on the ground after someone had just rushed up the stairs and run directly into her. She immediately looked for it, and her assailant did too.

"I'm so sorry, miss—" The person stopped abruptly, Emily's notebook in their hand.

"No. I apologize." Emily gratefully took back her possession and looked up.

It wasn't possible. Everything stopped. She'd often wondered if this moment would happen. What would she think, what would she say to her...but nothing came. Of all the things she'd thought over the years from anger, to sadness, to irrevocable joy, she expected something. She felt nothing. She couldn't decide if all those emotions had compounded or were absent at the present moment.

"The Thomas Jameson reservation..." Kate stated, not a question. Emily knew Kate could see everything she was thinking and tried to clench the fragments as they swirled around fighting for dominance.

"Sweetheart, I believe I found our person." Emily sounded out to Tommy, never breaking eye contact with Kate, her voice shaking.

"Ah! Grand. We were beginning to wonder—" Tommy likewise recognized her. He, however, was able to quickly mask and regain his composure.

"Why, Kate. What a wonderful coincidence," he exclaimed, but his expression betrayed him. Emily noticed his tight smile and wondered why he would be nothing but delighted to see an old, but brief, friend.

"How are you?" Emily asked. She hadn't stopped gazing at Kate but finally caught herself. She looked down at a suddenly interesting spot on the ground, waiting for an answer.

"Just fine. Thank you very much for asking." Kate clenched her response. Emily imagined she was likewise trying her damnedest to mask the shock that still coursed through her.

"Shall we?" Kate gestured onto the bridge.

Emily could not imagine the shade of her face as every bit of embarrassment and regret surged through her mind, accompanied by anger. Somehow she found that anger refreshing, and it gave her confidence. She was determined to get this over with, forget making memories or other such nonsense. She thought of every way to blame someone else for this sick coincidence, but nothing came to her mind that she could justify. No need to be angry at her mother, but, yes, perhaps Allie, who she was sure made the recommendation...Instead, she was determined to remind herself that she was being overly dramatic and that this was all for her mother's benefit anyway.

❖

A thick silence filled the next thirty minutes as they walked across the Brooklyn Bridge. Kate supplied the only conversation as she guided the couple into poses that under any other circumstances would have been completely romantic. Now they seemed to be merely part of an advertising shoot of some sort.

She was still in shock that this was happening and tried not to recall all the times she'd wished more than anything in her world to be able to fall into those eyes that had looked at her with surprise and then anger just once more. Now each time they exchanged glances, she felt how guarded those eyes were.

And Tommy? Kate sensed that under his forced smile at their greeting not only anger, but perhaps a sick sense of satisfaction at the current circumstance. She decided in that moment to do whatever was required to make it through the session. Later she would find a way to never deal with it again. *Goddamnit! This is the biggest client we've had all year.*

The beautiful couple would provide Kate with the material she needed, even with their forced smiles. She felt ashamed when she sensed Tommy was actually enjoying the process. Emily, however...Did Tommy not sense her feelings? Kate knew when her most fabulous smile was simply plastered onto her face instead of being the real thing. Kate knew the real one. Anyone who knew Emily could see it wasn't how she actually felt. She stopped herself from thinking of Emily but knew she needed to see her authentic smile again. *For the photos, of course.*

"To the park?" she suggested, leading the way to the train.

At this point, the afternoon lunch traffic was in full force. They waited on the platform until a fully packed train made its stop and only a few individuals exited. Kate and Emily didn't hesitate as they pushed their way onto the train, but Tommy barely made it onto the car as the doors closed. To compare their personal space to that of sardines in a can would have been a clichéd understatement.

At the next stop, yet another wave of commuters attempted to board the train, and to her horror, they pushed Kate up against Emily, who couldn't back away because of the large individual standing directly behind her, the child at her knees to her right, and the other five people surrounding her in every other direction. As the train jolted forward, Emily reached out to the pole to support herself and grabbed Kate's hand accidentally. She flinched and moved it, but by that point Kate found herself pressed from head to toe against the person she imagined wanted to be near her the least.

Being almost a head taller than Emily, Kate could simply look around and act as though she were observing others in the cramped space. *I'm a New Yorker. Who needs personal space? I should be used to this, right?* Her self-confidence made it no farther than the useless musings, but she also tried to ignore every sensation associated with being so very close to Emily Stanton. Emily Jameson, it would be soon…She stopped the thought and closed her eyes. *Why did she have to come back?* The train lurched forward once again, and Emily's hand was forced against Kate's hip. She recoiled as though Kate were made of fire. Closing her eyes, Kate took a deep breath.

Kate simply couldn't help herself. As soon as she opened her eyes, no one on the train existed save the woman in front of her. She couldn't resist as she waited to meet Emily's eyes. She knew it would happen, and it did. Even if they didn't want it, they both knew then, as their eyes met, that a piece of the other had been found, even if the rest of them had changed with time. Life and time had molded them into who they were in that moment, but everything they once knew of each other was still there.

❖

Kate led Emily and Tommy through the park, the day surprisingly cool for a New York summer. Lush greenery cascaded in arcs above the path before them, and children ran and played as parents observed from benches. Kate waited and followed the couple, snapping a few shots as they strolled along. Using her own style of documentation, she sometimes rushed in front of them, taking a few more. She caught Emily observing her.

"I'm sure I'll get at least one good one out of all of these, no?" Kate asked. She just *had* to see the real smile once today. Damn the consequences. Tommy looked skeptical and a bit angry at her presumptuous joking, but smiled down at Emily when he heard her laugh. *There it is.* It had only taken hours to lighten the mood. Emily's glance to her conveyed gratitude, but a reserved sadness lingered. Kate felt a primal need to remove even that small bit of sadness. Knowing not to stoke the fires of memory with Tommy, she tried another tactic.

"Do you remember when Art proposed to Allie?" Kate asked. "Tell Tommy about it."

The mere mention of the event set fire to Emily's enthusiasm. "Oh, don't you remember? It was actually right here in the park, a few weeks after you got here. Art had put the ring on a kite string…" Kate snapped a few photos of the conversation as Emily energetically rambled away, Tommy casually grasping her around the waist. He smiled down softly at her, and Kate could imagine just how he felt, to be listening but have the best of the story be in the telling and watching her.

You're being utterly ridiculous. Only a few hours into what should have been a professional atmosphere, and she was losing it to some sick infatuation with someone she had once considered the best of friends. It wasn't right now, and it hadn't been right to begin with, she reminded herself. She was on a job and had no business bringing up her own stories. These were her clients, and she resolved to be professional for the remainder of their time working together. Time she wanted to make as short as possible, she resolved.

"I think we got what we need," Kate said to them after they'd wandered the park a while longer.

"I'm sure they'll be wonderful," Emily said. Kate hated that the small compliment meant so much to her.

"Yes, we look forward to previewing a selection before the wedding," Tommy added in a tone that seemed excruciatingly awkward in its attempt to be cordial.

"You should join us for dinner tonight," Emily suddenly blurted, "with Allie and Art." She immediately blushed and found something else interesting on the ground. Kate saw Tommy's arm around her waist tighten. "Yes, I'm sure they would love to see you, Kate."

Kate occupied herself with storing her gear, contemplating. When she looked up, she met Emily's eyes and realized she would take any excuse to be near her. Emily looked as though she was fighting a battle between her heart and mind. Kate had seen it before. When her eyes drifted to Tommy, however, she saw an almost pained expression, as though he were attempting to keep control of the situation.

As her heart screamed for her to take the offer, to give in and take every moment with Emily that she could, she knew she shouldn't. She wanted to repair the damage they had both done, finish what was left unresolved. Every fiber of her pulled her helplessly toward the opportunity to just find out a little more about Emily, how the last years had changed her. But one moment would leave her longing for another until she drowned in the need to have her in her life.

"I…" She resumed her mindless fidgeting with her gear. "I need to get into the lab to process these. I should get a head start on it so they're printed for the big day."

"Yes, of course," Emily replied, blushing yet looking relieved, then—perhaps—disappointed?

"Enjoy the rest of your day. I'll have these prepared for next weekend." Kate forced a cordial smile and small wave. She turned and walked away before she allowed herself to reason further.

CHAPTER NINE

Four years earlier, 1942

Emily stifled the growing impulse to giggle at how nervous Art was, running through everything for the millionth time by mumbling to himself. Even Kate suppressed a grin at the nervous mess he was quickly becoming. They were at his parents' corner market, waiting on Art to get everything together for the event coming up in the park. He had mapped out each part, and although Emily found it a bit over the top, she wholeheartedly agreed to help, in part because the idea of a surprise proposal was hers to begin with.

When, however, Art refused any help in preparation at the last minute, she and Kate resorted to perusing the shelves of the store and pacing around the crowded space. It apparently was large enough that every time Emily looked over at Kate, she blushed and looked down at her feet like she was ashamed of herself, then found a corner to round just to avoid Emily.

Emily was still confused at what had happened since the afternoon she last saw her. After a week before, Emily had heard nothing from Kate and wondered what she had done wrong, so she resolved to find out.

"What exactly is your prob—"

"I can't get the right knot in this thing!" Art fumbled with the string of the kite he'd chosen. "How the hell..." He grunted as he fidgeted with the ring captured on the string of the kite, Emily and

Kate stopping their perusal as he struggled. Kate finally made eye contact, only to have an excuse to avoid her as they stepped over to investigate what the problem was.

"All right, give it," Kate commanded. Emily was glad, as it looked like Art was about to have a hernia. She didn't wait for a response before snatching it from him. "What's the plan again?"

Emily guessed Kate was feigning annoyance as she expertly tied a knot that would hold the ring and easily be removed.

"I plan to meet her after my shift ends here, or at least she thinks that…and walk her from her parents' apartment to the park. I have a speech planned about all the spots she likes on that route… we walk it all the time. But she'll suspect something, I just know it. I'm going to mess it all up! Who takes an adult to fly kites?"

"Okay. Here's what's going to happen." Kate cut him off. "Allie is so in love with you, and so used to all your romantic shenanigans, she won't blink an eye."

"Emily, this whole surprise thing isn't a good idea. Maybe I shouldn't try to make a speech on the way there—"

"No, you shouldn't," Kate said. "You should have a conversation with her. Tell her all the things that you've told her before. Tell them again. Just because you have the rest of your life to show her those things doesn't mean you can't say them every single day. Make this just another day. The moment will take care of itself."

Art quieted but still looked hesitant.

"She's your best friend, right?" Kate asked. He smiled self-consciously to himself and nodded.

"So have a day out with her and then ask her to be there to do the same thing every day for the rest of your lives. You don't really control moments like these. You just hope for the best, go with the flow, and make the most out of them. If you're doing it with the person you love, it's always going to be special. And the two of you?"

Kate's eyes lit up. "I can't wait to find someone I don't even have to think about loving…my best friend. The one who you don't ever truly take your mind off, who enriches every moment…They challenge you, they argue with you and infuriate you one moment, but you can't wait to do the same to them because you love that part of them." She accidentally looked over at Emily and blushed once again. "They're the one who makes your friends go on overly sentimental rants when you're about to propose to them."

Emily, the entire time, found herself listening raptly as Kate calmed Art. Kate had such grand ideas of love. Emily saw it in Art and Allie but never thought of it for herself. Tommy was practical, albeit quite charming when he chose to be or propriety called for it, but going to this measure to ask someone to marry them? He would never think it necessary. He wouldn't even come with her to this event, claiming he wanted to go into the office to meet with a few of the other partners and introduce himself. Like he wouldn't have that opportunity tomorrow.

But all this coming from Kate? She had already realized the hopeless romantic that was hiding under the tough persona of this woman, but it had never so purely been expressed until that moment. Her thoughts wandered farther toward Kate instead of thinking of the man she knew would soon ask for her hand.

She watched Kate finish the knot, her hands sure, and her face remaining lit. A sensation struck Emily quickly and unexpectedly—a surge of something that closely resembled jealousy. Who was Kate thinking of? And more importantly, why in the world should or did she care? Instead of managing to pull her thoughts away, Emily was drawn farther into the train of thought.

Who would be the right person to complement her? She had never mentioned anyone, not that she had even known her for that long. It would be someone adventurous, someone willing to step out of the norm and take chances. They would have to keep up with her, for sure. *Good luck with that one.* Even as she inwardly laughed at the poor sucker, Emily thought to herself how she wanted more of those spur-of-the-moment experiences. She'd known her, what, only a few weeks? But when Kate had dropped off the face of the planet, she'd felt a void she had no idea what to do with, especially as it came with no reason she could think of.

Then Emily suddenly realized she wanted to be the one to pick arguments with Kate, go on inane escapades with her, and it occurred to her that Kate was quickly becoming her closest friend. She didn't want to lose that, and she wanted to know what had changed. It had something to do with Tommy's arrival, she was sure of it, and once this whole event was over, she planned to find out just what it was. Then it struck her. Was Kate jealous of Tommy?

When she looked up from her musings to find Kate looking into her eyes, the heat of embarrassment instantly replaced the fire of jealousy. How much she liked it. She had never given it thought before. She fought to scramble the pieces that were falling together in her mind. No way Kate should have a reason to envy Tommy or be ashamed of her friendship with Emily. The fear of losing Kate as a friend, confusion at the craving her mind stirred to have Kate look at her the way she just had, and the embarrassment of letting her mind wander so wantonly at the thought of it all bombarded her senses and set her mind reeling. She swallowed hard and diverted her gaze.

"You should get going, no?" she asked Art. "We'll walk you out."

The three of them left with Art's gear in hand and set him on his way.

After an awkward, silent walk to the park, Emily and Kate scoped out their spot among the littered field on the warm summer day. Everyone with the luxury of a workless day had chosen this spot to unwind, if only for an hour or two. Blankets and picnics scattered across the grass, kites flew high into the sky, and dogs ran freely for sticks thrown by their owners.

After spreading out their own blanket, Emily pulled out her favorite fedora, sunglasses, and the latest *LIFE* magazine from her bag and put them on.

"Are you a trying to be private eye?" Kate asked with a grin.

Emily huffed. "Do you want Allie to see us and ruin the whole thing? You're the creeper with the camera."

Kate looked down at her camera and grimaced. "Touché." She

looked across the field. "Oh, there they are." She pointed a bit away as Allie and Art walked arm in arm to an open spot. Art's nervousness was visible even from their vantage point. Emily peeked over the top of her magazine. Kate smiled just a bit and snapped the shutter on Emily.

"Them! Photograph them!" Emily squealed with a scowl at Kate. She raised her hands in mock surrender and lined up the couple as Art nervously prepared the kites.

The amusement on Allie's face was as visible as Art's nervousness. He bolted off to get the first kite up in the air and in a matter of minutes had it flying. He handed over the spindle to Allie and prepared his own. Emily and Kate could see him take a deep breath and look down at the kite for the ring. But it wasn't there. Then Art clearly realized he had given the wrong kite to Allie, and at any moment she could find the ring before he was able to make the speech he had so thoroughly prepared for.

Kate had to stifle a nervous laugh watching his predicament as he took off even faster, hoping to get the speech off before Allie noticed the prize. But it was too late. Looking over at Allie, they both saw the moment she realized something was on the string as it flew up. She pulled the kite out of the heights and was already looking up at Art, ring in hand, when he turned.

Although Kate couldn't hear what Art was saying, they knew that it was from the heart and not a memorized exposition. When he got down on one knee, everyone within sight of the two turned to attention, and Kate snapped away. Cheers erupted moments later as the two dissolved into their own world for just that moment. No one else mattered.

"I think you got it," Emily said as Kate searched for a new roll of film. Kate quickly replaced the old for the new, and rolled her eyes.

"It's one moment I think they'll remember even without the photos," she said simply, continuing her work. "But it's nice to see two people who love each other so much and get to share it with other people." Kate simply stood and walked over to the couple, Emily running to catch up.

"You have to come with us to show my mother!" Allie insisted. Art was beaming, his arm around Allie's waist.

"I do wish I could, but Kate and I have somewhere we have to be," Emily replied, resulting in Kate's incredulous and confused expression.

"Do we now?" Kate asked.

"Yes. I need you to come with me somewhere, and these two need to have some time alone before dealing with Aunt Jane."

So after one more congratulatory hug, Kate watched the couple stroll away arm in arm, happier than anyone in the world in that moment, and wondered where the hell Emily was dragging her off to.

"You don't actually have to come with me, but I do have a thing I wasn't planning to go to but—"

"Sure," Kate responded. "I don't have anything better to do at the moment, though I can think of other things I *should* do." She probably shouldn't have accepted, as she was trying so hard to distance herself. Not that the last few days had been any help whatsoever in doing so. The whole day she had been trying to be cordial without giving in to every urge to taunt Emily just to see her smile, and that resulted in the distance she knew Emily was noticing. This…whatever it was…was wrong and she just needed to get a handle on it. So obviously the logical thing to do was go with the woman at the mere suggestion. But she was helpless to turn her down and she knew it.

❖

As she and Kate made the short trip to the Village, Emily contemplated how to broach the subject of Kate's distance without projecting her annoying and completely ludicrous suspicions. She couldn't assume anything, but she also wanted to know if she had done something to offend the woman or make her angry. Her emotion never seemed like anger, however, more a sense of embarrassment or hesitation that Emily simply didn't understand. She thought of her suspicion regarding Tommy and realized he hadn't crossed her mind yet today. She just needed to make things right with her friend, and that was more important than Tommy's excuse not to participate this afternoon. Why was she comparing them?

Regardless, Emily never got the chance to bring up the subject, and Kate even attempted a few jokes along the way, presumably to break the awkward silence, but they fell flat. "I suppose I should ask where we're going?" asked Kate.

Emily hesitated. "I don't actually know...I mean, I know the location, but not what for..."

Kate stared at Emily as if to say *why am I not surprised?* "Is it some anti-photographer cult, and I'm the annual sacrifice to the paint gods?"

Emily could only roll her eyes. They came to a stop at the small art gallery Emily had discovered a week prior.

Kate stopped. "You're joking, right?"

Emily was completely confused and growing more reluctant to go in. Who knew what would await, if anything. It could have been the ravings of an old man in a crazy shop, trying to randomly lure her back. Kate shook her head and charged into the store like she knew the place. Emily bolted after her, stunned.

Unlike the calm, almost abandoned nature of the store the last time, as Emily followed Kate to the studio area, she saw that every table in the small space was surrounded by a pack of children hovering over every manner of art supply. At least thirty children of varying ages were standing and sitting while creating art. Some talked with each other, and others were off in their own worlds. Emily recognized the feeling immediately as she noticed the young girl from her last visit, Mia, entranced in her latest work.

Kate walked into the room, tapped Mia on the shoulder, and gave her a high five. *What the hell?*

"You came!" Mia shouted excitedly to Emily when she approached them.

"Emily, meet my kid sister, Mia."

"Why *kid* sister? Jeez," Mia said.

Emily looked between the two of them and realized why Mia had looked so familiar. The similarities were uncanny, both in their features and apparently in their attitudes.

Emily looked around for the eccentric owner she had met last time and found him with a teenager at the back, demonstrating a technique in shading on the sketch pad he held.

"Ah! You made it," Alfonzo looked up and shouted above the commotion around him. Emily returned a polite smile. "Katie, I thought you weren't coming today," he added when he saw Kate.

Kate nervously rubbed the back of her neck. "Well, it seems you coaxed Emily here into coming and managed to get me here anyways, Gramps."

"Welcome, Emily. Kate, show her around."

She gave Emily a pleading look, apparently her only lifeline in her self-created sea of craziness.

Kate guided them away from the children for a moment, over to the wall of artwork and studied it. She pointed to the drawing pinned at the far side of the covered wall.

"How did you know that was mine?" Emily asked.

"I recognize your style, of course." Kate grinned. "Not that it's the newest addition up there or anything." She winked. Kate really had recognized Emily's style immediately though. *She's incredible.*

Emily had *so many* questions for Kate later. "And which one exactly is yours, may I ask?"

"Which one do you want to see?" Alfonzo reappeared. He pointed to what was (at least Emily suspected and hoped), a child's sketch of a camera.

Emily stifled her laughter, and Kate turned even redder.

"He finally let me hang something I *prefer.*" She pointed to the few small photographs in the corner. One was of a man under the chassis of a car, wrench in his hand, smiling at the camera. Emily looked at Kate, who was gazing at the photo with softness in her eyes, and pride. Emily thought he must have been an interesting person, Kate's father. Her sister and her grandfather no doubt were, she was already learning.

"We should get to helping, I think," Kate said.

She turned and nearly knocked over a little boy.

"He's been interrogating me about photography every weekend for the last year he's been coming in," Kate whispered to Emily. "Apparently your opinion means more than mine though."

He held up his drawing on the coloring pages he'd been given for Emily's examination.

"Uhh…nice job, bud," Emily said, looking down at what was a group of stick figures, a square and triangle house, and a meticulously drawn attempt at what Emily assumed was a dog. She pulled her focus back to his beaming face while waiting for her approval. He seemed harmless enough.

"Come over here with us!" He grabbed her hand and pulled her back over to his table. Kate left her then, entering a conversation with a teenager who was showing her something on a separate sheet of paper, letting the girl try it on her own. Emily watched with fascination until the little boy interrupted her musing.

"My dad has a camera like Kate's. He never lets me play with it, even though he doesn't take any pictures. He says it's not a toy and too expensive for kids."

"Because it's not a toy for kids," Kate responded. Apparently, he was trying to butter Emily up and get Kate to let him play with it. "But it's a lot of fun. I'm sure he'll let you when you get older."

"Are you an artist?" asked Mia from across the table.

"She's actually quite a talented one, as a matter of fact, but don't tell her I said so," Kate chimed in before Emily could respond.

"Hey, little man. I bet today's the day Kate shows you that camera, eh?" Emily said.

She watched terror sweep back across Kate's features, but with the briefest eye contact with her, she saw Kate squelch it.

"Sure," she responded with a look toward Emily. "But it's not as easy as *some people* think."

"I can learn fast," Mia exclaimed. "I'm coming too. You promised you'd let me try it finally." She jumped off her stool and followed Kate with the little guy, leaving Emily sitting alone.

After a while Emily ventured outside to the alley next to the store, where Kate was now surrounded by a few of the older children.

While she still wouldn't let the littlest one have her camera, she did let Mia. She held it as Kate pointed down the alley and gave her calm instructions. Every child who asked a question, regardless of what it might be, got a one-on-one explanation. It was obviously a chance for her to share her passion with someone who wouldn't judge or question it. Each of them had an eager mind, and Kate willingly passed along her knowledge. Emily noticed immediately that her earlier tension was gone, and in its place was the relaxed, energetic, engaged woman Emily enjoyed being with.

"So see if you stop the lens down and close the aperture, less light gets in, and…"

"A darker image," Mia answered. She was catching on quickly, just as she claimed she would. Kate surely realized her sister had very good instincts and could be quite talented at yet another art form.

"Now don't go letting her spoil all her talent on taking pictures all the time," Emily called over. Kate shook her head and returned her attention to the group.

Alfonzo came up to stand beside Emily. She said, "I thought you had 'people' who would be interested in my work," a question lingering there.

"It seems as though quite a few are interested, no?" he asked, observing the group himself. Emily still thought him strange. How difficult would it have been to give her the details about what he'd asked her to come for? Although she came anyway, didn't she, and she admitted he was intriguing, but very strange indeed. She liked the man.

"All right, everyone. Time to head home for today," he called out.

A chorus of groans sprang from the group, including a slight slump of the shoulders from Kate. Mia was the last to leave, walking over with Kate while she asked a continuous string of questions.

"Why are you asking me everything now? Calm down," Kate murmured in obvious annoyance.

"Because you're actually answering stuff and being all nice," Mia snapped back. "Trying to show off or something?"

"Go away." That was all Kate said.

Mia laughed and sprinted inside.

"Next week you should show her the darkroom," Emily suggested.

"It's all I can do to keep her from opening the damn door and letting light in all the time..."

"She seems really smart. And talented, for that matter. Must run in the family."

Kate smiled at the compliment.

"I mean, your grandfather has to be talented to own the shop, right?" Emily winked.

Alfonzo met with them inside. "You do this each week?" Emily asked.

"Sure do. We have a few artists who come in sporadically, but it's a wonderful creative outlet for the neighborhood children. Today was one of the first Katie was going to miss. Glad we got her here."

"Well, it's a wonderful idea." She could understand why artists would take time with the children she'd met today. She looked forward to coming here again to share what she loved and was overjoyed to see the brightness this experience had brought to Kate's eyes. Perhaps it was a small repayment for the wonderful times Kate had already shown her.

Emily guessed that Kate had apparently never had the opportunity to share the Saturday workshops with anyone, and now that she had someone to tell about it, she couldn't seem to stop talking.

"Mia is such a fast learner. She was already picking up on metering the light, framing..." Kate went on and on about each of the children she had been working with as the two of them walked up Fifth Avenue. Emily didn't have the heart to stop her enthusiastic rambling. "I mean, don't tell Mia I'm raving about her, or I'll never hear the end of it..."

She needed to confront Kate. She'd avoided her the last few

days, as she'd planned to earlier in the day, but at every opportunity to sway the subject, she would look over and see the spark in Kate's eyes, and all she could do was stare. She couldn't halt that happiness. She watched, listening as Kate went on and on about the talent each of the children had, and how they deserved a chance to pursue it.

As she spoke about the kids, Emily couldn't help but wonder if Kate was subconsciously thinking of herself. Kate deserved the same opportunities, didn't she? Kate worked hard each day for any chance to be the artist she truly was. She'd never met anyone as passionate as the woman beside her, and she thought of the opportunities Kate had earned. Not been given, no. For all the teasing about her craft, Emily could see such talent in Kate. She wanted nothing more than for Kate to be able to live that passion; to share her work, have people see and appreciate it as she did. So many lived each week, each day, hoping for moments of enjoyment. So few managed to sync their hearts with the necessities of life. Emily considered her own path, but she fought not to fall into that train of thought.

Instead, she tried to focus on Kate's words, but she was still chattering about the day. At this point her enthusiasm had found its way to the prospect of the darkroom and the promise of teaching how to use it, especially to Mia. Emily nodded politely and walked along the cool city street. A northern breeze blew in as the sky clouded and the sun was hidden behind the gathering wall of gray. Emily welcomed a respite from the sunny onslaught. She simply enjoyed being in the moment, and she specifically enjoyed being in the moment with the woman next to her.

"Perhaps we should catch the bus for a bit. It looks like rain," Kate suggested out of nowhere.

"I think we're okay, and it's so nice out. The bus will just be crowded and stuffy." Emily couldn't help but want to be in the middle of everything and, she admitted, to be with Kate a bit longer.

"I've been meaning to find out if we can get a supplier discount on film stock…" Kate picked up her train of thought and continued her musings as they walked. The sky darkened and the wind picked up, but Emily decided it was better than the bus alternative.

As she thought of finally changing the subject, she looked

over at Kate in profile and listened, realizing her constant stream of thoughts wasn't annoying in the least. She watched the sleek hands animate her enthusiasm, the camera in one of them simply an extension of her. They were hands that worked hard each day, meticulous ones that moved with purpose. *Hands that would feel wonderful—* Fire flashed through Emily, and she immediately looked away, shaking her head but unable to dispel the thought. Where in the world had that come from? Images assaulted her as she blushed profusely, Kate oblivious to it all.

Images of fingertips brushing across her cheek, arms wrapped around her waist like the day at the beach washed over her mind like a tidal wave, and every interaction they'd had suddenly took on a different light. Emily thought of that first night walking from the club to Allie's and how, although tipsy, she could hardly resist leaning into the strong form beside her. She was startled to think her fascination with those deep, dark eyes was something more than simple appreciation. It was all just coming from her ridiculous assumption earlier about Kate and her *jealousy*, nothing more. She wasn't actually thinking that way. *She* wasn't that way.

"What exactly was wrong with you the other day?" Emily cut Kate off mid-sentence. She immediately regretted the anger she heard in her own voice as she met Kate's startled expression. She looked helpless, like a scolded puppy, and Emily once again stifled the urge to trail her fingers across the nape of her neck, pull her in close and erase the hurt she'd just caused. That urge in turn made her even more agitated.

"I don't know what you mean." Kate dropped her eyes. "And where is this coming from?"

"Don't give me that," snapped Emily. "The minute Tommy showed up, you became a total stranger."

"Me?!" Kate snapped back. The two of them halted, now a roadblock in the middle of the Fifth Avenue sidewalk. Kate hesitated and then returned her surge of anger at being accused of whatever Emily was getting at. "I…I wanted to give you time with him…and not have to be your tour guide in the process." She fumbled for an argument but was quickly coming up very short.

"So explain why you dropped off the face of the planet for the next week."

"I'm not responsible for you. I have a life too, you know! You act completely helpless all the time, depending on someone else to walk you around and tell you what to do." The tiniest indication of pain appeared in Emily's demeanor before her glare returned. Kate wished back the comment, but her stubbornness kept her from apologizing.

She'd seen firsthand the independent, wonderful woman that Emily was. It was one of the things she admired most about her. That and the gorgeous eyes that were now filled with fury. *Not again!* She'd been fighting off the images her mind had produced all week. It just made her all the angrier.

Tension built between the two as they stared at each other.

Crack-boom!

"You have got to be joking!" Kate exclaimed as the thunder collapsed the sky around them, rain pouring down out of nowhere. The heated conversation cooled little with the rain, as their own charge held between them. Instead of standing in the rain and potentially doing something she'd regret, Kate looked around and grabbed Emily's wrist, guiding her down the block and up the stairs of the magnificent cathedral adjacent to them. Grand stone arches adorned the towering oak doors and provided an overhang from the falling rain.

"Can't even get herself out of the goddamned rain…" Kate mumbled to herself, pacing around with her own inner fury. Emily didn't miss the jibe and threw her the most vicious of glares. The other grumblings Emily must have caught pieces of included *small town…middle of nowhere…stubborn.* Kate held out her hand and looked up at the still-falling sky, then pointedly turned to face Emily, who stood arms crossed looking out at nothing. "Should have taken the goddamned bus like I—"

And then she stopped—because of the sudden, fierce, molten press of Emily Stanton's lips to hers. All sense of reason fled, and the only thought that remained was the realization that a beautiful, stubborn, and altogether intriguing woman was kissing her. Each of her senses was filled with the exquisite sensation, and she immediately wanted more.

She kissed her back. God, did she kiss her back. Emily had pressed them against the wall of the church, hidden in shadow. She wrapped a hand at the nape of Emily's neck as they melted into each other. When she felt hands reach out to her, grasping at her waist, clenching her drenched shirt, fire erupted deep inside her. A moan escaped Emily's lips, and Kate thought she might go mad with wanting.

In that same small, fleeting moment, all the world around them quieted. It was their moment, alone and sheltered from the storm around them.

As quickly as she had kissed her, Emily pulled back, and in her eyes Kate saw every possible emotion play out. Their gaze locked for what seemed like an eternity, their chests heaving in shock. Kate dared not move and break the spell. Emily's gaze flickered to Kate's lips, and she leaned forward a fraction, causing excitement to surge in Kate, who was still beyond reason. She wanted those lips again. But Emily, as if suddenly pulled from a trance, jerked back. They locked eyes once more, and then Emily turned and walked away.

CHAPTER TEN

The rain continued mercilessly for the entire hour of Emily's walk home, her thoughts as chaotic as the world around her. Crowds parted as she bolted ahead, earning more than a few sideways glances from other pedestrians.

What the hell did you just do? Have you gone mad? She was certain she had done just that. She had kissed another woman, in public, in broad daylight for that matter. That could not have been her own action. She tried to reason with herself. *It sure got her to shut up, didn't it? Yes, that was why I did it. Infuriating woman…For once I got the last word—well, in a way.* God help her, she wanted to do it again. She'd like to shut her up the next time she saw her and every time after that.

"Damn it!" she yelled to herself, drawing the attention of the mother and son walking past huddled under an umbrella. She blushed and covered her mouth. She surely looked like an insane vagabond at this point. On top of that, she'd sworn more in the last hour than she could remember ever doing before.

Arriving at the door, she paused. She couldn't justify her anger at Kate completely, as much as she wanted to. After all, Emily had initiated the kiss. She was angry, she was confused, she was nervous at what she'd done but, she realized, not at Kate herself. In fact, the thought of her smile, her antics, everything that was *Kate* sent warmth spreading through Emily. She truly was a wonderful, kind, intriguing person. What if she'd ruined that? But Kate had returned the kiss, no? *Why did she have to go and do that?* Kate should have put a stop to it as soon as it started. She claimed to be the responsible one…

Why did Kate kiss her back? *And boy, did she kiss me back… Stop it!* Emily thought back on their time together. They had become fast friends over the last month, and in all that time, Kate had been engaging and open, showing Emily the most important pieces of her world, and of herself. The last week, however, she had been shut off from Emily, and it hurt, although she supposed she had little room to complain. She had Tommy…Perhaps Kate really was jealous. Emily assumed it was a matter of friendship, since it didn't seem as though Kate let many people in, but maybe it was more than that.

Emily did not want to lose her friendship with Kate. They never had to talk about this whole ordeal again, for all she cared. She simply had to find a way to stop imagining those full lips moving against her own, the sleek curve of hips beneath her hands, deep, dark eyes staring back at her from across the room…She banged her head against the brownstone door. *What a nightmare.*

"There she is!" Emily heard her aunt say from the kitchen as she stepped in. She braced herself.

"Where have you been, darling—" Tommy asked, appearing from around the corner. He stopped abruptly at the steaming, soggy mess that was Emily.

"Emily, dear, are you all right?" Her aunt rushed in, looking her over from head to toe. "Allie, fetch a towel!" Allie appeared at the top of the stairs with a look of extremely confused amusement, made questioning eye contact with Emily, and produced a towel from the closet. Emily knew she would have to explain something to Allie in the not-so-distant future.

"I'm all right. Just got caught in the storm. It was quite sudden."

"Darling, it's been raining for the last hour." Tommy laughed. He was likely worried.

"What are you doing here, dear?" she asked, wanting nothing

more than to curl up and sleep away the remainder of the day. Looking at Tommy also terrified her after what she'd done.

"Well, I made reservations at The Forrester tonight, of course! Just the two of us. Don't you remember?"

The repercussions of her earlier actions were already coming to fruition. She was now faced with having to spend a romantic evening with Tommy, who had surely planned the whole evening in detail. Although he was for the majority of the time quite a distractible and all-around busy individual, he did occasionally take the time and heartfelt effort to romance Emily, and his charm was quite effective. But tonight of all nights? She just wanted to be alone.

"Of course, of course." She pressed a smile on her face. "I'll take a moment to put myself back together, but I'll hurry." She turned away from the group surrounding her as if in a trance and went to go get ready. She could do little to avoid the commitment without causing suspicion, or being rude for that matter. At least Tommy had made the effort. Perhaps this was a quick chance to turn around what she'd done and move past it. *No need to actually talk about it, right?*

But she had no moment alone, as Allie followed her into the bathroom. "So where is your *fiancé*?" Emily asked, hoping the question would distract her from being questioned.

"We're going out in a bit. He needed to help close up the shop." Emily looked over to find her twirling the ring on her finger. "It was the perfect day, wasn't it?" She had such stars in her eyes that Emily could barely contemplate it had occurred all in the same day.

"How was your afternoon? What did you invite Kate to?" she asked, leaning against the doorframe, arms crossed.

"Oh, um…An art…workshop. It was quite interesting." She fumbled through her sentence.

"Right. An art exhibition in the rain?"

"Why are you so inquisitive all the sudden?!" Emily snapped before catching herself. Allie was momentarily taken aback at the uncharacteristic edge but then seemed to realize something was wrong.

Allie's eyes widened as if she had been struck. "Just wondering why you look like a sodden street cat, and an angry one, I might add."

"I'm sorry, Allie. It really has been a wonderful day, just..." *with a pretty wonderful kiss*—she blushed in embarrassment and anger, "just...long. I completely forgot this date as well." Allie said nothing further, simply shook her head, gave her a look that said *if you need to talk,* and disappeared. Allie might be the one person she could share her rebellious thoughts with, but she didn't want to have them at all. *If anyone, I should be telling them to a priest.*

Finally alone, she took a minute to dry and warm herself. She quickly changed, fixed her hair and applied a bit of makeup, and scurried down to meet Tommy, who seemed to wait patiently, but Emily knew he was anxious to be on their way. He sat at the kitchen table with Allie and her aunt Jane, who conversed animatedly, Allie once again displaying her new ring to the other two. Emily caught a very smooth compliment to Allie from Tommy, who managed not to be presumptuous or flirtatious, but altogether charming. She once again contemplated the man's ability to compliment and make one feel like the most glamorous star to grace the earth.

"You look stunning, my love," he said and gave her a chaste kiss on the cheek. "I'm quite the lucky man," he added in a whisper. She blushed with shame at the thought of her actions and his oblivion to them, but he must have assumed her reaction innocent. The brief glance Emily caught from Allie as they left told her she would soon face another interrogation, even though Allie was having the best day of her life.

In true Tommy fashion, a town car waited for them as they left. Before she knew it, he was escorting her into one of the most celebrated dining establishments in the city, new and trendy. She knew that to Tommy it would be just another night on the town. Normally it would be for her as well, but now it didn't seem to hold the same appeal. She wanted something real, something simple for once.

"...And Mr. Jacobs, Ed, is pulling me over to the Reese case next week, although the court date is set for Wednesday with Allan. I never imagined being this involved so soon. Have I told you about the Reese case?" He turned to Emily, who had been staring out the window. She quickly looked over, realizing she had missed most of the monologue.

"Oh. No, you haven't." She slapped an interested look onto her face, once again feeling guilty for not paying attention.

"Actually? Never mind," he stated, a smile forming on his lips. "I'll tell you another time. Tonight is just the two of us, no shop talk." He put his arm around her and held her close. Although she understood his enthusiasm and genuinely wanted to know more about his days, Emily leaned into him, grateful for the opportunity to just be with Tommy the person, not Tommy the future lawyer.

The car came to a stop just outside the restaurant, and before the driver or concierge could, Tommy jumped from the car to open Emily's door with a sweeping, overly dramatic gesture. Emily laughingly took his hand just as a young man in a polished army uniform nearly knocked Tommy over.

The man in question was part of a huge group of people their age, decked out in military uniforms or sports paraphernalia, but all in an excited rush. Although the group barely noticed, and one of the girls yelled at him, the soldier apologized in passing. They hurried down the subway stairs, and Emily saw baseball gloves on some, others with ball caps. The shades of each blue hat were barely noticeable, as a few were the dark navy and white New York Yankees, while others sported the royal Dodgers emblem atop their heads.

"Darling, are you okay?" Emily finally asked after Tommy ceased to stare at the group as if in a trance. He looked to her for a moment, silently, before responding.

"Let's go to the game," he said. Emily was shocked. Tommy never deviated from his plans. Ever. "Come on." He smiled, grabbed her hand, and followed the crowd before she could agree. Into the subway, they followed the group.

Over the course of the crowded ride on the train, Tommy acquired a few friends from the group. Given the warm and unsolicited welcome offered Emily and Tommy, it was clear the group had clearly partaken of a few drinks beforehand. One couple gladly took the two of them under their wing, but were supporting opposing teams and tried desperately to sway Emily and Tommy to their side. After the stuffy, congested, but hilariously fun train ride, the masses emerged in front of Yankee Stadium in the Bronx.

"Grab your tickets and sit with us," Rita, the girl who Emily inferred was informally in charge of the group, told them.

"We—they'll probably be in the nosebleeds at this point," Tommy replied.

Rita's boyfriend Tate chimed in. "Ha! They can barely fill the lower decks these days. Half the regular season team is overseas."

"The Clipper's still around, better be on his game tonight, is all I'm sayin'." Emily looked at Rita as if she were speaking a foreign language.

"Joe DiMaggio. She'd leave me for him if given the chance." Tate grinned. "Surprised the draft board hasn't hauled him off yet."

Tommy stiffened. "Let's get in there, then."

Just like her first impressions of the city, Emily was fascinated by the culture of the place where she found herself. She had only ever been to one baseball game, in Boston, when she was eleven or twelve years old. The atmosphere here was so similar, even with fewer people swarming about. The war truly did interfere with the great American pastime but would never fully stifle it.

This game was also one of the very first games ever played after dark at Yankee Stadium. Over a thousand brand-new, cutting-edge-of-technology floodlights filled the stadium with the glow of daylight, keeping the small but excited crowd intrigued.

Her other sense of wonder came with Tommy's complete disregard for their previous plans and his willingness to drop them for a plan-less adventure. She couldn't figure out his change in fundamental personality in the moment, but also didn't wish to question it. She liked being impulsive, not knowing what to expect next. The trait was attractive—she unsuccessfully attempted to hold the thought of comparison to someone else impulsive she knew. *Focus.* Tommy was being endearing and wonderful tonight, and she refused to spoil that novelty. She really did wish to know what had spurred it, however.

They did indeed wind up with excellent seating, right in front of first base, only a few rows from the front, and in the company of genuinely welcoming individuals. The crowd was as diverse as the city itself, from the old to the young, people from every walk of life. And nearly a third of the stadium seats were filled with those in uniform. Emily looked at Tommy, only to catch him almost nervously glancing at each of them. Just as she was about to ask if he was okay, the announcer's booming voice filled the stadium with the lineup.

"Ladies and gentlemen, we would like to take a moment to remember our boys overseas and thank those joining us here tonight. I can see all our strapping young soldiers, sailors, and marines out there. Welcome! Thank you, gentlemen, for your service!" The crowd erupted in applause and cheers for all those around them. Emily cheered along until she looked again at Tommy, who had tensed like she had never seen him do before.

"Just a reminder to all you folks that a portion of the proceeds from this year's World Series is being donated to the National War Fund, USO, American Red Cross, and other organizations in support of the nation's war effort." The announcer went on to name just a few of the major-league players who had traded their bats and gloves for rifles. Thousands of minor-league players had made the trade already, and the list grew by the day. "Get out there and support our boys and our great U S of A!"

After the national anthem, the game began. During the singing, Emily glanced at Tommy, who stood with his hand over his heart while every one of the proud soldiers around him saluted. His expression was almost pained. Throughout the beginning of the game he was silent, a completely different person than earlier in the evening. Emily could tell he was utterly uncomfortable, even as they were having a wonderful time. Emily felt that, for the second time of the day, she needed to find out what was wrong with someone who was acting completely out of character around her.

"Hey." She leaned into him with an arm around his waist. He visibly tensed and sighed. He put his arm around her but remained lost in thought. "Thanks for the wild idea to come tonight."

"I went to the recruitment office," he said after a moment, looking out at the game. Emily gazed up at him, and he reluctantly made eye contact.

Every emotion Emily had imagined when Art told her he was enlisting came back, but now it wasn't just a friend or someone she heard about in the paper. She hadn't questioned his reluctance to enlist, as he was in school still, nearly ready to become the lawyer he'd always wished to be. It was his passion, but often she had to answer for him as to why he wouldn't join the rest of America's young men. She didn't feel shame necessarily, but she did find it difficult to explain at times. She thought that eventually he might be drafted and then have no say, but, this, choosing to go on his own, much like the night as a whole, was shockingly uncharacteristic.

Now she would be the girl back home waiting for him, the faithful little wife-to-be—she shuddered internally. But this wasn't about her. It was about Tommy making a decision that would change his life. Still, she was in awe that Tommy would actually enlist. He was charming, respectful, intelligent, but had never shown the courage or machismo she saw in so many others their age, many of whom had flooded recruitment centers the day after the attacks on Pearl Harbor just a few months prior. He had kept quiet about it, and frankly Emily assumed he would never serve voluntarily.

"I'm ineligible." Hands in his pockets, he stared out at nothing. "The last seizure and my medications put me past the disability acceptance percentage."

Emily had completely forgotten that factor as being a disqualifier for service. Tommy regularly and easily managed his condition. Anger and remorse for him flared up, and she realized how he must feel. She instantly felt ashamed that she'd assumed he lacked loyalty or courage.

"I tried, Em. I want you to know that. I knew they wouldn't take me, but I had to try. They even said if the war progresses, standards might change for eligibility..." He was silent for a moment. "I've always, and still want to be, a man you deserve."

She searched for the right response, her heart breaking for

him and the level of guilt she was sure he was enduring. "Look at me." She pulled his face toward her. "It's Uncle Sam's loss. I am so incredibly proud that you stepped up to volunteer." She kissed him softly. "It was a brave thing to do."

She took a moment, making sure he understood what she was saying. "Thank you for telling me. That took courage as well. It's nothing to be ashamed of."

He nodded, and Emily could see a huge weight lift from his shoulders. It wasn't the entire burden of guilt, she knew, but perhaps some of it could lighten his spirits. It amazed Emily how her view of a person could change with one revelation. She knew him well enough to realize he would feel ashamed each and every time mention of the draft or volunteering came to him, but she hoped that maybe he would confide in her a bit more about this and other things in the future.

By the seventh-inning stretch, both the New York Yankees and the Brooklyn Dodgers had respectively gained one fan each. Emily couldn't help but root for the Yanks, claiming they were the true gem of the city, while Tommy boasted that Brooklyners had a fiery spirit and superior baseball team. The entire group that surrounded them found both arguments ridiculous, but their differences entertained a lot of the nearby spectators. Multiple stadium beverages aided in the heated, ridiculous debate between them.

With every inning the lively stadium announcer took to the mic. "And some very exciting news for the world of baseball, ladies and gentlemen. Mr. Philip Wrigley has recently announced sponsorship of the newly formed All American Women's Baseball League, which will kick off its first 1943 season in the spring!"

"Well, Jim, this should be a great substitute for our boys in the minor leagues who are overseas." The stadium announcer's sidekick chimed in. "But is it *baseball?* Or softball? As a few fans know, there's a thriving women's softball league—"

"No, Bill. This is a league of lovely ladies playing by official baseball rules! But for now, we've got the Yankees up by two, starting at the top of the eighth. Let's get back to it."

As quickly as the league was mentioned, it was over, but many in the crowd continued to discuss the idea of women being professional athletes in America's most popular sport. Although not popular or well known, thriving women's softball teams played across the country and had done so for quite some time. Emily thought about their presence and enjoyed the idea of finding a way to do what you love professionally. She assumed, though, that those girls had other jobs to support them while they defied society's expectations. The idea was thrilling.

"I'm sure you have an opinion on that, no?" Tommy asked, for once knowing her thoughts quite well. "I suppose it's a daring thing to take up a man's job, especially an athlete's, don't you think?"

Was Tommy goading her? She took the bait.

"Well, apparently more than a few people think it'll work just fine, since they're funding an entire national league."

"We'll have to go to a game then!" he said with a grin, getting the response he expected. "We'll have some time before the war ends, I'd imagine."

"And what's the war got to do with it?" Emily knew the reason he'd give, but she wanted to question it. Unlike her banter with a certain someone she refused to name, she found herself legitimately angry at his goading.

Tommy seemed to be forcing the issues and acting as though he agreed, while she knew he was never fully invested in his opinions. He could easily be swayed one way or the other in a moment and then seemingly forget the conversation and return to his original way of thinking the very next time it was brought up. Still, she couldn't help but engage with him.

"Where do you expect all these players who're away from home to go when they come back? Are they going to be the new housewives?" He laughed, in a way that was obvious he feared he'd just inserted his foot in his own mouth. "But really. What do you expect? They're professional athletes. No one's going to have time to watch women's baseball once the minor leagues pick back up."

"And what about every other career that women have already stepped up to do since the war started?" Emily fired back. "They just lose jobs they've learned, trained for, and quite frankly did damn well at?"

"No!" He sounded nervous again. "They'll just have to make room, I suppose. It's not an insult for them to take up their responsibilities back at home once the war ends. Someone has to, and people respect mothers and wives, don't you think?"

"We're expected to make room from the positions we've worked for, then, and give them up if a man needs to take it, you're saying."

"Why are you worried? It doesn't really apply to you, does it? It's the way society is, Em, I'm not saying I agree with it!" He took a stance of innocence.

All the relief and endearment for Tommy that Emily had felt just a short time ago had vanished, and tension mounted in its absence. If they stopped now, she could get past it, and she didn't feel like arguing on a wonderful night such as this. She knew he didn't mean it the way it was coming out, but she also didn't want to let him off the hook.

"Look at your friend Kate, for example."

"What?" Emily flung her head around to stare at him, arms crossed. He really was going to keep it going, even though she knew he could tell she wasn't enjoying the conversation. He was by no means as helpless as he'd acted just then, but had clearly struck a nerve with this argument. He was trying hopelessly to prove his point, even as he dug himself deeper into the hole he'd created. This was the last turn Emily had wanted the conversation to take.

"She doesn't seem like a person to give up what she's worked for! She's a photographer, no? I saw the camera the other day."

"She's actually one of the shop girls you're so sure are going to be able to keep their jobs in the house in a year or so."

"Really?" He seemed genuinely surprised. "Photographers have to be in high demand these days for the papers. I'm surprised she hasn't pursued taking pictures as a career. It somewhat reminds me of you actually." Some of his confidence seeped back in. "Seems a wise decision to have a job or a career to support your passion. Look at you! You're going to be well on your way to a smashing career once you've graduated. That's finding a practical application for your art. She's apparently got her own practical day job and snapping some photos on the side."

"Again, she has one of the practical jobs you're so sure will be gone the minute the men come marching home. Also, she isn't just snapping photos. She's an incredible photographer."

As much as Emily tried to be angry at Kate and the feelings Kate stirred in her, her pique was diffused the moment she thought of the talented, wonderful person Kate was. She was angry with herself for her earlier actions as well, and now she was frustrated with Tommy, who probably didn't deserve to be the brunt of it.

"Look, Em. I'm merely saying that you're a smart woman and I think we're both on a great track in pursuing an education. People are doing what they have to right now, and we're getting a rare opportunity."

Emily stifled the urge to bite into Tommy about the difference between fighting in a war and getting an education, and how him lecturing her about women's work was the same as someone lecturing him about the military. She felt ashamed for even thinking of it, but the man was being so incredibly narrow-minded that she almost did.

"I'm happy I've been afforded the opportunity to pursue that education, thank you very much." Her anger quickly diffused.

"And so am I," he responded quietly. His flair for argument had finally abated. A moment of silence stretched out between them as the crowds simultaneously booed and cheered a line drive from the Dodgers. Emily put her arm around Tommy, her anger also dampened. She simply wanted to enjoy the rest of the evening.

"I just need a big, strong man to bring home the bacon for me, I suppose." Emily felt Tommy's chuckle and looked up to him shaking his head. He puffed out his chest in faux machismo and gathered her in his arms. They both laughed, and he kissed the top of her head. She relaxed for just a moment. She felt safe, cared for, protected, *stifled*...She refused to think that. Why did things like that keep coming up?

"Heads up!" one of the crowd yelled behind them. A Yankee

popped a fly ball right at their section, and everyone swarmed together toward it, hesitating when no one had a glove.

The reverberating *smack!* could be heard all around her as the ball landed painfully in Emily's palm.

Just as the ball had been sailing in, Emily had impulsively dove right out into the aisle, over Tommy, and grabbed it bare-handed. The only thing stopping her from plummeting down the stairs with said ball was Tommy reflexively catching her in return, and he now had an expression of utter confused fascination. Emily realized that she had been successful in her mad dive only after the excruciating contact sent pain streaking up her arm. Although that pain in no way abated, the thrill and excitement of the moment distracted her when she realized what she'd done. Everyone around her erupted in a cheer, seeming in awe of the feat—not only Emily's, but Tommy's catch as well.

Emily planted the biggest, happiest kiss on Tommy as they were still dipped over, much to the enjoyment of nearly everyone in the stadium. As she laughingly looked into his eyes, she realized that moment was the most real and truly happy moment the two of them had ever shared. Accepting the congratulations of everyone around and recounting the moment with them, Emily faintly realized that she wanted to share every detail with someone else.

CHAPTER ELEVEN

Four years later, 1946

It had been a long week and Kate had reluctantly agreed to get a drink with Allie and Art at the local beer hall. As they walked in, she noted that although nearly every table was full or littered with leftover glasses and garbage, the place wasn't nearly as bustling as it had been in the past. A jukebox in the corner filled in the spaces of conversation, and even on a weeknight, the dance floor had more than a few occupants. But without the war, the place wasn't packed to the brim as it once was.

Allie was talking her ear off about her nephews and how Art's brother was planning to take them all on a fishing trip, which she was dreading, when she overheard Art mumble, "There they are," and saw him wave to a table.

When Kate looked up, her expression instantly morphed into that of a deer caught in the proverbial headlights when she saw who was at the table. *This has to be some type of joke.* Once again, an unexpected reunion. Both Emily and Tommy sat practically squirming in their seats but quickly greeted Art and Allie with hugs. Kate's hopes for as little contact with the couple as possible were quickly dying.

"Look who we found! Although I hear all of you had a wonderful engagement session just the other day," Art said to the group.

"I thought I agreed to a drink to get you off my back about

working too much," Kate mumbled, greeting both Tommy and Emily with a small wave, ignoring Art. She had successfully avoided dinner the previous evening with this very party but had little willpower to fight every outing, even if she'd wanted to.

"And a drink we shall have! What would you like?" he asked.

"Let me get them," Kate said, already heading to the bar. "What would you like, Allie?"

"Oh, I'll just have a soda water," Allie said. Kate noticed a strange, small smile touch Art's lips, but she already wanted to escape this ordeal, and a trip to the bar was one small way to do it. She briefly looked at Emily, who only gave a small shake of her head, swallowed, and looked away.

As she ordered, she once again contemplated how she'd found herself in the current situation. She knew exactly how. It wasn't hard to see how, with mutual friends and a theoretical friendship with the couple herself...but she saw no way to remove herself with any reasonable explanation. She thought Allie was her only ally, but here she was, tricked into having a cordial outing with the very person she was trying to avoid. It didn't help that, more than anything, she also wanted to rebel against that avoidance.

"Where's the honeymoon again?" Art asked just as Kate returned.

Tommy jumped on the question. "We have five days booked in Rome, and then another four in Madrid, along with travel time, of course."

"Wow! And to think that ours, four days upstate, was the best trip we've had yet." Art looked to Allie.

"It's who you're with that makes it special, darling." Allie chimed in, giving him a loving kiss on the cheek.

"I need another drink," Emily stated, rising to go to the bar. Tommy stopped her, however, and went himself. She sat back, as if defeated.

"Have you visited anywhere around here since you've been in town?" asked Allie.

"We had a lovely photo session on the Brooklyn Bridge and in the park the other day, as you know." Emily strained a smile, her eyes flickering to Kate again. Kate chugged at her beer. "But reviewing everything for Saturday is quite time consuming."

"We should get to a Yankees game this week." Tommy handed Emily a fresh beer, from which she proceeded to take an obnoxiously long pull. Any other time, Kate would have been impressed.

"They're headed to the World Series again this year!" Art attempted a sports conversation, but Tommy showed little interest. "We should all go if there happens to be a game before the weekend, no?"

Emily nodded and had little to say as the conversation went on instead of tossing her normally cheerful input into any discussion. She seemed much more interested in the beverage in front of her.

Kate, on the other hand, decided to be as engaged and interested as possible, then find the quickest out possible to make this a short night. She could deal with her thoughts alone later and not give Allie and Art reason to drag her along next time. She resisted the incessant urge to crack the miserable exterior Emily was hiding behind. She felt guilt at potentially ruining Emily's night, although she couldn't see this as her fault. She hadn't even known Emily would be here.

As she looked over at Emily finishing her drink, she couldn't help but be warmed by the thought of just being in the same space with her. It had been that way each time they were together, and she'd missed it. She missed their friendship. She scolded herself for her wishful thinking, as she herself had been the one to ruin it, hadn't she?

For only a moment, they looked at each other. With just a glance, one of many weights fell from Kate's shoulders, just as a few had on the train a few days ago. Perhaps they could simply enjoy this time with those they cared for most and not over-analyze everything.

"…to dance?" Tommy's most charming smile adorned his face as he asked Emily to dance.

"Oh!" The movement obviously startled Emily, but she politely accepted. "Of course."

Kate watched them go, this time herself finishing her beer. Seeing Tommy place his arm around Emily and hold her close, she looked away, turning to Art and Allie. "Go join them. You don't get the opportunity often enough."

At Allie's telegraphed *we aren't leaving you here alone*, Kate added, "You know I hate dancing. Go on. I'll get us another round." She walked away to the bar.

"Hi there," an objectively handsome young man said to Kate just after she ordered drinks for the group. She sighed inwardly but put on a smile. She didn't have the energy in that moment for an eager boy to attempt to woo her, but he didn't know that. She turned to him, noting his perfectly combed dark hair, striking blue eyes, and a quite charming smile. "I saw you're with some people, but would you like to dance? I can take your drinks over for you."

"Why, thank you, but I pride myself on being able to carry all of them at once. I'm actually waiting on someone to arrive." She smiled her own charming smile back, hoping to ease the blow but also firmly put a stop to it.

He blushed the tiniest bit, slapped his hand gently on the bar as if contemplating saying something further, and instead remarked, "What a shame. Have a good night, miss."

By the next song, Kate had the drinks back to the empty table. She took a long pull from her own beer and tried to calm all the thoughts racing through her head. She closed her eyes for a moment, listening to the music. When she opened them, hazel eyes stared back at her over Tommy's shoulder as the couple danced to the slow song drifting over the room. *Goddamnit.* She hated nothing more than seeing them together like that and knew that she had no right to that anger. She quickly looked away, angry at her slip-up. She had to get out of there, if even just for a moment, to get control of her runaway emotions.

She burst through the side door and stood just outside, letting the cool evening breeze attempt to carry away some of what she knew was useless self-pity. She was frustrated by her inability to express the happiness she found in Emily's sudden reappearance. Her actions had caused pain, as did Emily's, but she still held resentment because of it. She thought that keeping her distance, allowing Emily to enjoy these moments as her own might atone for them in some small way, but her friends were hell-bent on making sure she was interfering with that happiness at every opportunity. And under all the negativity, her heart wanted the chance to reconnect with the very person she couldn't. She threw her head against the brick wall of the bar alley and shut her eyes.

The door creaked open, and Kate was sure she knew who it was, but she didn't look over. Footsteps grew closer, and she felt the person lean against the wall beside her. They stood there in silence.

"It's too bad Ralph wasn't in there to charm you right onto the dance floor," Emily said. Kate could hear the laughter in her voice. She didn't look over.

"Ralph is married, with one child and another on the way, I'll have you know," she replied lazily. She couldn't resist looking over for a reaction. And a reaction she got as she saw the disbelief on Emily's face. It was amazing how much could change in just a few short years, while other things never did.

"The truly unfortunate thing, however," Kate leaned back again, "is that at the rate you were drinking in there, someone might have to carry you home."

"I'll have you right well know that has never once happened. I'm perfectly fine." Emily rolled her eyes. Kate's shoulders bounced in silent laughter, but she didn't say anything else. She knew Emily had no responsibility to, and should not have had any desire to, but that she'd come out to make sure Kate was all right. She almost wished that Emily simply hated her.

Kate finally turned toward her and simply stared, looking everywhere at Emily but her eyes, studying her face before finally settling on them. "Why are you speaking to me?"

Emily paused, and Kate waited. She just needed to know what Emily was thinking.

Emily, however, avoided the question with another. "How did *you* become my *wedding photographer*?"

"Ha! I think we both know how. I assume Allie was terrified of your mother and gave her the only recommendation she knew, seeing as though I'm basically their personal-life photographer." She paused and turned toward Emily. "I didn't know, Em. Honestly.

The last thing I want is to make you feel uncomfortable for your big day."

"We both know it isn't your doing. My mother wouldn't have hired you unless your work was excellent." Emily paused. "But don't get a big head about it."

Kate honestly couldn't figure out why Emily was being so open and kind. This was the first time they'd been alone together in so very long, and Kate, although she hadn't expected it to ever occur, imagined Emily was taking out every ounce of pain she still held on her. *Assuming Emily's had even thought of me since then.* She was clearly happy and had found the someone who inspired that happiness in her.

"I'm so happy for you, you know...that you finally have your own studio." Her voice was soft but direct.

"When you don't take a risk and you've regretted it every day after, you tend to not let the others slip by." She looked at her feet, scuffing them on the ground, hands in her pockets. "I suppose you live your life trying to make up for it, doing the things that might not work out but that you love."

As they stood there, piece by piece, some of the bad memories were replaced with fragments of happiness, new moments replacing the old in their minds. They imagined the moments each had missed and thought they might finally be able to catch up on where their lives had taken them. The city honked, splashed, yelled behind them, but for just that instant, they could talk with each other. They had moved increasingly closer to each other until, before Kate realized it, she reached up to touch Emily, whose eyelids dropped, leaning toward the touch.

A gentle cough stopped Kate just before her fingertips brushed Emily's cheek. Like lightning the two of them separated, Kate's cheeks heating under the dim street lamps as she saw Allie standing in the doorway. Her fear softened as she noted that Allie's expression wasn't judgmental, yet cautious and confused. Allie said nothing but gestured inside, then walked in herself, leaving the two of them alone once more.

"Can we—" Emily said.

Allie stuck her head out once more. "Well, come along, or the other two will be snooping around out here in no time."

Kate followed Emily as they retreated inside in silence. She heard Emily sigh as their oh-so-brief moment alone ended.

The conversation upon their return was much more lively and less strained, reminiscent of their time together years ago. Emily drank much slower, once catching Kate's eye as if to prove that she could take care of herself and there would be no carrying home of anyone. Although cautious, Kate nodded in silent acceptance of Emily's seeming determination. Kate caught Allie when she glanced between the two of them and swallowed hard. The last thing she needed was to be reminded of a time when she'd confided in her one night. Allie didn't know their story, but Kate knew she wanted to.

During a lull in the conversation, Art started fidgeting and looking at Allie every few seconds, apparently waiting to say something. Allie smiled at him and began to speak.

"You are all our closest and most trusted friends. We hope you know that." Her face lit. "And it's so rare to have you in one place at the same time. We wanted you to be the first to know."

Art picked up from there. "You're going to be aunties."

"I'm your cousin, Allie—" Emily stared at her. "You're pregnant!?"

With a nod from Art, Emily stood straight up and screamed. Cheers erupted at the small table, drawing attention. Kate hugged them both, in awe of her friends. The news was exciting and unexpected, but it seemed so very natural for the two of them. Kate was beyond happy for her closest friends. Her family.

They spent the rest of the evening talking of their plans, celebrating them, revealing their hopes for their addition. It was the first time in years that all of them could take their worries and drama and put them on the back burner. Kate and Emily, even Tommy, were the people Allie and Art had wanted to know first, their best friends. It felt like the old times this way, and they all could stop thinking of themselves and truly celebrate.

When everyone acknowledged the time that had passed, they reluctantly agreed that they should call it a night. Although preparations for the weekend to come were under control, Emily and Tommy still had so much to do. Both Art and Kate had early morning obligations the following day as well.

Kate was particularly saddened to see it end, as it was the first time in so long that she'd had the chance to enjoy her time. She didn't spend all of it alone; in fact, she rarely had such moments what with clients, students, and Allie and Art. But this was the first time in so long that she had stepped back from the endless hard work in pursuing her passion and let herself simply be one of the gang. She refused to admit part of her happiness was the reappearance of the woman at the table and the fact that they were speaking.

"Kate, we should catch up before the weekend madness is in full swing!" Emily said, overly cordial, as they left the bar.

"I, well—"

"Darling, the madness is already swinging!" Tommy piped in.

Kate glanced at Tommy briefly. "I wouldn't want to waste what little time you have."

Kate needed to be the mature one here, attempting to remain cordial while distant, even when it crushed her to see Emily's hopes dashed. Not that either of them had succeeded in doing that in the darkened alleyway. No, perhaps they shouldn't be alone.

As the group walked down the street, Emily fell back to walk beside Kate in silence. Kate fought with herself each moment, words coming to the very tip of her tongue and promptly logjamming there. She rolled her eyes at herself when she realized this was a first with Emily. She didn't like it.

Emily finally spoke. "I'd like to examine some of the prints from the other day before the wedding." She paused. "So my mother can submit them to the papers, of course."

The hidden ask for time alone was exactly what Kate had hoped for, as well as dreaded. Kate knew she shouldn't accept, regardless of the logic in the request. Every time they saw each other, another piece would come back, pieces that would be broken and pulled apart again permanently in only a few short days. She glanced over and, God help her, found herself helpless to resist.

"Of course. I can have them prepped for tomorrow afternoon if you'd like to come by then." Each time she saw Emily she expected only anger from her and continued to receive none, so she decided to enjoy the companionship. After all, her past asinine actions meant she owed Emily a world of kindness, no matter how good her intentions might have been. Also, under all of it, she wanted it.

CHAPTER TWELVE

Four years earlier, 1942

Emily loved shopping, and the boutique dress shop they had chosen was, like all spaces in New York City, a snug little narrow strip of a building that provided very little room to move. Despite this limitation, Allie, Emily, and Kate, plus Aunt Jane and the two enthusiastic little old ladies who owned the shop, frolicked about looking for the perfect wedding gown for the bride-to-be. Dresses lined the walls and mannequins displayed the most colorful and stylish designs as everyone looked through the selections for one matching the criteria Allie had in mind.

Emily was having a wonderful time seeing Allie so content, but the least enthusiastic dress shopper in the room was Kate. She was, as usual, photographing the entire process instead, even though she had never mentioned an interest in fashion photography to Emily. She could admit, though, that the place was very photogenic. Every dress that Allie tried on earned its own photograph, and Kate promised to not let Art see a single one before the wedding.

The shop owners made suggestions, her Aunt Jane doted on her daughter, and Allie contemplated her choices in the mirrors surrounding her. Kate photographed it all, but Emily noticed she was not so strategically avoiding her. *Not this again*, although Emily agreed she didn't want to draw attention to herself with the other woman. Frazzled, she felt as though everyone knew what they had done.

Emily held the train of the current dress Allie was wearing, but her right hand flinched in pain, catching everyone's glance.

"Emily, dear, are you okay?" one of the shop owners asked. Emily nodded slightly, not wanting attention brought to her, but it was too late.

"This young lady decided to catch a fly ball at a baseball game bare-handed!" The story began, Aunt Jane filling everyone in on what she thought was the greatest story she'd heard in quite a while. Emily blushed and smiled innocently as the story progressed.

She hated that Kate was having to hear all about her date night, although it shouldn't be an issue, and she shouldn't have had any shame. She thought she had played it well throughout the day, greeting Kate cordially that morning, and had been kind and responsive to everyone, including Kate. Kate had established a clear distance that no one else could see through. Unlike Emily, Kate seemed to be trying desperately to avoid her, registering any interaction as inappropriate or flirtatious.

"I would have tumbled right down the stairs and onto the field if it hadn't been for Tommy!" Emily finished the story. "He snatched me right up, just as I caught it!" Her eyes flicked to Kate. "It was quite romantic."

The women in the shop all laughed and gossiped about how dashing Tommy was, and what a perfect couple the two of them seemed to be. Emily questioned why she felt the need to twist what she knew was a knife into Kate at the end of the story and felt guilty about it immediately. But perhaps choosing to forget her transgression was the better option, even if the constant references to Tommy hurt Kate a bit.

Emily watched Kate continued taking pictures, hidden behind her lens where she knew she felt guarded. Behind the camera Kate had a barrier, one where she didn't have to be exposed, and Emily wished in a way she had something like it of her own. Despite her efforts over the last week, all Emily could think about was that last moment, one that was, in her heart and mind, the most wonderful moment she'd ever had. But Kate deserved to feel safe in whatever way she chose to get past it all and spend time with Allie.

"You'll have to visit us one of these days when that young man gets his act together." One of the ladies, Sarah, teased Emily, patting her on the back.

"Your dresses are lovely. I wouldn't think of shopping elsewhere. How long have you been in the business?" Emily asked.

"Oh, we've been at this for nearly, what, Darla, forty years now?"

Darla nodded. "We even designed each other's dresses. We opened shop in '03, when Bill and George remodeled this little place, and plan to keep it open until our fingers stop sewing."

"Never thought of doing anything else, even after both our boys passed away," Sarah added, pulling at a place on Allie's dress and pinning it for alteration. The action was systematic, as was the flow of the two women as they worked around each other with a lifetime of familiarity. The two of them fascinated Emily.

She immediately thought of Kate and their instant familiarity. She didn't want to lose a friendship over a silly and completely inappropriate infatuation. She'd spent the last week convincing herself that she could forget her moment of insanity and keep things as they were. No need to get hung up on that one incident. These ladies were evidence of a great lifelong friendship. As quickly as she had this thought, she caught Kate with her camera raised, in her element, and her thoughts took another decidedly rebellious turn. *Damn it!*

"I think this is the one," Allie said excitedly as she looked at herself once again in the mirror. All attention went to her as she twirled around with the biggest smile on her face. Her chosen dress was a beautiful ball-gown with all the lace and satin one could possibly imagine. The train stretched out behind her as everyone looked on. She was even more beautiful from the happiness so clearly showing on her face. Aunt Jane was nearly in tears, both from her own joy and probably her fear of her husband's reaction to the price tag.

"Art won't be able to keep his hands off you!"

Allie blushed at Emily's teasing. "Okay, okay. Now that I'm set, it's your turn." Allie pointed at Emily and then Kate.

"No...no, no, no." Kate waved a finger. "Photographer. I'm your photographer, and I cannot take photographs in a dress like that."

"First of all, you are not our 'photographer.' No one needs photographs of the whole day. We only want formals, and you're in them, since second, you're a bridesmaid."

"When exactly was this decided?"

"Decided? Why would I have to tell you that? Who else would be?"

"Well, I..."

"Oh, please. You're her best friend," Emily said.

"I don't. Do. Dresses," came Kate's clenched response.

"For heaven's sake, Kathryn Ann. You will wear a dress and enjoy this day looking like the beautiful young lady you are." Aunt Jane put an end to the debate.

Kate stared at her, stunned, and Emily covered her mouth, but her shoulders shook in laughter. Kate noticed Emily's reaction, then looked over, blushed, and replied, "Yes ma'am."

Kate pried her camera strap from around her neck and examined a row of dresses as Emily looked at the other side. Emily was getting an absurd amount of satisfaction from the progressing events and couldn't contain her smirk. Kate clearly had no interest in trying on a dress Emily was sure she would never wear again. But seeing Kate tortured a bit was an exciting prospect.

"Oh! What about this one?" Emily found a dress and held it up to herself and then to Kate. "This would be lovely for you, with your height, and it should let you move well with your hands to press all those complicated camera buttons. Obviously that takes quite a bit of flexibility."

Kate looked down in terror at the piece of clothing but rolled her eyes. She whispered to Emily, "I avoid these things at all costs, I'll have you know. Completely impractical and uncomfortable."

That much was obvious to Emily.

"I wore my share as a kid, and as an adult I should be able to wear precisely whatever the hell I want. Damn propriety and dressing like a lady." Now Kate was on a roll, and Emily didn't stop her. "My uniform at the shop is apparently just fine, and I don't know why the hell I should have to put myself into one in the little free time I have either."

"Go try it on!" Raised eyebrows from Allie's mother were all the motivation Kate needed apparently, shutting down her grumblings. She scowled at Emily when she got no support. Emily was just holding back laughter.

Moments later Kate stood in front of the partition with the most uncomfortable look and shrugged. Hands on her hips, she waited impatiently for a verdict, or for someone to even look up long enough to notice her. When she coughed, everyone did just that.

Emily stood still as a statue, her mouth opening and closing, seemingly unable to put together a single coherent thought.

Comments burst from the women in the shop as all of them but Emily flocked around her. Emily heard only a dim hum as she gazed at her, awestruck at the transformation. She watched Kate shyly brush the strand of hair from her eyes, blush painfully, and look up directly at her. Emily's heart pounded wildly as any hope of acting as though she were not attracted to the other woman faded. Her mouth opened and closed, but she was unable to form a thought except, "You look beautiful."

Instead of the either sarcastic or aggravated remark she was expecting, Kate gave her a look of innocence, one of surprise that someone would think that of her. The thought melted Emily's heart then and there. She had no idea how truly beautiful she was. Emily swallowed hard, trying to get her muddled brain back in focus.

"Don't you dare!" Kate screamed when Emily picked up and pointed her most prized possession directly at her. Photographic evidence of this folly might be the worst scenario Kate could imagine, but Emily was loving it. She clicked the shutter and Kate grumbled, "I seriously regret teaching you how to use the thing."

Emily laughed and snapped it over and over again, while the other women poked and prodded her. Kate couldn't stop her. It seemed that the first dress would be sufficient, and she wouldn't have to try on others, much to Emily's chagrin.

After Darla finished her pinning and measuring, Sarah helped the others find a dress of similar color and style for Emily. Emily was still intently watching Kate until Allie looked over to see the two staring at each other. "What about this one, Em?"

Emily jumped and rushed over. She smiled and held the dress up to herself. "Let's see!"

"I see you've quickly learned something with the camera," Kate growled as they crossed paths at the partition. The roll of film was nearly empty.

"Anyone could figure it out," Emily replied.

"Glad I could give you the satisfaction."

Emily looked down, away from Kate's stare, and noted just before she crossed the partition herself, "You really do look beautiful in that dress." Kate blushed and looked around. "But it's not you."

The next twenty minutes as Emily tried on each dress, she watched Kate fidget with the camera and snap a photo or two of her, then promptly blush, sit back, and stay put in silence while everyone fawned over her. She raised an eyebrow at the gloomy woman in question.

"What?" Kate asked. "Allie is going to want to remember this, but I don't need four rolls of it. I'm budgeting."

Emily threw her hands up in defense and turned to change back into her street clothes.

"Could we purchase these prints from you to display here in the shop?" Sarah asked as they put the dresses away and cleaned up.

"Oh, why, I've never sold..." Kate panicked. Emily caught her eye from past the ladies and tried to pass her some confidence through her smile.

It worked, as Kate squared her shoulders and responded, "Yes, of course. If that's fine with everyone else."

"Great then! They'd be a nice addition to the shop, and perhaps we could even have you come by to photograph a few of our designs?"

Kate nodded dumbly. "I'd love to."

Emily and Allie smiled, and Kate walked over to them.

"Even with the dress torture, it appears you got something

productive out of it," Allie said with a wink. Kate straightened her shoulders in a small sign of pride in herself.

"Still not convinced *anything's* worth wearing a dress for," she mumbled.

Just then the bell on the storefront door chimed. "Hey, Mia, almost done!" Kate greeted the young woman as she entered the store, looking around in awe. She held a large sketch pad and satchel containing an array of sketching supplies and other artist paraphernalia, slinking through the rows of the store.

"These are beautiful!" She stared at the dresses across the shop.

"We've tried on nearly their entire stock this morning." Emily was happy but surprised to see Mia there.

"Oh, hi, Emily. Are you coming with us?"

Emily looked at Kate with no idea of what plan the two had, while Mia looked back and forth between the two of them in anticipation. She must have automatically assumed Emily would be coming, as the two of them must have seemed like best friends during their last time together at Alfonzo's. Kate, however, looked as though she were about to make up an excuse for why Emily couldn't make it.

"We're going out for a small photo session, and I'm planning to show her how to process the film afterward," Kate said. "She has her sketch gear, and I'm sure she'd love some tips for that as well while we're out. Would you like to go with us?"

Emily wanted to. Under her mask of indifference, Kate evidently wanted her there as well. Mia was so eager to learn, and Emily loved to teach.

"I'd love to, but—"

The bell chimed again, and they looked over as Tommy entered the shop.

Emily threw a regretful look, and Kate nodded.

"How did it go, darling?" he asked with a kiss on the cheek.

"Wonderfully. We're all set." Emily wrapped her arm around him but spoke to Kate and Allie. "Everyone's going to look beautiful."

"Of course you will!" he said. "And I'm sure Kate here took some wonderful photographs. I can't wait to see them." He clearly knew he needed to make up for his comments to Emily about Kate but didn't know how to. "Are you ready to go?"

"Oh, yes." Emily remembered herself then. "I'm sorry. We have a lunch date just now. I'd love to join you two some other time."

"We can reschedule!" Tommy suggested, seeming sincere.

"I thought Jim was meeting us."

"I can meet with him. You'll have plenty of opportunities to meet the rest of the firm, I'm sure."

Kate was currently examining the quality of the wood flooring, shuffling her feet and refusing to make eye contact, and Mia looked hopeful at the prospect of having two *real* artists show her their crafts. This would be the perfect opportunity to be with Kate but not alone, doing what they both loved best.

The fact that Kate refused to meet her eyes, however, told her it would be a mistake. The entire morning Kate had avoided her whenever possible. Perhaps they both simply needed a bit more time. She should keep her commitments with Tommy. She had to choose him.

"I'd rather meet him now than at a company party with everyone else, dear."

Kate flinched and nodded, her eyes dull.

"Next weekend, I promise." Emily smiled at Mia, then at Kate. "After all, I can't let her pollute your mind completely with that photography business."

"I'll hold you to that then." The light had returned to Kate's eyes. "The two of you can have a coloring session."

"It's not coloring!" Emily and Mia exclaimed simultaneously.

Kate threw her hands up in mock surrender.

As Emily walked from the store, her arm looped in Tommy's, she was as excited about that simple afternoon outing with Kate and Mia as she had been about coming to New York.

Chapter Thirteen

Four years later, 1946

Alfonzo and Mia were out of the studio for the day, and Kate was completely and irrationally panicked. Emily had scheduled a formal appointment to come see the prints of the earlier engagement photo session, as her mother was allowing her to select the photos that they would display at the wedding and for various newspaper announcements of their ceremony. Kate wanted this review to be as professional as possible, while at the same time she was squelching an overflow of happiness at the prospect of being with Emily.

As a result, she scrambled around the studio, straightening each work of art on the walls and debating which should be on display. The works couldn't possibly be the caliber of work which Emily was accustomed to and studied on a regular basis. Emily would never vocally judge, but Kate wanted to showcase her best. The photographs she laid out were her top quality. She had included some by Mia, which also gave her a great sense of pride. Not only was Mia becoming an incredible photographer, but she was learning to perfect multiple mediums.

On the table lay a selection of the prints she had created from their photo session a few short days ago. She arranged them first chronologically, by location, then clustered the shot types, thinking the couple could select based on the specific shot. After creating a fourth arrangement she realized her nerves had taken over, leading to a ridiculous obsessiveness. She forced herself to leave them alone.

Although Emily had, Tommy had never seen her work, and for some reason she needed to prove herself to him.

She went to the darkroom to get away from her compulsion. There was plenty of personal work that was long overdue for development, and she had some experiments to try out. Helping her grandfather with exhibition programming and pursuing her commissioned work, Kate had a precious few free moments and used them as effectively as possible. The couple was not scheduled to be there for forty-five minutes anyway.

As was her style, Kate clicked on the radio, cranked the volume, and switched on the red light. Methodically she set to work, drowning out her anxiety if only just for a while. Emily would be there soon, and her mood lightened. She relaxed as the dark room became her place of peace, as it always did.

"Mia! How many times!? Come on. You know better than that!" Kate yelled over the music, startling Emily after she'd opened the door.

"Sorry!" Emily yelled back, quickly slipping inside and shutting the door. "I knocked, just so you know."

Kate turned down the music.

"Oh, Emily. Uh, hi…Sorry. Mia has a bad habit of waltzing in whenever she pleases." Kate's looked down at her watch. "I seem to have lost track of time."

Emily watched Kate frantically scramble to collect her things from the station, throwing away the print she'd been working on, and Emily knew she'd ruined it. She felt a little guilty. Emily looked up at the drying prints in the red light, stunned at the beauty of the images. Unlike anyone else, Kate was able to truly capture the spirit and the personality of her subjects. In the past several years, Kate had truly become a professional.

"You? Late? No."

Kate stopped scrambling and shook her head, the tension in

the room immediately released. "Sorry. I didn't hear you over the radio."

"Not a problem. I know that's how you work," Emily replied with a small smile.

After a pause, Kate finished collecting her things and switched off the radio. She looked around the studio as if expecting to find someone else there.

"Tommy decided to stay at the hotel," Emily stated, anticipated Kate's unasked question. She didn't add that he'd decided this because she'd encouraged him to do so, or that she'd questioned herself as to why she wanted it to be just the two of them that day. Tommy seemed fine with her suggestion, if a little uncomfortable. But Emily was sure she was simply projecting. She also couldn't tell if Tommy not being there made Kate more nervous or relaxed, but it was coming across as some strange combination of the two.

Kate simply walked Emily over to the display counter, though she seemed rather fidgety.

"I thought we could catch up," Emily said. "Tommy would be bored out of his mind and try to pretend otherwise."

"Okay then." Kate visibly relaxed, and Emily stepped closer. "Here they are. I'm very happy with many of them." She instantly transitioned into her professional role.

Emily scanned the images and, as always, was astounded by Kate's talent. The images were like an observer in an intimate moment, like looking at memories of another friend.

"My mother told me to pick three, and we could send them to my cousin who writes for the *New York Times*, as if they'll write a story on the wedding or something. I honestly don't see the point..."

"I won't complain about getting my work in the *Times*. I'll tell you that!" Kate laughed.

"You haven't yet?" Emily asked, looking around. "I'm sure something here has been pitched. What idiot wouldn't take something you've shot?"

"I never said that." Kate flashed a grin. "The ticker-tape parade after the war got me a few published." She bounced away and snatched a catalogue from under another nearby counter. When she returned Emily could sense her excitement to show her work. *It's adorable*... Emily stopped herself.

Kate opened the book and slid the other images Emily was supposed to be looking at away to make room.

"Wow! You were right there!" Emily was paging through some of the prints when a thought struck. "You didn't take—?"

"Sailor boy dipping his lady? No. Believe it or not, though. I was right there." She turned the page and pointed to one of the photos to reveal a familiar scene, but from a different angle.

Emily recognized the scene from not so long ago, the day that marked the end of the Second World War, and immediately wished she could have been there for the celebration. She scanned each print, looking at the faces of joy for those who had returned, faces of relief at the end to years of tension, children enraptured by the happiness of those moments.

"Alfred Eisen-something or other snapped it right as I looked over. A bunch of others got different angles of it as well. But it's just that one that makes the memory." She pulled the *LIFE* magazine issue from inside the album and pointed to two of the smaller photos included in the article. "Made it in the magazine with that one and everything."

"I'm sure photographers were swarming everywhere."

"Not really. Everyone was so excited, even I took the time to enjoy it, really be there. Sometimes it's hard to experience things if you have the camera in front of you." She pointed to another photograph, and Emily immediately felt a longing to have been there when she saw Allie between Kate and a still-uniformed Art, all three with the most profound expressions of happiness on their faces. She wished for more time with all of them, knowing a piece of her heart had never truly left this city.

"You've really lived life these past years," she said.

"It's been hard work along the way. Hasn't been easy."

Emily looked up from the catalogue. Lines were drawn on Kate's face that hadn't been there years before. Lines of maturity, sketched from that hard work, lines crafted from the experiences she herself had missed out on seeing, although she was sure she had her own such marks. Kate had come into her own, and Emily wished she could have been there to see it happen.

"When did you take over the shop?" she asked, steering the conversation away from her thoughts.

Kate turned to the wall behind them and the work displayed there. "My grandfather is close to the most stubborn person I've ever met. It took pulling teeth for Mia and me to get him to 'retire,'" she said, holding up air quotes. "I started losing hours at the shop two years ago, and eventually I sold a few of my pieces and got recommended for portrait commissions of a few families, which I could take with the free time I had.

"Managing the shop was a frightening transition. I went for it though. For once. Scared the shit out of me, and I wondered if the work would continue, if I was good enough, if I could live just on the thing I love to do. I juggled the shop and work for a while and could barely handle all of it at once.

"The store kept getting messier, and fewer people would venture in. Mia and I were trying to help out more. He needed someone consistent around, as he's getting older. Works for us both. Mia is here regularly as well. She just graduated high school a few months ago. Anyway, he formally gave me ownership, but he's still living upstairs with Mia, although I'm hoping she'll get a place with me. Hired a store manager too, so we can do our own work and run the studio."

Emily stood beside her, listening. It was nice to hear about their time apart, and she was proud of her, truly.

On the wall she noticed what she was sure was a photo from their trip to Coney Island long ago, of Art and Allie, along with one from their wedding. She continued looking until she stumbled upon a print of a figure silhouetted on the Brooklyn Bridge and recognized herself as the subject.

"Uh...Gramps won't let that one get taken down." Kate blushed inexplicably when she realized what Emily was looking at.

"It's a wonderful photo. You never showed it to me."

"These are of a few of Mia's prints and sketch work." Kate once again moved away from the current topic.

Noticing the shift, Emily regarded the next collection. She was immediately in awe of the progress and true talent she saw in Mia's work. The thought of someone so young having a degree of talent that nearly matched her own both terrified and exhilarated her, instantly diminishing a few of Emily's tightly held inhibitions. And although she was proud of her education and thankful for the opportunities she had been given, she remembered a time when she'd wanted more. Looking at a few simple sketches left her itching to do more with her own work, to strive for something again.

"She's come such a long way," Emily said. "I'm assuming she's your assistant these days?"

Kate nodded. "She's making quite a name for herself already. I'm sure she'll be on her own in no time." She pointed to one of the prints. "She has a very photojournalistic style, so I'm hoping someone will snatch her up. Or at least that she'll take on personal commissions."

"Well, she has a wonderful mentor."

Kate turned her head, obviously uncomfortable with the compliment.

"Alfonzo must have taught her everything she knows," Emily said as she barely managed to hold back a grin. Kate huffed, and they both laughed.

"You really have accomplished so much already," Emily said seriously. "It's impressive."

Kate laughed. "I inherited an old junk store from my grandfather...What about you though? You have a college degree, for Christ's sake."

"One that I'm not sure I'll get to do much with..." Emily caught herself. "Though I am extremely grateful to have had the opportunity. I suppose I should thank you in some ways for that." She paused. "You asked why I was talking to you, and I think part of it is just that. You helped me see sense, logic, and I've made it where I am now because of those lessons."

"And soon you'll have a wonderful husband as well," Kate said. As mature as she tried to be, the fact of Emily's marriage still hurt, but she had been the one to allow it, aid it even.

"He's great husband material, that's for sure." *That's the best you can come up with?* Emily scolded herself.

"Took long enough to propose, no?"

Emily rolled her eyes. "He wanted to make sure we were all set and secure once we finished school, so we can settle in..." She shuffled her feet, arms crossed. "I was offered a fellowship in my department that is an incredible opportunity. I'd get to travel, teach, study...Make my own work again..."

"That sounds like a wonderful opportunity" was all Kate said.

"But," Emily picked up with a false bravado, "there's still time to figure it out, and no one but myself is stopping me from my own work, right?"

Kate nodded, looking directly into her eyes, and for once, the person Emily remembered being came back. For a moment, Emily believed herself.

"When you arrived I was working on—"

"I'm sorry I interrupted—"

Kate waved away Emily's apologetic interruption. "I was going to ask if you'd like to see some of the shots and finish printing them...If you have the time."

She knew she should ask for as little time with Kate as possible, that she had so many things to do in the two days left before the wedding. They had selected the three prints plus a few others to display at the reception, and their formal business was over. Emily didn't want to monopolize her time further or get distracted, but she was always tempted when it came to Kate.

Emily lied before she could stop herself. "Believe it or not, I have the rest of the day free."

❖

Emily could barely see in the muted red light of the darkroom as she placed a print into the second set of chemicals that would produce the image. Kate stood close to her at the enlarger, the large machine used to size the image by magnifying the negative it held.

"You remember quite a bit," Kate said. Emily smiled at the compliment but continued her work with focus.

"I think something is jammed," Emily said after a while. Kate leaned over, examining the machine and Emily. They were quite close in the cramped space as she leaned over to fix it. Must have been a common flaw with the gear, given how quickly Kate knew where to reach. Emily noticed how Kate made as little contact with her as possible, even in the tiny room, but close enough that Emily could catch Kate's unique scent. She never quite could identify it, but it was unique to the woman. Dark and smoky almost. She swallowed when she caught herself leaning in to Kate.

"All good. Happens all the time," Kate said, looking up at her in the darkness and holding her gaze a little too long. Emily backed up hitting the wall behind her.

"We forgot the radio. Let's have some tunes!" She ducked skittishly around Kate and lunged at the radio. Slow jazz filled the room for a split second before Emily twisted the dial until she found a station with the latest hits. She stood for a moment, seeming to breathe in the music. She took a deep breath and turned around, only to run directly into Kate.

"What are you—" Kate took her by the waist and lifted her onto the tiny counter, their faces inches apart.

"What I've wanted to do since the moment I saw you again," Kate murmured. She inched forward, agonizingly slow. Emily wanted her, in that moment, in that place. So damn badly.

"Oh! Leave it there. I love this song." Kate's remark from across the room startled her out of her haze. *God, what was her mind doing to her?* She was so grateful that the darkness concealed her blushing face.

"You know, I don't want to take over your station, but I have a really interesting technique I've been working on, if you wanted to help with it." Kate looked over at her enthusiastically, unaware of

Emily's lurid daydream. If they were actively working together on something, her thoughts would have less time to wander.

"I'd love to." Emily brushed off her sweaty hands and joined Kate.

Over the next hour they both lost track of time, working as Kate explained how to blend two negative images together, expose both for the printing paper, and position them. She showed Emily negatives she had double exposed in the camera and complex techniques she was experimenting with lately. Each one fascinated Emily, and she remembered how much she enjoyed the other person's company.

Before she took time to think, she said, "You have so much talent."

Kate stopped her work. "Thank you."

They continued in silence until Emily could no longer stand it. "So have you...Has anyone—special...no one has swept you off your feet?" She finished in a rush.

"Haven't had the time," Kate said in a clipped manner. "Don't see as though there are any fellas out there of interest in this town anyways."

Emily wanted to think that there had been someone, not a fella, but someone lucky enough to know Kate closer than a friend. But she selfishly fought the small surge of happiness that she held that place herself, at least she did in the past.

"I've missed you," she said, almost in a whisper.

Kate again stopped her work. "Some little piece of you comes to my mind every damn day." She turned around and leaned on the counter.

Just then a familiar song floated from the corner radio, the melody calling to both of them immediately. Emily thought of a dark bar, smoky and dim, that very song guiding them together. Kate closed her eyes, and before Emily could help herself, she ran her hands up Kate's chest and around her neck. Kate pulled her close and rested her cheek against Emily's forehead. They swayed ever so slightly in the darkness.

She gave herself only a moment.

Gently pulling Emily's hand from around her, needing to make physical space, Kate asked, "Can we just enjoy you being here? I don't want to cause a problem."

"I suppose I shouldn't, but I'd very much like even that." Emily looked at her and pulled away.

Kate turned back to the counter and pulled a fresh print from the last container. "Congratulations. I believe you finally have a useable print."

"We've been here for an hour, and that's the only thing to come of it?" Emily asked. "I'll never understand your patience for this madness."

"I'll say it again. it's not all point and shoot, anyone can do it, blah blah blah." She smiled and Emily laughed.

"Come on. Let's put it up to dry."

"Emily!" Mia exclaimed as they stepped into the bright shop and stormed her with a giant hug. "I can't believe you're actually here!"

"You, young lady, are so grown up!" Emily was amazed as she assessed the young woman standing before her.

"I thought you weren't coming in today, kid," Kate said.

Mia completely ignored her. "Are you excited for your wedding? I can't wait to be there with Kate and capture all of it. I bet your dress is beautiful, isn't it? I can't wait to shoot it. It's a new trend—photojournalism in daily life, at weddings. I can't wait!" She continued in a stream of excitement.

After a day of being with Kate, the reminder that her wedding was so soon made her chest tighten. But it was the reason Emily was there after all, and she should be as excited about it as Mia.

When Mia's steady stream of questions finally ended, Emily got a word in. "Now that you're old enough, I am planning to take Allie and Kate out for one last hurrah tonight, just us ladies. You'll have to join us, and I can catch you up on all the details then."

She looked to Kate and winked. *I shouldn't be alone with you, but we'll make the time we have memorable.*

"Before that, though, I want to hear all about these photos you've been taking and see what other *real* art you've been creating."

CHAPTER FOURTEEN

Four years earlier, 1942

Each day of the next week after the horrific dress-wearing incident, Kate worked relentlessly, picking up extra hours at the shop and working herself to exhaustion to avoid the chance of appearing at all interested in anything related to Emily Stanton. She told herself Emily was spending her time with Tommy, with Allie and her family, and was likely quite busy. As each day passed she admitted more and more that she missed being around her.

She honestly didn't know why she was trying, as it hadn't worked the last time she attempted to avoid Emily. Maybe now, though, since they had seen each other after the kiss—*extreme lapse in judgment*—they could get past it, forget it...And Emily had promised to join her this weekend, so she couldn't, and didn't want to, avoid her forever. She was resolved to simply make it through the week.

Regardless, she remembered she would see her even before their planned excursion, as Allie had invited her to dinner at the end of the week. She was excited to spend time with her oldest friend. Though exhausted from the week, she was looking forward to relaxing with the people she considered her chosen family. She was also running late and didn't want to hear about it from Emily, or give her dirt to use later.

❖

Kate waited expectantly at the brownstone door and rang the bell, anticipating Allie.

"...Tommy must have been held up at the office again." Emily Stanton threw open the door. "Hi, hon—"

She halted abruptly.

Every effort she had made in the last week to not react to the woman went promptly out the window when she saw the flustered look on Emily's face. Kate could do nothing to stop the irrational flutter in her stomach or keep the corners of her mouth from smiling when she saw her in the doorway.

"Hi." Emily said with a swallow. She suddenly wrapped Kate in a friendly hug, as if not knowing what else to do. "We've missed seeing you this week."

"We've been on overtime at the shop with a new shipment this week. Probably won't let up for another two at least," Kate replied. "Apologies I'm late."

"I'm not exactly surprised." Emily raised an eyebrow, and Kate rolled her eyes.

"Hold that door, beautiful lady." They both turned to see Tommy running up. "Sorry I'm late. Big case coming up." He handed Emily a large bouquet of flowers and gave her a kiss on the cheek.

"Hey there, Kate!" He was in an irrationally chipper mood, compared to what little Kate had seen of him. Kate managed not to stiffen when he pulled her into a large hug.

"Shall we?" Emily guided both guests inside.

❖

Dinner progressed at a lively pace, everyone in good spirits as they de-stressed from their week, enjoying each other's company. The round table allowed everyone to participate, Aunt Jane questioning each of them at one point. Allie filled the group in on wedding details as Art politely nodded, and Kate spoke about the mundaneness of the shop. She lit up when she spoke about a new photography project she was working on, and Emily seemed to be asking every question about it imaginable. Kate didn't mind at all.

"Do we still have an appointment tomorrow?" She clearly wanted to make sure Kate knew she had remembered. Kate grew excited that she wanted to go with them.

"If you're still available," Kate replied, "I thought we would go to Prospect Park in Brooklyn. It really is beautiful. After all, you haven't experienced New York really, just seeing Manhattan."

"Hey now," Allie chimed in.

"As long as it doesn't start in the middle of the damn night."

"Emily Stanton! Language!" Aunt Jane gasped, visibly trembling over her dinner plate. The table erupted in laughter.

"I suppose we can sleep in a bit," Kate said. "You can meet us there around seven." She grinned and Emily mock scowled, enjoying the banter. She was thrilled that Emily wanted to join them and compiled a mental checklist of places to take them the next day.

"And Tommy, how are things at the firm?" Aunt Jane inquired. "I'm sure you're charming your way right in quickly enough."

"With the hours he puts in…" Emily mumbled.

"Actually, I have some big news." He lit up. "Ed got me an associate position of sorts for the school year, at home in Boston. It's a huge opportunity."

"But it's only your second year. You don't have a degree yet." Emily said.

"Exactly. Think of how soon I could make partner after law school with this type of experience."

Congratulations spread across the table. Emily whispered what Kate assumed to be congratulations in his ear and leaned in to give him a firm kiss.

"Allow me to clean up," Kate announced. She needed to keep herself distracted and she shouldn't ogle the couple. Let alone think of the infernal kiss of her own that still plagued her thoughts. *Will it ever go away? Damn it!*

As most of the group retired to the living room, the kitchen door opened to Emily with the remaining dishes. Her heart rate sped up as Emily stood close to her at the sink. She picked up a towel to dry them as Kate washed and rinsed.

"That's exciting news for Tommy," Kate said after a quiet moment in their work.

Emily nodded. "I'm thrilled for him. I'm not sure how much I'll get to see him now though, with a full course load, and now he basically has his career in motion." Kate let her continue. "I'll have to think about my own work outside of the classroom, but he's ahead of the pack and going places. I suppose I'm along for the ride."

Emily stopped in her tracks and looked up at Kate. "Sorry. I can't believe I just rambled like that."

"It's all right. You should think about how it affects you, too," Kate replied.

For a moment only the sound of the dishes sloshing in the water filled the room until Kate added, "I'm happy you can come out with us tomorrow."

"I keep my word." Emily flicked water out of the sink at Kate.

"What the—I never said you wouldn't." She returned the gesture, and before she knew it, they were throwing water at each other like ten-year-olds splashing in a tub. Kate somehow managed to wrestle the drying towel from her.

"Don't you dare." Emily stopped her with a wagging finger as Kate was ready to strike. They were both irrationally grinning widely.

"Truce?"

"Truce." They shook on it, and while holding Kate's hand, Emily flung a final bit of water at her before running from the room, sticking her tongue out on the way to join the others.

"I should hope the kitchen is as clean as the two of you," Aunt Jane commented dryly.

After hours of conversation and alcohol, Kate decided to make her exit. She said she was afraid she'd fall asleep on the train and miss her stop at her current rate of alcohol consumption.

"I will join you, my friend!" Tommy said, likewise tipsy, quite drunk in fact, Kate observed, "Get us both to the train safe and sound."

Kate rolled her eyes, but knew he was joking. Or at least she hoped.

"Both of you *please* get home safe?" Emily said at the front door.

"Of course, my love," Tommy lifted her off the ground and spun her around, "I shall protect us both." He looked sternly at Kate and then howled in laughter. Even Kate couldn't stop from grinning at his enthusiasm, but the smile dropped from her face when he planted a long kiss on Emily. Suddenly her shoes were the most interesting thing in the room.

It got harder to watch every damn time.

Not wanting to linger, Kate walked down the stairs, proud of not tripping. "I'll be seeing you tomorrow morning, bright and early?"

"Bright. Meaning *after* sunrise."

Kate bowed and walked away, not waiting for Tommy to run after her to catch up. She didn't really care if he was there or not, she just needed to leave.

❖

"Wait up, Kate!" Tommy nearly tripped, and Kate caught him. He was clearly in a wonderful mood. Why wouldn't he be? *He has everything he could ever want.* Kate stifled her anger. She didn't know him, after all. She should give him a chance. Emily obviously saw something in him.

"She's amazing, isn't she?" he asked. "You two are sure gettin' to be fast friends."

Does he know something? Am I that obvious? Kate went into full mental panic. She nodded and instantly sobered up.

"God, I'm a lucky son of a bitch." He laughed.

"She's amazing all right." Realizing he was clueless, Kate was then worried this was one of those times that someone doesn't take the hint that the other is in fact not interested in the conversation and continues to talk endlessly.

"It's almost 'mpossible to keep up with her!" Kate was confused as he slurred along. "So much talent. Always workin' on somethin', her mind always churning out something creative and...meaningful.

All I do is work for my father…It's 'bout all I can do to make myself worth it to her. Damn! Ya' know? S'like she's bored of me already sometimes…"

"Buddy, you don't gotta keep up with her. You gotta help her go even further. She can handle herself."

"S'like I'm doing what I need to do so she gets all the stuff she deserves, n' if I wanna ask her to marry me, I gotta be worth it, right?"

Kate nodded again.

"She's so stubborn though. Just don't see why she's gotta study so much. She can paint and draw all she wants if I get a good job."

"She's more than capable of pulling her weight with her art." Kate couldn't be silent anymore. "You gotta let her stand on her own too and not be…a macho man."

"Me? Macho? Ha!" He laughed for such a long time. Kate wanted so badly to be done listening to his blind vision of who Emily was and what she needed.

"I'm a lucky son of a bitch, huh?" he repeated.

You have no idea.

"She's always sayin' good things about you too. Gets all defensive and…" He almost seemed to lose his train of thought but picked it back up. "Seems happy here, thanks to you and Allie. I like you!" He clapped her on the shoulder.

"You gonna be all right getting home, buddy?" They arrived at the train entrance.

Tommy held a thumb up and winked as they parted ways to go opposite directions at the station.

How could someone so seemingly responsible and put together have doubts like that? And how could he not know just how lucky he was because of how focused he was on being what he thought he needed to be and not what Emily wanted. Her brain was officially a jumbled mess, but she realized that, in spite of it all, Tommy was a good man who cared for Emily. They both did. *Damn it.*

❖

Emily spent nearly every free opportunity in the following summer days with Kate. Often they met with Mia and worked on their crafts and enjoyed group outings with Allie and Art. Most of the time, though, Tommy was preoccupied with work. He made time for dates with Emily each week but fell absent from much of the summer festivities.

No one seemed to question that the two of them spent all their time together. The pair never neglected their friends but made a point to see each other regardless of what everyone else was doing. Over the few short weeks their relationship shifted and became a type of friendship all its own, the guilt that plagued them before easing each time they were together. Neither would admit it, but had they even tried, they couldn't stand to be apart from each other. They never spoke of nor questioned that they simply enjoyed being with each other most.

Allie's wedding grew closer, and preparations continued for the small ceremony and reception. Kate was proud to show off her photo work in the dress shop as they went for final fittings the week before the event. She hesitated to enthusiastically showcase them but made it known that Emily had helped her with the prints. They had spent an entire day at Alfonzo's perfecting them, and Emily was once again amazed at Kate's talent, as well as grateful to her for sharing it.

Emily struggled, however, with an ever-present pang of guilt that she invested far less time in Tommy than she should have, but it seemed to bother him very little. He continued to invest his time at the firm, committed to going as far as he could, and Emily realized it was his passion much like she had hers. She wouldn't deny him that. They enjoyed time together as it came, and she attempted to make the most of it. Emily hoped she was managing to balance her relationship with Tommy and friendship with Kate, but when she doubted herself, she ignored the question.

❖

Emily had looked forward to the girls' night Allie had planned the week before her wedding. A final bachelorette celebration of sorts. She had planned dinner and purchased tickets to a show at the Apollo Theater in Harlem, another part of New York Emily had yet to experience, and invited Kate to go along with them.

Emily was also excited to see the vibrant, ever-shifting community where Kate had grown up and talked about often. It was where she had lived and seen the changes, the hardships, the struggles of those around her, and according to Kate it was a place a lot of outsiders missed out on. It would be another step in seeing the true New York City, and hopefully after taking in a show at the theater, Kate could show them around. Emily knew, however, that it was Allie's night, and she didn't want to put her need for sightseeing above that.

"Where to next?" Emily asked as they exited the theater. "What a fantastic performance!"

"Next? I don't think there's a next for me." Allie sighed. "My weekend is booked solid, starting with picking up the dresses in the morning. I absolutely cannot be hung over around my mother."

"Who said hung over!?" Kate asked. "Don't deny our Emily here a look at Harlem now."

"That isn't going to work. You two go. It never stops you any other time. You're always together. In fact, I should be jealous of how close you are." She shrugged.

"We—uhh, w—" They both stumbled for an excuse. Emily was suddenly self-conscious that their habits were so obvious.

"Go! Have fun for me. And pray for me…" She hugged them both and shooed them off. So much for spending the evening with Allie.

"Okay, where to, my ever-present tour guide?" Emily casually linked her arm in Kate's as they sauntered down the busy Harlem street. She found she couldn't help herself, needing the contact, and knew that no one would think the wiser of two young friends out on the town.

She herself, however, thought back to all the other times she couldn't resist. The times when she would lean gently against Kate's shoulder in the park, clasp her hand just before telling her good-bye, or stand just close enough that she could see every detail in her eyes when they were in the studio. She had convinced herself that she was simply an emotive, affectionate person. Kate pulled her ever so slightly closer, causing a swell of joy in Emily.

They strolled down the street arm in arm for some time, Kate gently guiding them through the lively neighborhood. More than once Emily caught herself looking up for a glance into the other woman's eyes, and tonight, she let them stay there. So, it seemed, did Kate.

When she did pull away, she turned to see what at first appeared to be a very young man in an alarmingly dapper suit with a beautiful young woman in company. The way the young man moved was not precisely masculine, Emily noticed, surprised. *I wonder how Kate would look in a suit, sleek and dapper.* The door of a rather nondescript building, with no sign, no lights, was held for the lady as they disappeared into it.

"Let's go there," she suggested on impulse. She needed to find out more about the stranger and was having a hard time removing images of Kate in a fine suit from her rebellious mind.

Kate, on the other hand, noticed where the couple had gone. She fidgeted, suddenly uncomfortable and altogether nervous. "That's not the sort of place you should be," she mumbled.

"No place *I* should be? And just how do you know?"

"We. No place *we* should be." She was practically begging, yet Emily persisted.

"Why ever not, silly? Those two looked completely respectable. I don't see the problem."

She grabbed Kate by the hand and pulled them toward the shadowy entrance.

"Em…" She finally begged.

Her name being called so softly stopped Emily. She turned to stare at Kate and saw her fear up close. She understood what the place might be then, that the young man might have been no man at all.

She decided in that moment, even if she didn't realize it, to follow her gut, to throw care to the wind, and to go for something. For some reason, she longed to find out more about why Kate shied away. She felt a strange comfort in seeing the couple that had gone in there, seeing Kate's reaction…It sparked a curiosity she couldn't resist.

"Just for a bit," she whispered. "Where's your sense of adventure?"

❖

It was a bar Kate had narrowly avoided in the past weeks, during her time growing closer to Emily. More than once she had found herself in the very same spot, contemplating entering but lacking the courage. She longed to go in, to know the place, see what it held, who was inside.

She'd heard about it a long time ago, in school. Kids talking. She hadn't known if it was the one they mentioned or if it was still there. But with the war waging in her mind, she'd walked right to the entrance, watching the few others go in and out. She'd wondered if she could find someone to help her with the feelings she'd realized she was coming to have. Someone like her.

The bar was dim and smelled of old booze and cigarettes, a permanent fixture to any dive bar. Music drifted softly from a piano in the corner, one of the only lights in the place provided for the player and his music. The bar and lone bartender stood immediately in front of the entrance, with a scarce number of shadowed individuals scattered down it. Figures swayed along with the piano, gathered close to one another, while others huddled in conversation, and while at first glance the place seemed seedy and sparse, rather nondescript, an undercurrent of energy was there.

The bartender and nearly everyone in the space looked up when Emily and Kate entered, as if startled and wary of some foreign presence entering. Everything seemed to have frozen except for the notes continuing from the piano. Kate swallowed hard as Emily guided them to the bar. The feel of her hand clutched in Emily's was both a lifeline and an anchor pulling her down into the unknown. Fortunately, no one took further notice of their presence as they sat at the bar, silent, stiff.

Emily looked for the couple they had followed in and found them at a table near the piano. The young man stood, held out their hand, and asked the lady to dance. Emily remained mesmerized for some unknown reason and watched the two in a lovers' embrace, swaying along with the music. She couldn't pull her eyes off the person in the suit, the way their movement was gentler, their stature distinctly less masculine than most men she knew.

Kate meanwhile avoided any connection with others, instead staring at the shelved wall of alcohol.

"What'll ya have, loves?" the bartender asked. Emily and Kate jumped. The bartender was a petite black man, an older gentleman with eyes that stood out even in the darkness. She could somehow sense a kindness about him, his gaze welcoming and accepting.

Just then, the couple Emily had been studying so intently appeared at the bar next to her. The suited person gestured for Emily to order in turn and smiled at her. When she looked back to Kate, there it was—the realization that they were among those who had nowhere else to go, who let themselves free there. And though she expected to feel shame or disgust, her heart sped up, and she felt a part of this place.

"You're safe here, babies," the bartender whispered as he handed over the drinks Kate had ordered. He smiled and turned to the other couple.

Oh no. I'm in more danger than ever.

"Did you know what this place was?" Emily didn't look at Kate, instead watching others intently as she had been for what seemed like a lifetime of silence that stretched between the two of them. Kate picked at the label on her beer bottle. "Did you need to come here?" Perhaps it was a question for herself as well.

The answer was written with intensity in the eyes that gazed into hers. Emily realized she herself needed this place just as Kate had and felt the terror in that realization mingle with the overwhelming comfort that she wasn't alone.

"I needed *you*," Kate whispered. "I need you."

Kate sat as stone as a statue, fearing she would shatter if Emily came too close. But she did come close, their bodies nearly touching as she moved to Kate, gently pressing between her legs. Kate wanted nothing more than to wrap her arms around the other woman's waist, pull her in close, and never leave.

Their eyes never left each other, and with the terror of breaking the spell they cast upon each other as the guiding force, Emily held out her hand and waited for Kate to join her. And Kate did.

The sensation of their hands held by the other and the pounding of their hearts made the world fade from view as they moved into each other on the dance floor. The smallest touches of their fingers, the gentle press of Kate's hand on the small of Emily's back, and the look in her eyes were all that kept them grounded as they gently swayed to the notes drifting across the small room. Time slowed, and with each step, the barriers that had held them apart fell away in the small haven they had found. Together.

> *Where in this wide world can I find someone*
> *To hold me like you do*
> *In our secret place, our quiet space, to hold me*
> *The whole night through*

Kate needed the press of her body against Emily. Her resolve to deny this woman slowly broke into pieces, her last remnants of control on the brink of shattering along with it. She guided Emily's hand to her chest, capturing it over her heart and covering it with her own. Their cheeks pressed against one another. She took in the scent that was so uniquely Em and felt the soft caress on the nape of her neck, fingers beginning to run through her hair.

> *I've never wished upon a star so bright*
> *As the one I see in your eyes*
> *I'll find you here, I'll find you there,*
> *To hold me in the deep night skies*

Fire traced down Emily's spine at the acceptance that she finally, after restraining all her incessant fantasies, was touching this woman. She pressed her leg hard between Kate's thighs, needing to be closer, wanting to feel her desire. She dug her fingers into the thick black hair, tasting her neck with the smallest of kisses until Kate could take it no more.

Kate closed the distance, kissed her the way she'd been dreaming of for weeks. She felt the press of Emily's tongue begging for entrance. Cupping her neck, she opened herself and drank in Emily as she'd wanted to for so long. She couldn't seem to get close enough to this woman, wanting more and more of the sweetness of Emily's mouth. She had never felt something as spectacular as holding her in her arms.

Emily clutched anything of Kate she could get her hands on. She never wanted to stop kissing this woman. She felt she was about to practically climb her like a tree, the intensity building each moment. Her hips involuntarily ground against Kate's leg until she was practically begging for release right there on the dance floor. *My God. I'm out of control!*

But, as much as she wanted to, Kate knew they needed to slow down. Regardless of the *type* of bar, they were still among others. She gently pulled away and lifted Emily's chin to meet her eyes in the dim light. With only the smallest smirk from Kate, both fell into laughter—the joy of finally giving in winning out. Forget the outside world. They were going to be with one another in this small sanctuary.

Hours passed as they swayed along, held one another, gave in to the kisses they both so desperately needed. Patrons came and went around them. As yet another song began, Kate took in the sight of their hands entwined together, felt the softness of Emily's cheek against her own, heard the music playing softly around them. And in that moment, she accepted she was hopelessly and completely in love with Emily Stanton.

❖

Emily sank into the comfort of the arms holding her.

"Last call, folks," the bartender called from across the room, the pianist finishing the final notes of his song. *Not yet. I'm not ready to let go, to go back to fighting this.* Emily kissed Kate again, simply because she could, and led them back to the bar. They never stopped holding hands, needing to touch each other.

We should talk about this. It can never be a reality. Emily pushed away the doubts. *Not tonight, not yet. Maybe there's a way. Maybe we can have the summer at least.*

Strong arms wrapped around Emily from behind, as she was about to open the door. A soft kiss on her neck followed, and she turned to look at the most beautiful woman she'd ever seen. She tripped and tumbled head over heels in that moment. It was the moment Emily had hoped she'd never feel, because she would give up everything she knew in her life if it meant nights like these with Kate. *Damn it.*

I'm in love with her.

CHAPTER FIFTEEN

Kate shuffled down the stairs and grabbed her camera from the entryway table, as though it were her safety blanket. She pulled at the dress she was currently subjected to, attempting to adjust it enough to make it anything other than a dress, unsuccessfully.

"We need to be out this door in two minutes. Does everyone understand that!?" Allie yelled across the brownstone. "I absolutely refuse to be late to my own wedding."

The sounds of scurrying upstairs continued while Allie's father sat in the living room reading the paper.

"I'd rather get this going than sit here in this thing." Kate pulled again at the fabric.

"Almost ready," Emily called from upstairs. Kate absent-mindedly glanced up, waiting for her to descend. She'd replayed the feeling of every inch of Emily for the last week, constantly on a loop in her mind. She craved her now, wanted to be with her, to take on the world. But today was about Allie. She would put her wandering thoughts aside for just a bit longer.

All hope disappeared when the object of her fantasies hurried down the stairs, nearly tripping—just as Kate's heart did in her chest at the sight.

"Ready—" Kate snapped the shutter and waited for the look. Emily feigned annoyance, and Kate loved it. Emily froze though when she saw Kate in the dress again, and Kate watched as she scanned her from head to toe. As uncomfortable as she was, she enjoyed the effect the dress was apparently having on Emily. She saw Emily adjust her own dress, a lovely blush growing up her neck, and Kate hoped that it had something to do with what she hoped were thoughts they had in common.

"You are aware that I'm the one getting married this afternoon, correct?" Allie held out her hand, breaking up their moment. "Give it up."

"We aren't even—"

Allie had her arms crossed, hand out waiting for the camera.

Kate trudged out the door, Emily close behind, laughing as they climbed in the car at the street corner. What would it be like to be on her way to her own wedding—to Emily?

Kate hadn't been to many weddings, but this one she would never forget. The ceremony was intimate, at a quaint little church just over the bridge in Brooklyn—the same church Art's family had attended since his grandparents had stepped off the ship in New York Harbor fifty years before. The small chapel was filled with an air of love and hope for the new couple as they said their vows to one another.

Kate and Emily stood by Allie, while Art was accompanied by two of his younger brothers. As the oldest of five, he held a great deal of responsibility, but all his younger siblings looked up to him and saw what he had with Allie. She was already part of their clan, the ceremony only making it official for the rest of the world. It was a day of celebration, and everyone was joyous on their behalf.

The reception was what everyone was truly looking forward to. In lieu of using the church's reception hall, Art's parents had insisted on using their backyard garden and opening their home to everyone. Toasts abounded, food was abundant, and drinks overflowed as the night kicked off.

Kate had never really thought about marriage, but if she did, it would have been like that one. A day surrounded by those who truly mattered to her, those she knew by name and those she'd easily be able to meet. Not like what she knew Emily was destined for, a grand proceeding and spectacle made into an extravagance by her mother (who was currently in animated conversation with Allie's mother on just this subject). Regardless, she hoped on her own wedding day she would have the same glow Allie did in that moment.

As if conjuring her, Emily walked across the yard in front of Kate, and she took the opportunity to… *Click—*

Kate had been reunited with her instrument and was lasering in on Emily. Giving her a wink, she moved on to frame up her next victim, one of Art's uncles and his wife. Directly behind Emily, though, was Tommy, holding out his hand for a dance on the makeshift dance floor. Her stomach clenched, fearing she'd been caught. As usual, though, he seemed oblivious. *God, she wanted to dance with Emily again, to have her in her arms.* Instead she'd have to watch Tommy do just that.

Kate watched them go, the now-familiar stir of jealousy rumbling inside her. Instead of giving in to it, she threw back the shot of whiskey she'd snagged from the makeshift bar, determined to have a good time.

"You look right well lovely tonight, Kate."

Ralph. Damn it. Well, what the hell? "Let's go, my friend." She pulled him along, surprising him as a shocked grin shot across his face.

With a shared look across the dance floor, the two couples joined the throng and danced away. But Kate and Emily had their own dance, stealing all the glances they could manage as they were spun around, smiling to each other over the secret held between them.

They stopped only when the small band took a much-needed break, Kate realizing this was the first time she hadn't attempted to pawn Ralph off on another lucky lady. He wasn't such a bad guy after all. As a matter of fact, everyone else probably thought she should have given him a chance.

"Enjoying the party?" Emily startled Kate. She was close to her ear, close enough she could smell her fresh scent, feel her breath on her neck.

"I've had better dance partners," Kate replied. After another stolen glance, Emily blushed profusely. Kate blamed the alcohol. They needed to be careful.

Emily snagged a piece of the freshly cut wedding cake and took the biggest bite possible. Kate raised an eyebrow, no doubt wishing she could kiss the lips Emily had just licked the icing off of. *God help me.*

"Kate, dear, would you mind bringing out the case of wine from the kitchen?" Allie's mother beckoned from the makeshift bar that they were all periodically tending to.

"Sure thing."

Kate fought her way across the tiny kitchen space through a particularly inebriated group of Art's high school buddies to the crates of wine stacked in the corner, rejecting three macho offers of assistance. *Damn dress. No. Damn testosterone.*

"Does the lady need some assistance?"

Kate nearly jumped out of her dress. "Is that your new thing? Startling the shit out of me?" She couldn't help but let her eyes wander down the woman she'd been stealing glances of all day. Emily had caught her red-handed and smirked.

"And destroying the last shred of control I have around you?" Kate asked.

The room had emptied, faint sounds of the party outside wafting in.

"It's the only thing keeping mine from snapping," Emily whispered into her ear, her tongue slipping along the edge.

Just a taste. Kate's hands took on a wild mind of their own, wandering along every inch of Emily's body as their mouths fused, tongues hungry for one another. She wanted to take her, feel how hot and wet she knew she was right there in that kitchen. She pulled the dress high and let herself enjoy the silky thigh beneath as she inched higher and higher. Emily spread her legs, just enough for Kate to feel her wetness soaking her panties. She whimpered.

"I'm sure they can lift the wine themselves." Tommy rounded the corner into the kitchen.

"Do you think they need more red, or the white from the

cooler?" Kate was visibly out of breath, Emily tugging at the hem of her dress.

Tommy was silent a beat too long for comfort.

"Mrs. Miller asked me to also acquire a liquor refill and help you as needed, Kate."

How formal.

"Ah, yes, well. The liquor's there on the counter if you'd like to make a selection."

"And I shall *acquire* the chardonnay." Emily chimed in with an exaggeratedly pompous accent.

Following this incident, the new goal of the night for Kate became staying multiple feet from Emily at all times, which was nearly impossible given the ever-shrinking size of the party. As the night continued, the older the person, the sooner they left. The younger crowd continued to celebrate, filling the dance floor under the light of the lanterns and moonlight above. With everyone who left, Kate and Emily had one less reason not to be around one another.

Many of the gents remained close to the makeshift bar, dedicating yet another round to the newly married Art. It would likely be one of their last times together before many of them went off to basic training.

"Get over here." Art grabbed Kate by the arm and bounced a shot glass into her hand. He wrapped his arm around Allie, the stupidest grin shining on his face, and held up a toast. Kate purposefully focused on the toast instead of Emily, who stood next to Tommy.

"*My wife* and I..." He looked lovingly at Allie, and Kate's heart almost melted. "Wanted to thank you for making today, and this summer, so special."

"You have brought such joy to our lives, and we hope that all of you find a love that takes your heart, holds it tight, and keeps it as home wherever you might be in this world. Cheers."

The five of them lifted their glasses, a toast to the couple, to friendship, and to a summer of memories.

"So eloquent," Kate said, playfulness seeping into her tone. They all laughed.

"Emily and I have thoroughly enjoyed our time with you and wish you all the happiness in the world. I can only hope that we one day have a ceremony as wonderful as this." Tommy threw his arm possessively around Emily's waist.

"You'll have to work on an equally romantic proposal then," Kate blurted, beer in her hand, before realizing she'd commented aloud.

Tommy bit off a glare, Kate avoiding eye contact at the sudden turn in his demeanor. "Indeed. Shall we dance, my love?" he inquired of Emily, turning on the charm. With a handshake to Art, he pulled Emily to the dance floor.

Kate wanted nothing more than to steal her away for herself, erase all the complications, and get them out of the mess they found themselves in. A mess no one else knew of, or so she desperately hoped.

The night wound on, the ladies dancing away, chatting on the dance floor, the copious amounts of alcohol providing more than ample conversation material, and the band played on, nearing their ending time.

Kate stood, minding her own business, when "Oof." Someone nearly took her to the ground. Looking down...*of course.*

"Come on. We have to get Allie through all the smelly men and rescue her husband." Emily slurred her words, drunk but without a care of any sort, it seemed. She clung to Kate, apparently having forgotten their need for distance.

Kate had a hand around her waist to stabilize Emily before she could decide against it, unable to hold back a laugh and a knowing look at Allie when she was nearly knocked over by the cheerful but sloppy woman now in her arms.

"Never fear. I can get him from their clutches, I'm sure." Allie walked away.

Damn it, Allie. Emily's head had to be spinning.

"Mmm. You're not smelly though." Emily sagged against Kate a bit, likely more tired than drunk.

"I should hope not." Kate laughed. She wanted nothing more

than to hold her upright but was increasingly nervous of Tommy's glances her way.

"Allie is married!" Emily exclaimed. Kate smiled at the fact as well.

"And you are drunk," Kate replied, attempting to spin Emily around, resulting in them almost tumbling to the floor.

"Where's Tommy?" Kate asked. Perhaps letting Tommy take care of her was best, even if it was the last thing she wanted.

"...don't care," Emily mumbled. She leaned into Kate.

...I've never wished upon a star so bright
As the one I see in your eyes...

Kate tightened her hand still around Emily's waist infinitesimally, recalling their night that felt too long ago as the same song played softly. She closed her eyes for just a moment, escaping to their haven, taking in Emily. She knew Emily heard it too, feeling her grip tighten as well. Neither moved for a moment, just listening. But when Kate opened her eyes, Tommy was walking over cheerfully from across the yard. She stood up straighter.

"I fear we'll have one less set of hands for cleanup," she nervously joked, guiding Emily into his arms.

"Let's get you settled inside until we're ready to go, my love." He practically ignored Kate, smiling down at Emily.

She watched them go, wanting nothing more than to be the one caring for her. But she wasn't hers to care for. She watched them stumble into the house and occupied herself with clearing up the discarded bottles that scattered in abundance around her.

❖

Finally, mercifully, the last of the guests made their way home, leaving the immediate family cleaning in their wake. In spite of Allie's insistence that they could leave, Kate and Tommy remained to help, while Emily still lay passed out on the couch inside.

Kate walked past the living room searching for any remaining garbage scattered about and saw Emily asleep. A streak of moonlight crossed her face, shone over her shoulder as she lay on her side, illuminating her soft hair as it fell across her cheek. Kate took in every feature. She wanted nothing more than to crouch beside the couch and brush her hair behind her ear. She wanted Emily to reach for her, smile softly when she realized she was there. Take her home and keep her safe...

"It was lovely today, wasn't it?" Tommy startled Kate.

She turned to the kitchen and took on the monstrous pile of dishes filling the kitchen sink. "It was. Very romantic. And a great party."

"I'm sure you got some wonderful photos too, no?"

"Hopefully. Allie held my camera hostage for a big part of the day."

"Any good ones of Emily?" He set down the crate of empty wine bottles he'd been organizing.

Kate hesitated. *What was he getting at?* "I'm sure I did."

"She looked beautiful today, don't you think?" He leaned against the counter. Kate scrubbed the dish harder and tried not to imagine her asleep in the other room.

"Well, I should hope you'd think so." She smiled nervously.

"I think she's the most beautiful lady I've ever met, and I feel like the luckiest son of a bitch alive." He paused. "I can't wait to ask her to marry me one day soon."

Kate momentarily stopped washing, caught herself, and continued. "I'm sure she'll be overjoyed."

"I'm not sure. Since I've been here, she seems preoccupied."

"I'm sure she's enjoying her summer, getting to know the city." Kate proceeded carefully, fighting down the anger bubbling inside her. "Maybe she's focusing on herself for a change."

He waited a moment too long for comfort but picked back up, as if trying to get to his point, mildly ignoring Kate's analysis, "I know I've been preoccupied as well, working a lot of the time. But I feel lucky that I'll have a career to support her. Have a family one day...Let her lead a healthy, *normal* life."

Kate finally looked up at him.

As dominant as he was attempting to be, his gaze faltered, and he looked away. Silence stretched unbearably between them. "I don't know what's going on between the two of you, but it can't lead to anything good." His eyes met hers again, his confidence returning. "I care too much about her to let some strange infatuation tarnish what she's working toward."

"And what is that?" Kate asked, red finally seeping into her vision. "Being a cute housewife with two point five children and a white picket fence?" She nearly broke the glass she was still scrubbing, surprising herself that she was far angrier than scared of him. "When have you ever asked what *she* wants?"

The accusation seemed to diffuse him a bit. "I want her to be happy."

"Happy? Or making her into whatever is convenient for you?"

That comment sparked his anger anew. "I'm working my ass off to provide a life for both of us. Maybe it isn't glamorous, but it's something real. *Convenient* is doing whatever the hell feels good in the moment and without thinking about the repercussions."

Kate laughed bitterly. He could never imagine how inconvenient the depths of her feelings for Emily were. Or how precious.

"She deserves better than sneaking around hoping for some perverse fantasy to come true."

He stormed from the room, leaving Kate with only the sound of the running water. She stood frozen, contemplating how the few small shreds of hope she had held onto had snapped in an instant.

Perverse fantasy... Was that all she had to offer Emily? In what world could her love possibly amount to anything more than that?

CHAPTER SIXTEEN

Four years later, 1946

"Did you see the look on Tommy's face when he had to help your mother out of the restaurant?" Lauren, one of Emily's close school friends, laughed as they meandered through the door of Allie's small Brooklyn apartment.

"She was such a flirt, I thought he might jump out of his skin," Annabelle, her other invitee and school friend, replied.

Allie chimed in. "With all the charm he lays on her to get his way, I think it serves him right."

Emily followed them in, smiling and secretly agreeing with Allie. At least her mother had finally loosened up and agreed to let all the girls have the evening without everyone else around, including Tommy. After all, he was dropping her mother at her Aunt Jane's place and heading out with the boys for his own celebration. She deserved the same, and they had managed a fabulous bachelorette evening amongst themselves.

They had dinner, went to a bar, danced with so many young gentlemen, and had finally decided to head out before the evening wore on for too long. Now they were all spending the night in Brooklyn together, the apartment to themselves.

Surrounded by her closest friends, Emily couldn't have been happier. She was elated that Kate and Mia had been able to join them as well. Having Kate in her company made her remember the fun person she enjoyed having around, how funny she was, and how she could get along with nearly anyone. She had such an easy personality, at least when she wasn't mercilessly teasing her.

Emily watched Mia tail along through the front door and shook her head in disbelief at how she had become her own young woman. It was amazing how it seemed so long since she'd met those two, but how quickly the time had gone by and changed them. She'd changed as well...But tonight, they were all together, her worlds colliding, and they were having an incredible yet simple time together.

"Bring out the wine, this night's not over," she announced to the group. Allie laughed and, although she herself wasn't drinking, held up two bottles from the kitchen, part of the stash for the wedding in two days. Surely no one would realize. The group cheered, already tipsy.

"So has Clarke mentioned the lecture position again?" Lauren asked as they conversed.

"She did at graduation. I hadn't even talked with Tommy about it," Emily replied. Another thing she had to think about, even if it could wait until after the wedding. She hadn't forgotten her professor's follow-up on an offered position, or that she'd yet to discuss it with anyone except her two closest friends at school.

"What's the position?" Kate chimed in. She'd been fairly quiet during the latter part of the evening. Emily noted she'd made the effort to get to know her friends from school but never drawn attention to herself.

Emily's attention was immediately drawn to Kate, however. She really wanted her opinion. "It's an assistant position within the department to my mentor, Professor Clarke. I've been studying with her for a few years now. She travels quite a bit, so I'd have an opportunity to lecture and permanent studio space at the university. I'd likely get to travel with her as well, every now and then."

She paused. "She travels here to New York University quite a bit, actually." Her gaze flickered to Kate. *Perhaps I could see you again?*

She wanted the position and didn't really know why she was hesitating.

"Sounds like an amazing opportunity." Kate looked as if she was holding back a question.

Allie piped up. "Tommy will support it. He seemed excited when you mentioned it last month."

"He seemed surprised by it, for sure." Emily hesitated. Tommy never meant to hold her back, but she said, "He's made so much progress himself. I don't want it to get in the way of that."

"Your career wouldn't get in the way of anything. Why does yours matter less than his?" Kate looked surprised at what she'd just said.

Emily grew defensive. "I didn't say it wasn't. He's just worked so hard, and it's a lot to think about." *It's just how things are, right?*

"I'm sure you've worked just as hard," Kate replied. She stood and gave Emily a small, perhaps knowing smile. "Who needs another round?"

They eventually broke into smaller groups, the alcohol consumption slowing, while the conversations continued. Allie talked with Lauren, and Kate quietly chatted with Annabelle.

"So, my high school graduate." Emily bumped shoulders with Mia. "What are you up to these days besides making much more beautiful art than your sister?" The comment earned a scowl from Kate, who looked up at them from her spot on the floor.

Mia blushed. "I have a waitressing gig at the diner down from the studio. Mostly nights right now, since I'm low man in. Trying to be in there as much as possible and helping Kate whenever I can."

"I did the same thing once I started school. My mother thought it was ridiculous and that I should focus on my studies," Emily said, noticing that Kate had started listening. "But I think it kept me occupied and helped me have a sense of accomplishment."

"Kate keeps offering to get a place with me, but it's hard to leave Gramps. We'd have to find someone to help watch out for him. I want to pull my weight."

"Gramps wants you out." Kate smiled, finally chiming in.

"And you just want cheaper rent."

Kate shrugged and returned to her conversation with Annabelle.

"Are you sure you want to live with that one?" Emily asked, grinning.

"She's all right, I guess."

"I think it would be a great step. Give you some independence and help you feel like the young adult you are." Emily cupped her cheek, amazed once again that she'd grown up this fast. "Plus that way you can hang all your work around the place and show her up." They giggled together.

Mia quieted. "You know, I missed getting to see you off when you left."

"I know. I'm sorry for that. Everything was a bit…hectic."

"It's okay. I think Kate was really bummed out though." She lowered her voice. "She got all broody for a long time that fall."

Emily was silent, and Mia looked at her. "She really missed you."

"I've missed being here," she replied, not allowing herself to reveal any more than that. But she meant it. She loved being in that place, with those people. "And I promise to keep up with you, young lady. You're going to go far. I know it."

❖

"Can I help?" Emily asked Allie in the kitchen. Everyone had gone upstairs to prepare for bed, and Allie was straightening up the rest of the house, finishing in the kitchen.

"Stay and chat?"

Emily pulled up a stool from the corner while Allie finished wiping down the counter. She felt like a patron seeking advice from a bartender at last call.

"Thank you for tonight. It was nice to be relaxed before the rehearsal dinner tomorrow and then, well, the wedding."

"I'm happy to have everyone. I miss girls' nights. With all of Art's brothers over all the time it's a regular den around here." A trace of endearment seeped into her words.

"Ever have Kate and Mia over?" Emily casually asked.

She laughed. "Those two are regular workaholics. Mia took

right after her sister." Her smile dimmed a bit. "Kate pulled away a bit a few years back, really put her head down and immersed herself in getting her own business going. Not that she hasn't always been a hard worker. So it's difficult to pin her down, but we try to have the two of them over as much as possible."

A few years? As in four years? Everyone was pointing that out tonight, it seemed.

"She's really making it for herself though, huh?" she said, attempting to stay on a comfortable level of conversation and not drown in guilt.

Allie nodded. "We try to be there for her. Give her someone to share her time with outside of her work, get her to live a little."

Emily dropped her eyes. "She needs that even if she'd never admit it."

"Tell me about it. She talked to me some after you spent the summer here last time," Allie said codedly. "Not much, though. As though she wanted to but couldn't. She's stubborn."

Why was she coming back to that?

"We all know she's stubborn. And I mean she is your best friend. I was only here for a few months. I'd hope she always talks to you," Emily replied, trying to escape Allie's implications.

"I think you made an impression on her while you were here. I remember how close the two of you got." She paused. "I tried to keep her updated on you whenever you called or we visited, but she didn't seem to want to know." She pinned Emily with a stare. "She wouldn't tell me what happened between the two of you before you left."

Emily shifted uncomfortably in her seat.

"Regardless, I'm glad you've been able to reconnect, it seems, while you've been here." She let her off the hook.

"Seems a small world that she'd end up our *photographer*," Emily replied, getting slightly annoyed with Allie's persistence.

"Yes. Well, I recommend only the best, and I couldn't very well have no suggestions for your mother."

"True, I suppose. It was quite the surprise though."

"What surprise?" They turned just as Kate entered the kitchen, holding an empty glass. She stepped behind Allie to refill her glass from the faucet.

"The small-world occurrence of you just *happening* to be my wedding photographer."

"Ah. Yes. I thought the same thing. Such a small world that includes your mother and…perhaps Allie?"

"Guilty, okay?" Allie threw her hands up in mock surrender.

"I'm headed to bed. I'll see you upstairs," Emily said.

Her eyes met Kate's for just a second, and Kate wondered what they'd talked about that would put a well-hidden look of sadness on her face. She followed Emily out of her line of sight, and when she looked back, Allie was watching her.

"What?" she asked, suddenly defensive.

"Nothing at all." Allie went back to wiping the counter, even though it was spotless. "Have a good time this evening?"

"Indeed."

"That was enthusiastic." Allie laughed while Kate chugged her glass of water and refilled it once again.

"It was a lovely time, and I hope Emily enjoyed being with her friends," Kate said.

"She seemed happy you were here."

Kate didn't respond, just kept drinking more water. She was determined not to talk about Emily and not to have a massive hangover in the morning, although she wasn't nearly even tipsy at that point.

"Glad I could drag you out tonight."

"You don't have to *drag* me out often, and you know it. I just don't want to be intrusive with your family things."

"Family isn't always blood-related," Allie said quietly, giving Kate a pointed look. Kate turned and leaned on the counter next to her.

"Plus, we're going to make sure you come around since you're at the top of the child-sitting list. I'll tell you that much." Allie smiled and bumped her shoulder.

"You'll regret that when you see all the photos you'll have of that child."

They laughed together.

"What about you? How many do you want?"

"How many!? Who says *any*?" Kate huffed. "I suppose you should be asking Emily that next, no?" This time her laugh was hollow. Emily would have her own family, one she'd never be a part of, blood-related or not. She swallowed hard.

"Well, I was asking about *you*!"

"I haven't really thought about it. Don't know that it's in my future, and besides, if you're secretly trying to coerce me into becoming your au pair for your sure-to-be-minimum of five children, I think I'll have enough on my hands."

They stood in silence. It was amazing the paths their lives had taken, diverging in the most seemingly drastic ways, yet they could still be there for each other. No matter what, being who they were or destined to be, whether mother or no, they'd remain the closest of friends, truly family. Allie threw her arm around Kate's waist.

"Are you okay with the wedding coming up? Being there for it?" Allie asked boldly.

Kate immediately flashed back to nearly crying, wanting to tell Allie everything after Emily left. Every time Allie had probed during the months following her departure, she'd wanted to tell her how her world had walked out on her, after ripping her heart out and taking a piece of it with her back to Boston—how she'd pushed away her best friend, someone who'd ignited something in her she hadn't felt since. But she could never do that. It had turned out to be nothing but perverse fantasy after all. But Allie knew, didn't she? Damn her. Why was she being so nosy?

"Why are you bringing this up again? You always think there's something more to everything than there is. I was hired for a job. I'll do it. Emily is your cousin, we were friends for a while years ago, and now she's a client. Simple as that."

Allie paused, clearly unfazed by the backlash. She took Kate's face in both her hands and looked into her eyes. Kate's bottom lip rebelliously quivered, but she refused to let anything out. *Alcohol makes everything dramatic.*

"Don't make yourself hurt any more than you have to."

All she could do was nod and sink into Allie's embrace.

❖

Everyone was sound asleep, bunked up either in Allie's room or the spare, soon-to-be-baby's room, except Kate, stubbornly posted on the couch downstairs. Emily, however, tossed and turned, nearly waking Allie up multiple times as she lay in the dark of her room. She blamed her restlessness on the wine, and refused to believe it was the pressure of the coming activities tomorrow, the wedding, or all the thoughts that plagued her endlessly, as they had in the last few days. Were these the feelings all brides had before their ceremonies? She remembered preparations with Allie for her wedding and how, despite the stressfulness, she'd constantly had a smile on her face.

She didn't deny, though, that she'd had fun in her time here. Being in the city with Allie, her family, with Mia, and with Kate had been a treasure. This evening had been charming too, a great time with all her closest friends, her worlds colliding. *Until Allie stuck her nose in things she didn't need to.*

Once again her thoughts drifted, as they so often did, to Kate. Seeing Kate again…The shock of literally running into her, moments of pain, finally being able to move on and enjoy being around each other. She smiled, thinking of the quiet time they'd spent together in the studio getting to know each other again, spending the evening with everyone, yet in each other's company. She dwelt on the moment in the alley when she wanted nothing more than to remember how soft and demanding Kate's lips could be. She wanted to connect again, but that could not, and would not, happen. *You're getting married in less than forty-eight hours, for Christ's sake!*

Determined to relieve herself of the endless processing, the screaming of her bladder from the copious glasses of wine she'd consumed that evening distracted her. She squirmed just enough to cause Allie to roll over before she gave in.

At the end of the darkened hallway, however, she spotted the squared-off line of light seeping out of the bathroom, which was clearly in use. Emily waited patiently, and sleepily, for the door to open. When it did, it took a moment for her eyes to adjust to the bright light as the occupant silhouetted within exited.

"Jesus Christ!" Kate jumped back, hand on her chest.

Emily covered her mouth to contain her laughter.

"I would apologize, but that was pretty entertaining."

"I'm sure…"

They stood for a moment. "Can't sleep?" Kate asked.

She shook her head. "Too much wine." *And thoughts of you.*

Kate raised an eyebrow. "Still a lightweight, it seems?"

"I was perfectly mature this evening, thank you very much!"

Kate apparently still loved getting under her skin. "Indeed you were. Thank you for inviting us. It was a nice evening."

"I'm happy you came. Wouldn't have been the same without you."

Silence again. *When were we reduced to this level of small talk?*

Emily danced uncomfortably. "I really do need—"

"Of course." Kate moved aside and Emily stepped closer. Emily could feel the heat coming off Kate's breath. Neither moved.

"Good night," Kate whispered, seeming to search Emily's face before stepping aside.

Emily took her time, splashed cool water on her face, and tried not to stare too long in the mirror. *Just go the hell to sleep and tell Allie to mind her own business tomorrow.* She opened the door.

Kate stood there, leaning against the wall, looking at her.

"It wasn't the wine," she said, her voice low. "I couldn't sleep either."

They stood in silence, studying each other for a moment. Emily leaned against the wall beside her, their shoulders brushing. She simply couldn't help her need to be close to this woman.

"Are you excited for this weekend?" Kate asked.

Emily couldn't quite decipher the look on her face or the intent of her question, but she would take the time with her, small talk or not.

"I'm looking forward to the party." She didn't feel like lying.

"It's a lot of fun to have everyone you care about with you and celebrating."

The corner of Kate's mouth turned up in a small smile. "That's good then. You deserve it."

Emily laughed. "But in reality, it's all for my mother. Go against her on any of it, and she nearly has a hernia. She's sort of sucked a lot of the fun out of it. You'd think it was her own wedding all over again."

"You should care a little less what she thinks. It's your life, after all." Kate paused. "And your wedding."

Emily's gut dropped. She never felt as though she were in control of things, of her choices, anymore. *When did that happen?* She nodded. "I should care a lot less about what people tell me about a lot of things lately," she whispered. She slid down the wall, sitting against it. Kate joined her, knees to her chest, clearly looking at Emily for more. "I really want the position I mentioned earlier."

Kate put her hand on her knee. "So take it."

"It's complicated." Emily was fixated on the hand touching her. She couldn't help it when she placed hers atop it. She stroked the soft skin.

"I'm sure you've earned it. You're an amazing artist, and you deserve to make your own choices with your talent." She wove their fingers together.

"I'm not just thinking of me though. Tommy deserves what he's worked for. What if it gets in the way of that?"

Kate pulled her hand away and looked into the darkness. "He should love you enough to make it work, to stop thinking of just himself," she whispered. Then, she added, "If you keep doubting it, the talent you have, and never take a chance, then you can be sure it won't happen. You'll just keep trying to please someone else."

Silence spread again.

Kate finally spoke. "I want you to be happy." Their eyes met. "It's all I ever wanted…for you to know how amazing, and talented, and beautiful, and strong, and wonderful you are. And for you to believe it."

Emily dipped her gaze to Kate's lips just before she kissed her.

She kissed her love, the one who saw her like no one else seemed to, because she simply had to. It was a kiss that spoke of the want they both still held, of missed chances. Emily felt Kate put everything into it. The desire to be closer overtook her, and she deepened the kiss. She grabbed fistfuls of Kate's shirt, and shifted, feeling Kate's hands on her hips as she straddled her, sitting in her lap. Sweetness turned to heat, igniting between them. They pushed each other, farther and farther, testing their limits as the passion flamed hotter.

Kate broke their kiss and whispered frantically, "Get up."

Emily froze in fear that she'd gone too far but stood quickly. Kate stood as well and immediately pressed their mouths together again. *Damn it all.*

Kate pulled them into the bathroom.

God, had she missed the heat of those lips. So much better than all her memories of the last time she tasted them. Kate pressed her tongue, begging entrance, which Emily happily gave. Emily was suddenly lifted and was sitting on the sink, mouths still fused, still clutching Kate's shirt. She grabbed tighter, pulling up on the fabric, only letting go to slide her hands underneath it.

Kate grabbed her ass, sliding up her back as she took Emily again and again with each kiss.

Emily's hands traced a fiery path up Kate's back, sliding one hand around to cup her breast. She didn't hesitate, squeezing her nipple. Kate's breath hitched and she moaned softly. Not to be left out, Kate unbuttoned the first button of Emily's night shirt and fused her mouth to the silky skin there, nipping not so gently. Emily gasped.

"Need something?" Kate was teasing. Their eyes met, and Emily saw the mischievous grin that haunted her dreams so often adorn her face. She kissed her again, deeply, letting all the passion bubbling in her boil to the surface.

Emily couldn't possibly process a witty retort, not now, when she needed Kate so much. "Kate…" she whispered in her ear. She took Kate's hand and guided it beneath the waistband of her panties. Their eyes met. Emily kissed her softly, realizing she needed more than her touch but wanted even that so desperately.

Kate kissed her back with equal fervor, but just as softly. Her hand slid lower, agonizingly slow until her fingers dipped into Emily's heat and through her wetness. Emily whimpered and pressed into her hand as Kate slowly stroked her.

But then she stopped.

Emily nearly cried out, breaking their kiss when Kate took her hand out, making her nearly go mad. She stared at Kate, confusion and disappointment filling her, overwhelmed by her primal need. She still had her hands pinned to Kate's nipples, but then Kate brought up her hand, popping a soaked finger into her mouth. Emily licked her lips, eyes locked as Kate cleaned her finger, and she hungered for that mouth on her.

As if reading her thoughts, Kate lifted her from the sink and pulled at her drawers and underwear. She dropped to her knees, and Emily watched as Kate raised her legs one by one onto her shoulders and looked up at her.

Emily ran her hands through the thick locks below her. Kate never moved her gaze from Emily's as she edged closer, and Emily could feel her breath kiss her just before her tongue snaked out, licking her. She gasped and covered her mouth to stop the sounds she so desperately needed to make. She held on as Kate licked and sucked her endlessly, pleasure building with each stroke. It built and built, better and better until she felt the orgasm nearing. And then, just as she was about to come, Kate met her eyes and she lost control.

Emily pulsed in her mouth as she came for so long, feeling as though it would never end. Kate kept sucking, Emily savoring the feel of her hard clit in Kate's mouth until it was too overwhelming. Her hands that had gripped the thick hair below her so tightly shifted and were pulling the hot mouth away.

After an eternity, Kate stood and kissed her again, letting Emily taste herself on her lips.

"Oh my God, baby." Emily panted, still reeling from the aftershocks of her orgasm and the incredible feeling of wholeness that she didn't know she'd missed. Damn, the woman was talented.

They stood there in the night, holding each other, Emily

desperate to feel more, to let this never end. She reached down, her hand at Kate's waistline, wanting to touch her so badly. But just as she moved in, a hand stopped her.

"I can't." Kate met her eyes, and Emily paused when she saw tears glistening in them. Emily held a frantic need and a question in her eyes.

"I can't…be touched by you…claimed like that. I can't pretend you're mine," Kate whispered.

Emily understood then that she needed so much more than her touch and knew she couldn't have it, so having her for even just those fleeting moments would have to suffice. Kate's eyes fluttered shut.

Feeling selfish but knowing it was true, Emily gently cupped her chin and held her head up to look into her eyes. Eyes that held her captive and laid everything bare. Eyes that wanted her but held fast for not wanting to be hurt. Emily ran her thumbs across Kate's tearstained cheeks, memorized every detail of her face. She nearly kissed her again but instead brought their foreheads together, smiling softly as she closed her eyes and threaded her fingers into Kate's hair. God, it hurt, yes, but holding each other was the sweetest of moments.

Emily moved first, collecting herself. Without words she took Kate's hand and guided them past her room, through the darkness, down the stairs to the makeshift couch bed. She sat and pulled Kate down beside her, their shoulders brushing.

"Maybe we needed that." Kate spoke softly.

Emily smiled weakly. "Releasing the tension, I suppose." She could still feel Kate's mouth. *Liar.* That very mouth turned upward in a smirk. Emily shoved shoulders with her.

They inched closer once again, the gravity that always pulled them together holding strong. Finally, they moved, lying the rest of the way down on the narrow couch, their fronts pressed together. Kate wrapped Emily in her arms as her fingers gently roamed through her hair.

Emily wanted to say something to make this easier, to make going down the only path she could see as the right thing. She didn't want to hurt Kate. Maybe, if nothing else, they could have closure that night—sharing themselves with each other once more and letting it become a memory they cherished, but setting them free. She could remember what they had long into the future, be the person Kate helped her be. She was grateful for that and planned to live up to how Kate saw her.

"I want nothing more than for you to feel every one of the things you think I am. It's what I've always wanted," Emily whispered. "You deserve someone to show you how talented and strong, funny and *difficult*, and amazingly beautiful you are as well. Because you are." She once again traced the lines of Kate's face, taking in every detail she could absorb.

"I don't know how to let you go again," Kate admitted, eyes watering. She pressed their foreheads together, pulled Emily even closer. "But I can't keep you, can I?"

Emily gently tilted Kate's chin up again to look into her eyes. She kissed her gently but passionately. *I wish I were brave enough to be yours alone, like I was once.*

"I don't know how."

"And you love him?"

Emily paused, not meeting Kate's gaze. *He loves me. He's a good man. He cares for our future. It's comfortable, the one simple thing I have in life.* "I do." *But not the way I love you.*

Kate nodded. She wiped her eyes, taking a breath, "You have to take that damn position, though. Be the badass woman that I love."

Joy returned to Emily's heart, taking in the encouragement, the knowing tone of the words, the confirmation that Kate truly still loved her. She smiled. "I have never once stopped loving you."

"I will *always* love you, Emily Stanton," Kate whispered.

Emily traced Kate's cheek in soft strokes with her thumb, neither speaking. Kate's eyes slowly closed. Emily watched her drift toward sleep.

"You are going to be the most beautiful bride," she mumbled.

Emily remained awake, watching Kate sleep, painting a picture of her in her mind. God, how she wished Kate could be the one waiting for her at the end of the aisle.

It was a strange feeling, she thought, to be looking right into heartbreak—knowing it was coming and desperate to avoid it but lacking the strength to do anything to stop it.

She had tried it once. Tried to step away from it all, follow her heart. It couldn't work then, so how could it now? Kate hadn't let her then, had put what she thought was best for Emily ahead of anything they could have had together.

No, she knew where she needed to go, what she'd chosen, and she wouldn't make this any harder on the amazing woman lying with her in the night. She deserved better, and maybe by not giving in to what she wanted, she could show her that.

Chapter Seventeen

Light filtered through the front windows, and Emily blinked into the morning. She quickly closed her eyes again and tested if she felt the telltale heaviness behind her eyes or queasiness of a hangover, but she felt neither, for which she was grateful. Then she realized she was still on the couch. Alone. Her gut dropped and her heart constricted. She took a deep breath.

"She left just as I was getting up." Allie stood in the doorway with two steaming cups of coffee. She handed one to Emily, who refused to meet her eye. She was waiting for something, for Emily to confide in her, deny any reason that she'd ended up on the couch, anything. Emily refused to do either, staring instead into the cup of brew.

She had thought it was a dream, her hazy memory of moments earlier. How Kate had crouched down, reached out, and brushed a strand of hair that covered her face behind her ear. Kate had leaned in and pressed the softest of kisses to her cheek, stroking her thumb along her jawline. Emily had smiled in her sleep, moving slightly into the touch. She heard her say, "Bye, love," and then was gone.

Did Allie see that?

"You don't have to tell me anything. But the two of you are my closest friends. I don't want you to make decisions you'll regret," Allie said carefully.

"And just what would I regret?" Emily asked, suddenly defensive. She'd never regret a single moment with Kate. Was that what she was getting at? If anyone, she'd hoped Allie would be the last to judge.

"Regret not following your heart, baby girl."

Emily laughed. She actually laughed. "Not all of us get a fairy tale." *Like you,* she didn't have to say. "Falling for the love of our lives and it happens to be perfectly convenient and wonderful and everyone accepts it. Some of us have our hearts pull away from our minds, knowing what we want, who we want, versus what we have to do, who we have to be..."

Allie didn't comment, just let her speak.

"God, I sound pretentious, don't I?" She laughed bitterly again. "I have everything. I'm getting married tomorrow in a goddamned cathedral in New York City. A wedding I didn't have to work for, a man who would give me the world. I've never wanted for a damn thing my entire life!" She stopped, looking up at Allie finally. Her eyes teared up, but she stopped herself.

"So of course I can't have her." She was done. She wasn't letting anyone sway her from her decision. She'd ripped her heart and mind apart, but she knew she could do this, and she could be happy, and she was done wishing for more. "I know you mean well, Allie, but leave it alone."

"All right then." Allie pulled her to her chest and squeezed her in a tight embrace. "Let's have you the best wedding you could imagine."

❖

That night, after a day of brunch with the wedding-party ladies (during which Emily was pleasantly entertained by her mother's obvious hangover), final checks for the following day's details, and being herded around the city to sightsee with the large gaggle of women, Emily was exhausted, and it was time for the rehearsal dinner.

Another in her mother's set of elaborate wedding details, the dinner included both her and Tommy's extended families, along with

LATE CITY SUMMER

the entirety of the wedding party. She'd reserved the Oak Room of the Plaza Hotel, the cost of which Emily refused to contemplate, but it was truly immaculate.

Tommy was there when they arrived, chatting with Emily's father. She was grateful the two of them got along so well, despite their obvious personality differences. She loved her father's ability to listen, only speak when he had something significant to contribute, while she also enjoyed Tommy's ability to keep a conversation engaging and moving.

"Hello, Daddy." She gave her father a kiss on the cheek and turned to Tommy. "Hello, darling."

"You are a vision, my love." Tommy smiled at her, giving her a chaste kiss.

"Has he talked your ear off yet?" she smiled, asking Tommy. Her father's naturally stoic expression broke with the edges of a knowing grin. "Tommy was filling me in on a case Phil has him working on."

"Tommy, reviewing a case? I'd have never guessed." She put her arm lovingly around his waist and leaned into him.

"Shop talk over, scout's honor." He held his hands up. "Have you seen the ballroom though? It's all set up for tomorrow. Ann gave me a walk-through just a few moments ago." He was obviously excited.

"I should join your mother." Her father kissed the top of her head and sauntered away.

"Well, are you going to escort me to the ballroom like a gentleman, then?"

He held his arm out, his eyes absolutely glowing. Apparently his excitement for the following day had finally kicked in.

They managed to avoid conversation long enough to escape the room. Tommy held the door to the darkened ballroom and ushered her in. Even in only the square of light flooding in from the open doors, it was magnificent. Grand stone arches lined the perimeter, rising to meet the high vaulted ceiling adorned with a grand chandelier. Tables circled the main dance floor, candles on each one already placed and waiting to be lit. Place settings were aligned at each chair with precision, and their own table for two awaited at the front of the room. *Just like everything in my life seems to be.*

Tommy wrapped his arms around her from behind, resting his chin on her shoulder.

"Why do you want all of this?" she asked. She had to know. He turned her in his arms.

"Me? Why do *I* want all of this?" He nearly laughed but turned serious when he evidently realized she wasn't joking. "If anything I'd think you'd be scolding me for a lack of enthusiasm about it all!"

She kept her gaze pinned on him. "Why do you want to marry me?"

"Why ever would I not? We've been together for nearly six years, you've planned for this for over a year, your mother might have a hernia if one of these salad forks is out of place when she arrives tomorrow. Might as well make it worth her effort, no?" He was trying to joke.

"I don't mean the damn wedding." She was frustrated and doubting, needed him to ease her mind. "Why *me*?"

"How can you ask that?" His expression gave away his disbelief. "I want to build a life with you. Who wouldn't want to be with you? You're beautiful, talented, determined…you make me excited about our future." He lifted her chin and kissed her softly. "And I love you."

She kissed him again, putting all her passion into it. "I love you too."

"Since you're asking, why me? How'd I get so lucky, huh?"

She thought for a moment, perhaps a moment too long. "You're the best man I know." *I can do this. He's who I should be with.*

She took his hand and pulled him back to the party.

❖

Emily enjoyed the rest of the night, filled with fun, laughter, food, and alcohol. Toasts were made to the couple, well wishes sent all around. Memories were shared of the two, all in celebration of the two people who were meant to be together.

Tommy stood to make his own speech. "Thank you all for coming tonight. Emily and I are so very excited to share tomorrow with you all. Earlier this evening Emily asked me why I wanted to marry her."

Emily blushed profusely. A few people laughed.

"And I've been thinking of her question all evening. I know we get to say our vows tomorrow, but I have to let everyone here know why they should be jealous that it's me who gets to make you my wife." The group laughed heartily. He turned fully toward her. "They should be jealous, Emily Stanton, because you are without doubt my life's greatest treasure. I'm the luckiest man in this world because you are the most unique and wonderful woman I've ever met, and you are my rock. No matter what I try to do in this world, I know I can because you'll be there to catch me if I falter. I cannot wait to marry you."

Cheers erupted as he leaned down to kiss her. She ignored the guilt that threatened to erupt in her and shifted it to gratefulness. She truly was lucky to have his love, and she'd try her all to return it in kind.

Four years earlier, 1942

Emily stood among the horde of people at the bus terminal near Port Authority, gathered around Art and Allie. It was surprisingly quiet, the waiting. The entirety of Art's family had joined them, and the most noise came from some of his younger brothers who played on the sidewalk nearby. The bus arrived precisely on schedule, and a touch of dread spread throughout the group.

Art was scheduled to ship out to army basic training for thirteen weeks, after which Allie planned to attend his graduation and visit. He'd have a few weeks' time before further training, and likely a rapid deployment overseas, especially with the ever-increasing pace of the war.

Kate jogged up, slightly out of breath. She stood near Allie, who clung to her husband until he was pulled away for hugs and final well wishes. Emily smiled at her across the group, and as she felt the familiar melting, Kate politely smiled back. There it was again, the cycle of avoidance and awkwardness coming between them again. She wanted to ease it but had no idea how. At least Kate wasn't avoiding her this time.

"Glad to see you made it. You're usually so prompt," Emily joked, sliding over beside her. Tommy quickly followed.

"Got out of the shop late, as usual," she replied cordially. Emily instantly sensed the distance beneath it though. "Evening, Tommy."

"Kate, glad you could make it." Neither of them looked at the other.

What the hell?

"I should get in there before I really do miss him." She pushed through the crowd and gave Art the biggest hug. She watched as Kate said something to him, something she knew was comforting, encouraging. Kate was good at that. She also saw her, as usual, snap a photo of the couple before he left. Never without the camera.

Emily watched her, wanting badly to find a moment alone with her, but Tommy seemed stuck to her. She suspected he was feeling a bit insecure, knowing he wasn't getting on a bus himself. He wouldn't leave her side. They'd had their own good-bye with Art just before, during which Tommy had given his firmest handshake.

"You're doing what not everyone can. Remember that. Be safe," he'd said. Emily realized this situation really must be eating at him.

But then with one last epic kiss for Allie and waves to his group, Art boarded the bus and set off on his journey.

"I was thinking we could do dinner, the three of us?" Emily asked Allie and Kate after much of the group had dispersed. She remembered Tommy was still beside her. "You have drinks with your uncle and the boys this evening, don't you, darling?"

"I'm actually helping Gramps with a project at the store this evening." Kate jumped in before Tommy had a chance to reply.

"Perhaps another night this week?" she suggested. Emily was instantly suspicious.

"Ah. I was planning to stop in tomorrow anyway. I'll see you then?" Emily asked.

"Oh, uh, sure thing. You should bring Allie along, let her meet some of the kids," Kate suggested.

She doesn't want to be alone with me. "Oh, okay…Good idea. We have to keep Allie company now, right?"

Tommy seemed to take a breath for the first time in their brief conversation. Emily looked back and forth between the two of them.

"I should head out." Kate waved, hugged both Allie and Emily (carefully and quickly), and shook Tommy's hand. Then she was off.

"Looks like it's just you and me, Allie." Emily wrapped her arm through her cousin's and smiled. She'd just have to wait for another time to talk.

❖

And so it went. Each day and each time Emily saw Kate, she was completely kind, attentive, and cordial, but Emily found her as slippery as a fish in water when it came to getting her alone. They spent time at Allie's new home, as Emily had moved her things and decided to stay at Allie's for the rest of the summer. The two of them helped her make it just that, a home, while adjusting to life without Art around. They'd spent time at Alfonzo's, teaching their crafts, everything they enjoyed doing together, but they never had a moment they could actually talk, and the lack of private time was taking its toll on Emily.

She had only a few short weeks left in the city, and she wanted so badly to be around Kate, really talk with her, *touch her*. She had thought there was a small ray of hope for them, in some beautiful universe, and she didn't want to waste any time they might have had. She needed to know for sure, and if she weren't mistaken, she would swear Kate was once again avoiding her, in the most sickeningly sweet way possible.

But now she was done waiting.

That led Emily to stand on a train platform late on a Friday night, scanning the crowds as each train unloaded. She'd managed to siphon Kate's infernally ever-changing shop work schedule and train commute out of Mia, lied to both Allie and Tommy about being with the other, and was determined to find a single moment alone with Kate no matter what it took.

After nearly an hour of waiting, she began to worry she'd missed her, that it would have been the one time she'd gotten off her shift early, or she'd escaped her in the crowds. Nearing her wits' end, she was still there only because she hoped there had been train delays. Emily decided to wait for one more train.

It arrived, even at the late hour, filled to the brim with late-evening commuters. Attempting to stand her ground and watch the exit staircases, she heard grumbling from those forced to walk around her until she spun in place, having been elbowed by an old man with no patience in his direct path home. The spinning was immediately followed by someone else knocking the air out of her.

"Sorry!" she mumbled, getting her bearings and turning around to make sure she didn't miss Kate.

"What in God's name are you doing, exactly?" Kate asked, appearing bewildered that she had once again run directly into Emily.

"Oh! Hi—"

"I imagine stalking isn't as satisfying when you get caught." Kate deadpanned, but Emily sensed she was happy to see her. She had to believe that.

"Yes. Standing on a crowded platform blatantly looking for someone is the most effective method of stalking, I'm sure." *She'd done it!* She had found her. God, she loved looking at Kate.

The hordes had finally dispersed, leaving the two of them quite alone for the first time in nearly two weeks.

"What are you doing here, Em?" Kate asked, her tone somber.

"I've missed you." She didn't look away.

Kate put her hands on her hips, looking exhausted. "We've seen each other quite a bit lately."

"And that's been good enough for you?" She took a step closer, invading Kate's space. Kate stepped back though, looking frustrated. "It has to be, and you know it."

Emily was confused. She thought they could at least talk about this thing between them. "I thought we could…spend time together. I don't have much longer before I have to leave."

"Exactly! And then what? I'm just supposed to be around until you go back to your life? Why do I *always* have to be the logical one?" She stormed off.

"And why are you *always* the one walking away?!" Emily bounded after her.

Although she'd managed to get her hands on Kate's train-station details, she had no idea where she actually lived. It was a muggy night, even at such a late hour, and Emily nearly ran to keep up with the definitely frustrated, on-edge other woman. Her own anger grew with every step.

"Oh, you're really going to ignore me then?" Emily continued trying to get her to talk as she struggled to keep up with Kate's long stride. "Not this time. I'm not letting you walk off and then act like everything's fine the next time I see you. No, ma'am."

Kate came to a dead halt, turning to face Emily. Shocked, Emily stopped abruptly on the dark side street.

"And do you plan to sleep in front of my apartment door?"

"Well, it won't be that long because we all know you'll be back up at an ungodly hour in the morning headed right back to the shop you came from."

"Then why waste your time!?" She stormed off again until she reached a nondescript building and flung the street-level door open. Emily squeezed in the door behind her, climbing the three flights of stairs above the small market. She was completely out of breath by this point.

"Because being with you is never a waste of time," Emily answered to Kate's back.

Kate stared at the key in the lock.

Emily said, "You truly are the most aggravating, boneheaded person I know."

"Boneheaded?" Kate opened the door and stepped into the doorway as if prepared to slam it in her face. "I'm the one who followed someone to their doorstep and is refusing to leave? Oh, wait. Here you are. Talk about stubborn."

Emily challenged her, stepping forward far into her personal space. "Do you want me to leave?"

Kate sighed. "Why do you want to stay, Emily?" Her gaze dropped.

"God damn it, because I love you!" *Shit, I said that out loud.* She swallowed hard.

Kate stared at her, her focus shifting between Emily's nervous eyes.

Then, just as Emily had so hoped she would, Kate closed the short distance between them with her lips to Emily's.

❖

The moment the door slammed shut, Kate had Emily against it in the darkness. With hands pinned to each side, bodies pressed against each other, she let go of any hesitation, of any fear, and gave in to the longing she had suffered through for too long. The kisses in the dark bar, the touches they shared were no longer enough. They pressed their lips together with a hunger unknown to either until that point, but with an underlying gentleness that drew them closer to one another.

Emily yielded eagerly to the kiss, allowing them to explore each other with their lips, their tongues, their hands. Kate deepened it and grasped the nape of Emily's neck as her mouth wandered away from her lips, desperately needing to feel her against every part of her. Her senses pulled in every direction, she tried to take in each sensation that was Emily. Emily's fingers tightened in her hair, her breasts tense with arousal and hips pliable beneath her wandering hands. She smelled the fresh scent that was uniquely Emily. She heard her breathing, the small moans escaping her mouth. She was surrounded, drowning in this woman she knew she loved too, but thought she could never have.

She continued her explorations, still not close enough to her. Emily curled a leg around her, pressing her center over Kate's thigh in a slow rhythm, inviting Kate to take all of her. Kate pulled her closer, wrapped both of Emily's legs around herself, and lifted her from the floor. Wild hunger simmered, and the painful pressure to take her fast and hard eased into moments of passion as she held Emily suspended in her arms. She took a moment to slow the kisses, exploring the depths of her mouth, drinking in the unique taste.

Emily broke the kiss and whispered in her lover's ear. "Put me down, baby." She needed Kate completely, as soon as possible, but not up against a door. Hesitation and fear crept into Kate's expression, probably thinking she had gone too far or done something wrong. Emily smiled sweetly and pulled her to the bed of the small studio.

As they tumbled down, this was, she realized, what true passion felt like. She was giving herself to someone who deserved better than her but wanted her more than anything. She straddled Kate, looking down at this beautiful woman, and discovered she was truly doing what she wanted for the first time in her life with the person who inspired her most. The person who she meant the most to in this world, who cherished her for exactly who she was. Kate.

Kate sat up so that Emily was sitting in her lap, her arms around her, and she could look up at her, their faces close.

"Emily Stanton, I've been in love with you since..." She paused, gazing into her eyes. "Well, since the first time you yelled at me for running into you."

Emily laughed out loud and pushed Kate down onto the bed. "You, my love, are truly the worst." They smiled at one another, and Emily leaned down to connect their lips again.

"I do love you, so very much," Kate whispered in her ear. She was done denying herself this woman who clearly wanted her. Her love was not perverse, and she would give them both as much of it as she could, in the little time she had.

Emily didn't have to say anything in return. Instead, her hands found their way beneath Kate's shirt as they finally, hastily, removed their clothes. Craving her skin to touch Emily's, and being so close, Kate flipped them over, pinning Emily to the bed. She moved her mouth agonizingly slow, a trail of kisses laced across Emily's chest. She reached around to unclasp her bra and kept trying, unsuccessfully.

"Need some help there, stud?" Emily finally asked. Kate growled in frustration as Emily reached back to unclasp it herself, laughing at her.

Kate pulled it from her arms and looked down at the exquisite woman smiling beneath her. Streetlamps filtered light in through the open window, casting rays across her naked, gorgeous lover. She'd never seen anything more beautiful. She stilled for a moment. A touch of nervousness snuck in, and Emily caught it.

"What's wrong?" she asked, suddenly self-conscious.

"I, uh, I've never..." Kate mumbled in return.

"Oh." Emily was relieved and gave Kate a small smile. "Neither have I."

Emily stroked the face above her, memorizing each detail. She smirked, the woman's vulnerability somehow even more attractive to her. "I'm sure we'll do just fine." *And I'm so happy it's with you.*

Kate hastily unclasped her own bra, and Emily surged up and captured a nipple between her lips. Kate gasped in apparent surprise.

Emily couldn't wait any longer. She once again flipped them, needing Kate beneath her. She let her hand wander across the softest skin she could imagine as Kate's callused ones roamed across her back, reaching around and cupping her breasts. The contrast in textures as she explored Kate amazed her, just like the woman herself did. Sometimes calloused, sarcastic, tough to the world, but there and then melting softly to her touch.

She returned her mouth to a nipple, unable to get enough of the soft weight of her. She was living for the sounds Kate was trying to hold back as she let Emily have her. Her passion grew hotter, knowing Kate was holding back, letting her have her way with her. It was *her* that she wanted. Her touch, no one else's.

Her hand made it to the soft patch of curls at the base of Kate's deliciously toned stomach. She stopped and looked up at her lover. Her eyelids were heavy. Emily had never seen such want before now as she finally dipped her hand lower.

Kate gasped again as Emily ran her fingers through her wetness and tentatively pressed inside her. Her hips surged forward until Emily was running circles across her hard clit.

Emily grasped Kate's neck, pulling their mouths together in a deep, demanding kiss as she continued to circle her fingers.

"Oh my God, baby. I'm going to come," Kate breathed out.

Emily slowed her fingers. "But I need to taste you. I've wanted to for so damn long."

It took every ounce of willpower Kate possessed not to fall into oblivion as Emily slid down her body, tongue trailing across her curves.

Emily spread her legs, pulling them onto her shoulders as she kissed the soft skin of her inner thigh. She spread Kate open with her fingers and looked at her for the first time. She had no idea what she was doing, but she didn't care. She would find a way to keep Kate making those intoxicating sounds.

This is going to be fun. Emboldened, she delicately ran her tongue up the length of Kate's sex.

"Oh, God, yes!" Kate screamed.

Emily took her time, savoring Kate's taste, caressing her with sure strokes.

"Emily..."

She looked up and their eyes met. Kate was flushed, panting, and so close to coming undone. Emily smiled slightly and latched her lips to Kate's clit, sucking while she let her tongue continue to muse, strokes growing quicker and quicker. She never wanted this to end.

But then Kate's hips surged to meet her, a tremor started beneath her tongue, until Kate's long legs tensed around her. Emily nearly came herself from the taste and sound and feel of it all.

"Yes!" Kate moaned, and then she was shuddering in Emily's mouth until she collapsed back onto the sheets. "Holy mother of God."

Emily grinned and slid back up the sweat-sheened body beneath her.

Kate licked her lips. She found something fascinating about

tasting herself on Emily's lips, remembering what she'd just had done to her, and she needed more. She nearly pounced on her, kissing her roughly until Emily was the one breathing heavily. Kate's hands seemed to have a mind of their own, and her mouth followed, her tongue exploring the shape of Emily's breasts.

Kate's hot mouth settled over one nipple while the other she gently rolled between her fingers. *Was she teasing her?*

"Go inside me, please," Emily finally whispered, desperate for her touch. She grasped at Kate's hand, trying to pull it down to her most sensitive spot.

With so much care, Kate slid into her easily, but gently, testing what Emily wanted. Emily pushed her hips forward to meet her, and Kate slid farther in, a second finger following. And then they were pulsing, together, in and out in their own rhythm. Emily grabbed a handful of Kate's hair, pulling her down as their mouths fused, but Kate continued to drive into her.

Kate shifted her hand so her thumb could work her oh-so-wet, stiff clit. She ran circles around it while continuing her fingers within, curling them into Emily and making her go mad with pleasure.

"Fuck!" Emily hissed as her hips drove up again, and again until she could no longer hold back. Once more, and she was coming around Kate's fingers, shuddering violently, her screams swallowed up as Kate kissed her.

"That was amazing," Kate told her.

"My line…that's my line."

"I can't believe I could give you that kind of pleasure." Chuckling, Kate rolled over, pulling Emily tight against her front, arms wrapped around her. Her lips at Emily's ear, she whispered, "You. You are amazing."

Emily turned her head and kissed her. As Emily lay there, feeling Kate press gentle kisses up her neck and with her strong arms secured around her, she thought she would never want to be anywhere else in the entire world.

❖

They made love late into the night, testing, learning new things from one another. They napped curled into one another, they laughed, they were silent at times. They were simply with each other.

Emily stirred as the morning light filled the room. She was curled up against Kate, arms around her, one of Kate's legs draped over her hip. Her mouth was inches from a supple nipple waiting for her, and she couldn't believe when her sex clenched with need. She had never thought she could experience desire that intense, but she wanted the woman again. Resisting, however, she nuzzled just under Kate's chin, soaking in the warmth of the embrace.

"Shit!" She jumped at her second realization and startled Kate awake immediately.

"Work! It has to be nine, at least!" She scrambled for her watch.

Kate flopped back face down into the pillow and mumbled, "Off day…no work."

"Wait, what? Are you serious?! You were going to let me sleep like a dog at your front door, thinking you'd be up at your usual ungodly hour?"

Kate's shoulders bounced in laughter, but she didn't even open her eyes.

"You!" Emily climbed onto Kate's back, sliding her own naked body over every inch of her. She ran her hands up Kate's sides, sliding to her breasts.

"Mmm," Kate mumbled in clear delight. "At least you're waking me this time. Shall we tour the city again?"

"I'd rather stay right here with you," Emily whispered. She was struck, though, with the reality that she couldn't do just that, as much as every fiber of her wished to.

"Obligations as usual?" Kate asked, obviously sensing her shift.

"Allie is at work today. I sincerely hope she doesn't realize I'm not there this morning. And Tommy and I planned to have lunch this afternoon." She paused. "He leaves next week."

They looked at each other, silently acknowledging the potential ease that put on things, at least temporarily.

They sat up, still close and needing to touch one another. Emily pulled Kate's arm around her shoulders and nestled into her warmth. They sat in comfortable silence for a few moments.

"I want to be with you. Whenever we can. I'll find a way."

Kate knew they were putting off the inevitable, that in three short weeks Emily would leave. It was selfish to sneak and lie to those around them in exchange for each extra minute they could have together. *And it will be harder to say good-bye.*

"School starts mid-month?" Kate asked. She couldn't answer the unasked question just yet.

Emily nodded. "The week after I get back. I have a professor who wants me as a teaching assistant this semester."

"Already making those connections, eh?" Kate wove their fingers together, admiring how they looked entwined. "So very smart, you are."

"It isn't set in stone," she said under her breath.

Was Emily contemplating finding a way out of it all? Did she want to? Kate was desperate to have her life continue, to feel anything like she did in these moments. "It's only three weeks." God, how Kate wanted more. She knew they were spiraling into heartbreak, full steam, but all she wanted right then was to be consumed by Emily.

Emily sighed. "Yes."

Kate looked down at her lover. She wanted to think she would give her the world if she asked. She ignored the doubts creeping into the small of her mind. *We'll find a way, together.* "Then each day of it, what time we have...you're mine." She connected their lips and pulled them back down into the sheets.

She had three weeks to fill herself with all the light and warmth that Emily gave her and save it for the dark times she knew would come once Emily left.

CHAPTER EIGHTEEN

Tommy was to leave town the following Friday, and with each small precious piece of time that Emily was able to spend with Kate, she grew one step farther away from Tommy. She nearly resolved to sever their relationship. She couldn't endlessly keep up a charade of being enamored of him while she spent each night longing for Kate's touch—to hold her, talk with her, be with her. But it could wait, and should. He deserved a longer conversation and to not have her throw him away as he was leaving. She also didn't have a reasonable explanation.

As he caught the bus, he'd given her a chaste kiss and his most genuine, yet oblivious, smile. Her guilt surged for a moment, knowing hard conversations were to come. She was determined to make her life what she wanted and to be happy, to find a way. She admitted it was a relief for him to leave. She had one less person to hide from, if only for the moment. Oh, how she hated the deception she was caught in.

As Emily walked home, she wondered if a day would ever come when others could accept, even celebrate her love for Kate. For now, she didn't even know a way to be with her love, hidden or not. She intended to find one. And so, for the next fourteen days, she would let herself be consumed with a glimpse of what she truly wanted.

They spent each and every moment possible together. Often Kate would visit Allie's new home, the three of them conversing late into the night, only to have Allie offer Kate a place to stay as opposed to traveling home. They would wait long enough for Allie to fall asleep and make their way together into the guest room. Stolen kisses, lovemaking deep into the night as quietly as possible was theirs.

Emily began visiting Kate during her lunch breaks, which were mercilessly short. Kate excused herself from the group of other women she normally ate with, finding an unused loading dock where she could sit with Emily. Despite the brevity, they sat talking with one another as close as possible for as long as they could. Each would feel a rush at the small points of contact they shared, remembering the touches they'd had the night before, longing for the ones to come.

As much of a risk as it might have been, neither could resist tasting each other for only a moment, a small kiss holding them over until they saw each other again. Even in its secrecy, their being together was bliss.

"My God, you're so beautiful," Kate said reverently, looking into Emily's eyes just before they parted.

Emily blushed. Kate had no idea how much she thought the same of her. The woman was so incredibly sexy in her uniform, a grease smudge across her chin. She wanted her right there on the shop's loading dock. "Allie has dinner with her in-laws the night after next. I could come to your apartment, tell her it got late and I'll just stay with you."

"Please?" Kate said. It might be their last night together.

"Can't wait, my love." With another small peck, Emily scurried away, looking forward to a few hours of solace, just the two of them.

❖

Kate put the finishing touches on her abode, enacting her plan for the evening. She tugged at the floral fabric strip wrapped around her neck, questioning how bold she had been when she'd purchased it earlier in the day. Despite the rush it gave her, looking in the mirror and seeing, truly liking her masculine reflection pulled at her insecurities, and she feared Emily would think she looked ridiculous. She'd bought the damn tie in a split-second decision, telling the cashier it was for her father. She didn't dare think of buying a suit jacket. Now she was worried she looked more like a waiter than anything else and nearly took it off as the bell rang.

She clutched the doorknob nervously, taking a deep breath and steeling herself for potential embarrassment. That breath was immediately taken from her as the vision of a woman standing in the doorway took her breath away. She couldn't even form a sentence.

Emily blushed. "Kate Alessi, pull me into your place this instant before I make a scene in this hallway," she whispered into Kate's ear.

Kate wrapped Emily in her arms and lifted her, spinning them into the apartment. Laughing, Emily grabbed a handful of Kate's tie and pulled her into a searing kiss.

"This..." she still held the tie, "this should stay on later." She promptly brushed past Kate into the apartment.

Kate wondered if they'd make it through dinner.

When she could force herself to move, she followed Emily into the small living area, where dinner waited. Emily turned to her and snuggled in close. She gave her another kiss, softer this time. Kate placed her hands on Emily's hips and savored the taste of her.

"Hi," Emily murmured. She wrapped her arms around Kate's neck and leaned into her.

"Hi, love."

"I didn't know you could cook."

"It's one of my many other secret, non-button-on-the-camera-pushing skills," Kate quipped.

"Oh, I know some of your other secret talents."

Definitely a chance of not making it through dinner. Kate grinned.

But somehow they did. They talked with each other, sat close, held hands through most of it. Emily seemed truly impressed with everything Kate had done to make the evening special.

Both of them, however, avoided mentioning that this was their last night together before Emily's departure. Neither seemed able to bring it up.

Kate went to the other side of the room and raised the needle of the record player, and the now-familiar melody of the song they knew was theirs drifted across the room.

The world will turn and turn again
But my heaven is here with you
Your light will never end, my dear
In my heart I know it's true.

Kate held out her hand. "Dance with me?"

Emily slid easily into her arms. Kate never wanted her to leave them.

As they swayed along in the tiny space between the table and the bed, holding each other tighter by the minute, Kate's thoughts drifted inward. Everything she had avoided reminded her of her fears, creeping to the surface.

She deserves better than hiding each day. What in the world would she tell her family? She'll be famous someday, and you'll just hold her back, hold her in the shadows. What kind of life can you offer her?

"You know I have quite a few breaks when it comes to school... Excuses to come to the city for galleries, to see Allie..." Emily whispered. She laid her head on Kate's shoulder, arms tight around her.

Kate pulled her tighter. "You have to focus on school. I'm sure your studies are going to get much more intensive." *God, this can't be easy, can it?*

Emily mumbled, seeming to lose some of her confidence, "Of course. But we could see each other. I could find the time..."

Kate answered noncommittally. "We should just see. You'll likely be busier than you think."

"I wouldn't necessarily have to tell Allie. I could just stay with you."

Until someone comments or catches us. What if Mia finds out?

"That wouldn't be fair to Allie either."

Emily held her tighter, snuggled in closer.

As they swayed along together, Kate admitted a lot to herself. She was scared. But even more, she had to put Emily first. Before her wants, before her need of the woman, she'd make sure she could do her part in letting Emily have success, even if that meant being without her. Emily was her adventure of a lifetime. But God, how impossible it would be.

Yet those thoughts were not for that night. That night they would be together, even if it was their last.

❖

Emily stirred, the room just out of darkness, the blue light just before sunrise beginning to creep in. She was wrapped in warm arms, felt every point of contact between her and the woman surrounding her, flesh warm and pliant against her. She knew by the steady rhythm of breath against her cheek that Kate was still blissfully asleep.

How do you say good-bye to someone you love? It wasn't like Allie and Art, knowing, hoping that your love would come back soon, although she and Kate lacked the danger of losing them physically. It was simple. She'd see Kate each time she came to the city, enjoy her time with Allie and be with Kate when she could. And then after school she could change her plans, be there with Kate, find a way to make it all work.

Yes, she would have to break things off with Tommy. Her mother would question her about why she would choose to end things with such a eligible, wonderful young man. And he was, she admitted. But the woman beside her? That was who she wanted her future to point toward, whether in New York, Boston, or wherever they wanted to go.

Kate must have felt her stir as she did so herself, pulling Emily in ever tighter.

"How long do we have?"

"Allie and her parents have brunch planned before my bus, which leaves at two. And I need to get my things from Allie's before then."

Kate was instantly awake. She leaned over Emily and, with a look of longing, intensity, passion, and sadness, kissed her. Emily cupped her cheek and kissed her back, giving her everything she felt.

"I can't wait to see you again. And we can talk every now and then, right?"

Kate swallowed hard. "Em, I wouldn't plan on anything. It'll be harder if you don't make it down here when your classes pick up."

Emily recoiled and sat up. "Why don't you want to plan? I want to see you, and we need to figure out how to."

Kate got up out of the bed and threw a shirt on. She now refused to make eye contact with Emily, and the shirt seemed to provide some protection from Emily's unguarded stare.

"I just don't know if it's the best idea," Kate managed to mumble while putting pants on.

"What in the world are you talking about?" Emily pulled the sheets up to her chest.

Kate sighed. "You have a *life*, Emily. You have responsibilities, you have *potential*. Why always be worried about when you'll be able to sneak off with me on breaks when you could be genuinely exploring, getting better at what you do? Living?"

Emily deflected. "Oh, and you're happy working at the shop? You want to do that the rest of your life? Is that living?"

She stared at Emily, knowing what she was asking.

Kate let her head fall between her hands. This wasn't about her. She didn't want to make it that. "Don't you think I want out of there? The shop...It pays for my luxurious abode." She gestured around her studio apartment. "And with everything happening overseas, I'm sure the work won't let up anytime soon. No real way to jump ship."

"Why are you so scared of taking a chance on something different?" Emily nearly yelled.

"So what? I just quit? Even if I do, I'm going to end up taking care of my grandfather's harebrained store and becoming just like him, never leaving this goddamned city anyway." Kate looked right at her.

Emily didn't know the feeling of being responsible for someone, having to care for someone you hadn't chosen. She appreciated and realized that it must be difficult, but she didn't truly know how it felt. She dropped her eyes, and some of her anger dissipated. She wanted to take that burden from Kate.

"You, on the other hand, have everything you could need. You can do whatever you want, and you're going to keep studying other people's work? You should be doing your own, using your talent, making something of yourself on your own!" Kate said. "You shouldn't be hiding away with me," she added under her breath.

Emily's anger sparked anew. She got up and threw on her own discarded undergarments. "And exactly how much say do I have in that? I know what I'm doing with my life, thank you."

"Emily, I just think—"

"You *think*. What about what I think?! Everyone in my life believes they know what's best for me. My mother, Tommy…You were supposed to be the one person who didn't decide things for me. I never asked you to think you're *caring* for me too."

"I'm not! I mean, I do, care for you…" Kate shouted. "I just want you to have everything you deserve."

"Bullshit. You're scared shitless that I want you so much." Emily had steeled herself. She stood on the opposite side of the room.

The tension in the silence that spread between them was thick. Kate took a tentative step forward but stopped and looked right at Emily. "I want the day when I realize I can't live my life without you. I want to get to the day that, if I ever could in this world, I'd ask you to marry me. I want to think about waking with you every morning and holding you as you fall asleep every single night. I *want* all of it. But it would stop you from having all the things you deserve in life, and because I love you so goddamn much, I refuse to let what *I want* be more than what you *need*."

Seeing a tear swiped hastily away from Kate's cheek nearly

did Emily in, yet she knew if she tried further, she would cause yet another round of pain. Kate had set up a stone wall between them, resolute in her decision, and Emily had never felt this level of hurt, never realized how heartbroken she felt, until right then. She had finally fallen into it, right then and there.

The woman she loved with all her heart, who hours earlier she had envisioned some sort of future with, striving for all the things Kate said she wanted too, who she *knew* wanted a future with her, was standing only feet away in the physical space, but a canyon stretched between them.

"God damn it, Kate. Don't do this," she whispered. *Stop being scared.*

"I'm just no good for you."

And that's what it really was about. Emily crossed the distance and cupped Kate's cheek. She forced her to look her in the eyes. "You are *everything* good, Kate. I hope you see that for yourself someday soon." Emily pressed the softest kiss possible on her cheek. "I love you."

After Emily closed the door gently behind her, she hoped with every step she took that Kate would come after her. She never did.

Chapter Nineteen

Four years later, 1946

Coffee. Emily smelled it before she opened her eyes, and when she did, Allie was sitting at the foot of the bed holding two cups, one outstretched to her, with a smile. She sat up and graciously accepted it with a smirk of her own. It was her wedding day.

"Time to get at it before your mother knocks on that door."

They'd stayed together the night before in the hotel room, while Tommy chose to stay with Art in Brooklyn. Allie had taken full advantage of the posh night in the hotel and looked refreshed and ready to fulfill her maid-of-honor duties. They sipped their drinks in silence, a few moments of respite before it all began. Emily thought of the day ahead and everything that needed to be done, and while she was nervous, she was also excited.

"We have breakfast waiting downstairs, then hair, last looks at the reception hall, and then you'll be able to get dressed right at the church...and." Suddenly she sounded cautious. She pulled out an envelope from her pocket. "Someone asked me to deliver this to you."

Emily took it, smiling at the thought that Tommy had written her a note, surprising her with such a small romantic gesture. She should have thought to do the same herself.

But what she found didn't seem to be a note, even though she saw writing on the envelope's contents. It was on the back of a photograph, one with worn edges, a fold line across its center. She glanced up at Allie and back to the photograph. Allie took a large drink of her coffee, not looking at her.

She pulled it out to read it.

Never lose your sense of adventure. I truly do wish you all the happiness you can fathom. And you, Emily Stanton, are everything good.—K

With trembling fingers she flipped the photo over. It was the image of the two of them on the Wonder Wheel, faces pressed together, hair blowing in the wind, and the brightest smiles on their faces.

She found another photo there, one of their group at Coney Island in front of the Wonder Wheel, the four of them. She smiled looking at it and handed it to Allie.

"Look at those baby faces," she said, reflecting. "It really was a great summer, huh?"

Emily had focused again on the first photo, running her thumbs across their faces. Allie didn't comment or ask to see it.

Knocking at the door brought her out of her reverie. Allie went to answer it, and in poured her mother and the rest of her bridal party in full cheery mode. The madness had begun. As calmly but quickly as possible, she tucked the photos back into the envelope and put them in the top of her suitcase.

Amelia at that moment swooped in and pulled Emily across the suite to the vanity, where the hair stylist had already begun to set up. Time to get to it.

❖

I shouldn't have given her the damn photo. Of all the selfish, stupid...the group one, though, that makes it less awkward, right? Kate growled to herself in the studio as she rushed around prepping her gear for the twelfth time. *Give it up. You said your good-bye, you promised yourself.*

"Are you ready yet?" Mia yelled from the doorway. "I thought you'd want to get there early. They're your friends too, after all."

Kate gritted her teeth. "They're clients today, Mia. We have a job to do."

"Okay…" Mia walked back into the room and leaned against the counter Kate was finishing packing her gear on.

"What."

"Why are you in such a foul mood? She's your best friend. You should be happy for her."

She glared at her sister, enough that Mia almost recoiled. Kate sighed, not wanting to bring more attention to herself. "*You're* my best friend, you goof."

Mia smirked but didn't settle. "I have to be. It's a requirement of living with you."

Kate smiled. She was happy to get to live with her sister again, and that was the all the acceptance of her earlier invitation she needed. It was a brief spark of happiness in the day she was having so far. They'd talked about it multiple times, and Kate had been trying to get her to move in with her, take a step toward independence. They both knew the responsibility of taking care of Alfonzo and that they'd figure it out together. And, perhaps after Emily left again, this time for good, she wouldn't be so lonely.

"It's okay with me, you know." Mia looked right at her. "That you love her."

Kate froze. She certainly hadn't seen that statement coming.

"Does she know?"

Kate ground her teeth together, lips pursed. She blinked once and tried to still her breathing. Her mind raced. No sense in denying it, she supposed.

Her voice was barely audible. "I should hope so."

Mia actually laughed. "And you'll just let her marry someone?"

Kate looked up at her. "What exactly do you imagine I should do? When they ask if anyone objects, I run in and swoop her away? You might not mind, but a few other people would. Besides, she wouldn't be able to live with it, always hiding."

"Have you asked *her* that?" Mia asked, treading not so carefully. Kate gave her an even deeper glare, but she didn't back down.

Kate paused again. She'd never spoken to anyone about any of it, as much as Allie had attempted to pry. Mia had never said anything, just been there in her own way, a constant, usually annoying little sister. Kate trusted her as much as she was often annoyed by her constant stream of questions.

"She tried once, that summer. She wanted to…to be together," she whispered. "I couldn't make her do it. Like I said, she deserves someone she can be proud of, someone she doesn't have to hide. She'd eventually grow to resent me."

"Oh, please. She looks at you like you hung the moon."

Kate looked wide-eyed at her. "Well, that's even worse, isn't it? If she *can't* hide it…"

"What do you want from her then?"

"You don't know how any of this works!" Kate yelled. She was frustrated and now running late. "I can't believe I'm having this conversation, especially with someone who hasn't even been in love before."

"But I know you, you ass." Mia defended herself.

"It's impossible, okay? I finally let it go. I'll be fine. I have you to worry about and make sure you don't go falling for some stupid boy one day soon."

"Kate." Mia grew serious. "You're always taking care of someone. Me, Gramps, Dad. You deserve to be someone's someone."

Kate flung her bag over her shoulder and walked toward the door, Mia following her. "Well, it's too damn late for that now, isn't it?"

Mia stopped her at the door, looked her in the eye, and pulled her into a tight hug, "I mean it though. I love you." Kate squeezed back just a second before pulling away.

Just get through today, and find a way to be happy, Kate thought. Maybe she did deserve that, not holding on to Emily or holding her back. Maybe they could both be happy.

❖

"You look absolutely stunning!" Her mother reeled, dabbing her eyes in a dramatic display for the crowded room just outside of the chapel where Emily and the other women were gathered. They scurried about, acting as though none of the preparation throughout the day, or for the last twelve months for that matter, had made any difference. They were all in a panic. The church continued to fill, the wedding coordinator ran back and forth from the room, and music came from the grand organ and filled the room with a faint undertone of the coming procession.

Emily stood in the far corner of the room by the mirror, gazing at herself. Her mother rushed over to adjust her veil, her dress, the train, all for the hundredth time. The madness all seemed to orbit around her. Emily tried to keep up, smiling along, having an occasional good laugh at Allie's teasing or a shared look between them at something ridiculous her mother had said. But all in all, she realized she was simply going with the flow of the day. She perked up, reminding herself to be fully invested.

But as hard as she tried, standing there, she thought of the ceremony, of the faces of those waiting to see her walk down the aisle. She saw her parents watching proudly from the front row, Allie at the front standing up with her as she made this commitment. She saw all the faces staring as she passed, even though she couldn't name half of them. But this was to be the happiest of times. This was the one event that signified not only a commitment, but a public declaration of the love she shared with the one who was supposed to be her soul mate.

As Allie handed her the bouquet and smiled at her, she tried desperately to give a genuine smile back, even as the seriousness of it all came crashing down. Allie knew what she was thinking though, didn't she? Emily pictured the next moments. She would walk down the aisle, along with her father. Thinking about that moment in particular brought a smile to her face. She imagined the front of the church, the priest waiting, and her father lifting her veil and kissing her cheek. She would turn to meet her love, her best friend.

"Everything is ready out there when you ladies are," Kate said from the doorway, interrupting her reveries and scrambling to fit her lens on the camera around her neck. Emily nearly laughed at her colossal fumbling, her camera bag also still over her shoulder, two lenses being shuffled around. Kate finally managed to get it together and look up, freezing in place.

Emily caught Kate's eye across the bustle of the room. It was like a moment in stories when everyone in the room vanished and only the two of them remained. The madness ceased just for a moment.

Those are the eyes, thought Emily. Those are the eyes I want to look into at the end of that aisle. Those were the eyes that with every part of her being, she wanted to promise herself to. This was her best friend.

"Your mother and I will see you out there," Allie said, looking between the two of them. She pulled Amelia toward the door. "Your father is waiting just outside."

"Thank you, Allie," she responded, forcing a smile. Allie turned and gave her a fierce hug and a kiss on the cheek. She touched Kate's shoulder on the way out. Then it was just the two of them.

"I just thought I would get a few shots before we start," Kate said, carefully stepping into the room and setting her bag down.

"Where would you like me?" asked Emily. *In your arms? For God's sake, keep it together.*

"Here by the mirror is fine," Kate replied, avoiding eye contact.

Emily leaned forward to adjust the flowing train of her dress as a loose strand of hair escaped her flawless hairstyle. Kate stepped in to aid with the dress. *It's so hard to move in this thing.* They both looked up at the same time. They were so close now, or at least it felt that way. Realizing this, Kate took a quick step back, putting distance back between them. Emily fingered the loose strand of hair and sighed. It had taken so long to get it perfect, so of course it would fall out. She reached up to place it back in its proper position.

"Leave it." Kate stopped her with her words. She stepped over and took Emily's hand away, and Emily felt her fingers brush ever so lightly across her cheek, lingering a bit too long to be an accident.

She thought of the hazy touch of fingers in her sleep the morning before, remembering Kate doing the same thing. *Oh, God, please don't let this be the last time she touches me.*

Emily saw the pain in Kate's face as it echoed in her own heart. All the mental prep she'd put herself through had vanished. As much as she tried to hide it, Emily could see that Kate was fixated on her, looking at every part of her face, though she never met her eyes.

Kate's touch, her hand lingering, felt like fire. She pressed closer into the warmth of those fingers, closing her eyes to take it in even as the instant passed. When she opened them, it was into those of the one she wanted to open them to every day, the ones she wanted to look into whenever she wished, and the ones she knew would be looking back at her each time.

Kate stepped back, removing her hand and separating them. It was the only possible way to make this more bearable. She lifted her camera to take another shot when tears gathered in Emily's eyes. The camera came back down.

"Don't go and cry on me," Kate teased her, giving her a genuine smile. Emily could see that she was about to cry herself, and couldn't help but smile back. Even at a time like this she made jokes.

Just thinking how she would go on once again without everything that came from the woman standing in front of her—from the way she challenged her, inspired her, their conversations, the spark she felt whenever her thoughts drifted to them—even the sarcasm and arguments they shared—

And then Kate was there, rushing in and cupping Emily's neck. She pulled her in close, aggressively, but Emily welcomed her as she kissed her and pressed as close as she could, seemingly never close enough. Emily thought of nothing but this moment as she put her arms around Kate and returned the kiss with everything she had. This. This was their moment—their last moment, yes, but it was theirs. She thought of their first moment so long ago, standing in the rain just outside that very church. Kate nearly lifted her off the ground as their lips pressed together and gently broke the kiss as a small moan escaped Emily.

They stood there, foreheads pressed together and arms around each other. Emily was stunned when Kate turned away abruptly to wipe her eyes.

"Now who's crying?" Emily smiled bittersweetly in spite of herself. Kate turned and stepped forward as if to come back to Emily but stopped. Emily saw the inner battle she was fighting and wanted desperately for Kate to lose that last shred of control, of logic. But she didn't. Emily watched her walk to the door and compose herself, but she didn't turn back.

"You should get out there," she said.

Emily couldn't let her go just yet.

"The photo. Have you carried it this whole time?" Emily asked, Kate's back still to her. She saw Kate's shoulders sag. She nodded. Emily could barely hear her.

"I came after you that last day, you know." She turned then, but still didn't look at Emily. "Argued with myself the entire morning and decided to meet you at the station, if anything just to be there so you knew we could try…And damn it if I didn't show up as you were pulling away."

"I told Allie that you had to work that day when she asked why you weren't there," Emily replied. She laughed a little. "Glad we got our stories straight."

She stopped smiling when Kate walked back in and looked her squarely in the eye.

"Don't go in there." Her voice quivered. "I always thought I might not be the one who deserves you, but I want you. You make me feel like I just might be worth it, and if anything? I want you and I *need you*. The way you wanted me then. Emily, you are the best thing that has ever happened to me.

"I don't know how to make it work. I don't know how to hide how much I love you from the world every single day, but I want you to know that my heart is yours, and I want to know that no one else has yours. Even if no one else in this world knows. Just us."

Emily stood as still as a statue.

"I know it's selfish, asking now. I'm sorry for that, and I'm sorry for not being who you needed before, who you wanted me to be. For being too scared to try. But God, I love you more than I ever thought I could, and I want to show you that instead of just telling you." She waited, searching Emily's eyes.

"Everything okay, sweetheart? It's time." Emily's father appeared in the doorway, startling her. She and Kate never broke eye contact.

The processional. The overly loud and intrusive organ blared around them, breaking the spell. Then Emily did look away. She looked at her father, smiled, and brushed past Kate to take her father's arm as Kate stood there in shock.

❖

Emily felt nothing. She didn't feel her arm in her father's, she didn't feel the breeze of the doors opening grandly in front of her to reveal the cathedral, she didn't see everyone who had to be looking at her. She just replayed every word Kate had said to her over and over again with each step she took down the aisle to the front of the church.

She barely saw Allie smiling at her or caught Mia looking around as if confused and walking to the back of the church. She did see Tommy though, waiting for her. He smiled proudly, so happy to be waiting for her. She felt her father pull back her veil, barely felt him kiss her cheek. He shook Tommy's hand. Emily robotically put her hand in Tommy's and knelt at the altar with him before the priest.

I want you. She had begged Kate all those years ago, and today? Of all the days, today was the day she...she what? Was asking her to walk away from her wedding? *That! Of course she'd wait until the last minute and do...that! It has to be hands down the most infuriating thing that woman has ever done.*

And damn it if she wasn't going to have to do it.

❖

Kate stood in the back, still not believing that she had finally found the courage to pour out her heart to Emily and that she'd quite literally brushed her off without a word. She didn't cry, which surprised her. Not in that moment. Strange. She'd simply stood there in the room alone.

Seeing Emily across the room moments ago had floored her. While the dress was beautiful, and Emily was as close to angelic as a human could get, Kate's heart drifted to the other moments of beauty she'd seen. Emily asleep in the soft morning sunshine, her head thrown back in pleasure, or the smile she tried to hide when Kate teased her. She was instantly back to square one, at Emily's mercy, transfixed, and then she'd gone and opened her mouth. And then Emily left her.

That is until she heard Mia's voice. "What exactly are you doing? We need to be out there."

"I have to go," she mumbled. She pushed her camera into Mia's hands and walked past her. A hand on her arm stopped her.

"What just happened?" she asked.

"She's getting married, and I can't be here anymore. Take some photos."

Mia let her go.

❖

"Of all the…uhg!" Kate slammed her hands down on the work counter in the darkness. The old enlarger had gotten jammed once again, and she had zero patience left. It was well into the night, and Mia had still yet to return. *Must have been some party.* She might just stay in the darkroom forever at that point if she had the choice. She growled again in frustration. At everything.

"Yo! You hiding away in the cave?" She heard the voice over the record she was blaring.

When she walked out, Mia was pulling gear from both their bags, laying out the cameras and then the film rolls next to them.

"I took a few with the Rolleiflex but mostly stuck to thirty-five." She slurred her words a bit.

"Are you *drunk?*"

"I will have you know I am within a perfectly legal age to do so." She giggled but sobered at Kate's scowl. "They're all yours." She gestured to the film and walked away. "G'night."

Kate sighed. Not tonight. She couldn't deal with them and didn't need to. But she didn't want to sleep either. If she went back into the darkroom she might smash the ancient, frustrating machine to bits. *It's time to buy a new one, that's all. I'll order one tomorrow.* She plopped down on the old worn couch in the back corner and waited for the time to pass.

❖

She woke hours later and rubbed her neck. It was going to be killing her for half the day. She bought a coffee and a sandwich next door, taking her time and avoiding dealing with the work. Finally she was back, well into the morning. At least she could develop the rolls. No need to worry about the prints just yet. Perhaps Emily would send her mother to get them in the end and save them both the embarrassment of seeing each other after her colossal faux pas.

She scooped up the rolls and set to work. As she had to prepare the film in complete darkness, she fumbled around with the first roll, got it into the developing tank, and finished it. She put in the second, from Mia's camera, and processed that roll as well. But when she went for the third, it wasn't used. It was a fresh roll. *Mia! Drunken fool couldn't even separate the unused rolls.* She fumbled for the next, and then the next, until she'd gone through all the others Mia had set out for her. Two rolls used? What?

She took everything back out into the light, the first-roll negatives ready to view. She held up the long strand of film against the light, only to find only four small negative images. She recognized the few, of Emily standing in her dress by the mirror. But then they stopped, the remainder of the long strip as blank as when it went into the camera. She grabbed the other strip, expecting a full roll, only to likewise find nearly half of it empty.

She sighed and dug through the bags, finding nothing else in them. *Where the hell are the rest of the shots?* She heard the door open.

She yelled into the room, secretly wanting to rip Mia a new one. "Mia! Where did you throw the rest of the stock? You're supposed to be the organized one!"

When she didn't get a response, she stomped to the front of the store. "I swear, if your hungover ass forgot—"

But it wasn't Mia.

Emily stood across the room from her. And she did not look happy. Well, thought Kate, at least someone is going to get ripped a new one.

Emily held out an envelope. "That is the remainder of your fee for the event. I didn't want to give it to Mia last evening, as she had a few drinks."

Kate noticed then the bags under Emily's eyes, how a bit of color was missing from her face. "Seems like it was quite the party."

"You could say that…" Emily replied under her breath.

"This isn't due until you receive the prints though," Kate pointed out. She tried to hand the envelope back. She needed to find the rest of the images first. Emily didn't take it, instead crossing her arms and staring directly at Kate, who nervously fidgeted with the envelope.

"I don't imagine I'll need the ten prints that you both likely got in total."

"What? Mia was there the entire day!"

"Indeed she was, with Allie and me."

Kate scrunched her brow in confusion. And then realization seeped in. She squelched the small grain of hope bubbling inside her chest. Silence sat heavy between the two of them.

And then Emily went off. "Of all the selfish, harebrained moves either of us has ever pulled, that was an all-time new, Kate Alessi. What in the *world* were you thinking, pinning me like that right before I had to walk into an event that cost more than you could ever imagine, in front of every person I know in my life?"

Kate didn't look away. She wasn't ashamed of what she'd done. She was proud of herself, happy that she'd had the courage to pour out her heart. In fact, she was pretty angry that she'd been blown off, and she told her so.

"And you just stomp off and do it? Would you rather me never have said anything? Bump into you—ha! We've done that enough. And just act like everything is fine for the rest of our lives? I'm just supposed to know that the love of my life is someone else's and that I didn't do anything to stop it? God!"

Emily huffed. "*You* get to be angry about this? You stubborn—"

"Yes! I do get to be angry. You're an expert at causing it. You should know that by now, because you've done it enough."

"Well, it's mutual!" she yelled back.

Kate threw the envelope forward into her hand. "Fine! Take the money. I didn't finish the job and clearly neither did my airheaded sister."

Emily pinched the bridge of her nose. "You are the densest—open the thing."

"What?" Kate pulled it open, finding a check. *Okay...* but then she noticed along with it an old worn, folded-up sheet of paper. She cautiously pulled it out and unfolded it.

"I've spent the last four years hiding that thing and resisting looking at it because it was all I had of you." Emily still had her arms crossed, still had her brow furrowed in anger, but she'd softened her tone.

Kate looked at the image. It was a quick but detailed rough drawn sketch of herself. Emily must have sketched it one morning before she woke, a morning they were together. Peaceful.

"I'm no one else's. You difficult, maddening woman."

Kate looked up to meet her eyes.

"My mother is a mess, threatening to disown me for causing such a scene. Thank God she doesn't actually know why. I'll never hear the end of it." She got riled up again, "If you could have just been on time for *once* in your life, been there at that bus stop, you could have stopped doubting yourself and what you meant to me..."

Kate stepped forward. She reached out, brushing her fingers across Emily's jaw as it relaxed from its tension.

"I won't doubt it ever again." She stepped even closer, wrapping her other hand around Emily's waist. "The being-late part though...I can't make any guarantees."

Emily shoved her, a smile quickly breaking across her face. Kate held her close though.

"I'm all yours, Emily." She moved in, waiting for Emily to close the distance. Emily did.

For the first time, they kissed knowing that they were together, that there was no one else but them, and they would be together no matter what. They kissed, remembering all the others and looking forward to so many more.

"Finally!" The voice ripped them apart like lightning. Mia trudged past them, one hand clutching her head.

They both relaxed a bit but knew they would have to navigate their hidden affection. They were still touching each other, hands held, both needing the contact. It was nice for someone to know, someone to trust.

"So where were you last night?" Kate asked Mia.

Emily spoke up. "Shots at a bar are very therapeutic when you bail on your own wedding and manage to escape your ranting, whaling mother."

"You got my little sister drunk?" Kate asked.

"She and Allie were *consoling me*, thank you very much. For something *you* caused! I couldn't very well talk with anyone else. At least I had those two."

"Don't worry. I'm never drinking again." Mia walked back in the other direction with her camera. "We should start looking for apartments." She held her head again. "Tomorrow."

"Lots of water helps." Kate nearly laughed at her.

Mia scowled. "See you around, Emily?"

Emily lit up. "Yes, you will."

Mia smiled at that.

Then they were alone again, standing in the middle of the space. "Come on." Kate pulled Emily by the hand to the darkroom. She turned on the bare bulb, lighting the dim space, and pulled Emily close to her again, kissing her once more for good measure.

"When do you have to head home?" she asked when they finally separated.

"Who says I'm going anywhere?" Emily replied.

"You have a job waiting for you, and you shouldn't turn it down. I meant it when I said you should take it."

"I don't want to leave you." She nestled into Kate's chest.

"You won't. Wherever your heart is, that's right where I'll be," Kate whispered to her. She kissed the top of her head. "And you need to work on finding excuses to be down here. You wouldn't want to completely uproot yourself and really give your mother a hernia."

"I love you, Kate." Emily smiled.

Kate vowed then, to herself, that she would always be there to make Emily laugh, even if she infuriated her more often than not, to keep going with her life now, the one she had a piece of left and had worked so hard for. Kate would work toward the one she wanted for them together. Her heart swelled, knowing Emily believed in her, in them, and that they'd figure out being together, even if it took time. It would be worth it.

Two years later, 1948

Two years. Two years of short visits every few months, visits shared with their friends, and small moments of intimacy. Two years of phone calls, often hidden and short, and of letters written, sent, read, and hidden away, each waiting for the next to arrive. It was two years of longing, working, and waiting, but it was two years of growing closer, knowing more of each other, and of the longing to be with each other increasing every day. And then their day was there.

Throughout those two years, Emily had begun a thriving career of her own, traveling often not only to New York but across the country. Even as an assistant she'd had the opportunity to lecture and hold workshops, and she'd managed to continue her own work as well. After two years, she was finally ready, having the connections she needed, to begin on her own, and she had chosen to do so in New York.

Much to Amelia Stanton's dismay, Emily had convinced her mother that she was independent and was choosing to have roommates, as opposed to them purchasing her a place of her own. Regardless, her mother had micro-managed the entirety of the process of moving her to the city. It did, however, mean that she had thought of everything she might need for the move, leaving Emily to simply be excited for the next chapter of her life.

Emily had changed in the last two years as well. She'd grown ever more confident in herself, what she wanted in her life, and who she was. She had something to look forward to, and she had someone who was waiting for her. Emily had let go of the lingering guilt of running away from Tommy, realizing that she was running toward Kate, and that it was what she had to do to live her life fully.

She was happy that Tommy had recovered, or so it seemed. It was impossible for them to avoid each other completely, seeing each other with a glance at her father's functions occasionally. She had actually seen him with a lovely woman at the last dinner party they had attended, and he seemed to look at her in a way Emily wasn't sure she'd ever been looked at by him. She truly did hope that he had found the type of happiness that she now knew.

❖

Kate had counted the days until Emily would be there, preparing the new apartment in Brooklyn that she and Mia had acquired. She cleaned, reorganized, settled, and then reorganized nearly every room, much to Mia's annoyance but also slight amusement. Kate hadn't once stopped smiling at the thought that she finally, after all the years of wishing, hoping, and longing, would get to be with Emily in the same place, the same city, the same life.

Kate had worked hard each day that they were away from each other to build a foundation that they could grow into together. She and Mia had fully taken over the store from Alfonzo and remodeled it, accommodating two additional artists who shared the space, and although it was endless work, they were never without clients. Kate often worked endlessly to help pass the time until she saw Emily again.

But the time had come. Kate forced herself to stop fidgeting, instead sitting on the floor with Allie and Art's baby girl, Margie, as they all waited for Emily to arrive. At just over eighteen months, Margie was lightning, and the cutest thing any of them could have imagined. Kate loved being part of the family they'd all created together and couldn't wait to see Margie become one of the strong, wonderful women she was being raised by. She took the opportunity to play with her while she had the chance, as she often thought that Emily was more excited for getting to spend time with Margie than herself.

The horn on the truck outside signaled Emily's arrival, and Kate's pulse jumped. It was really happening! She swooped up Margie and held her, letting the baby fidget with her hair. Art bounded outside, and moments later they came in with the first of Emily's things.

Allie rushed over to pull her into a giant hug. Kate caught Emily's eye over Allie's shoulder and smiled softly at her, even as Margie pulled at her ear. She squeezed Allie tight and released her, quickly walking over to Kate.

Kate spoke softly, but her excitement was clear. "Welcome home."

Emily wrapped Kate in a similar hug. They were practiced now around others with their affection, letting out their true close friendship for others to see and hiding everything more. Kate was genuinely happy to see her though, and she showed it. Kate immediately, as the only way to stop herself from kissing Emily, offered Margie into her waiting arms. Emily grabbed her and had the baby laughing and covered in kisses in seconds.

"Let's get the rest of it," Kate said to Art. Emily needed to catch up with her newest favorite cousin. Kate quickly greeted Emily's father. "Hello, Mr. Stanton."

"How are you, Kate?" he asked, a bit more upbeat than with others. Kate was always a bit nervous around him, but he seemed to like her, and she liked him well enough. They were often both quiet and in their own way just…got along. It was nice to see.

With all hands on deck, they had Emily situated in little time at all.

"I'll need to get back to the hotel. I'm still impressed you managed to persuade your mother to stay there." Emily's father looked at his watch.

"I'll let her come over tomorrow to do some organizing," Emily said.

Mia covered her mouth to stifle a laugh, and Kate scowled.

"And we'll see you this evening. I'm going to get something made up this afternoon, and we can have a little housewarming dinner tonight, all of us," Allie said. She collected the scattered toys from the floor while Emily continued playing with Margie. Reluctantly she handed her off to her father.

Eventually they took off after last hugs, leaving the three new roommates.

"I, uh, should get some time in at the store today," Mia said vaguely, finding a reason to excuse herself. "I'll see you both for dinner tonight."

Then they were alone. Alone in the room that was supposed to be Emily's, the one Amelia would inevitably bombard and rearrange the next day. Boxes were stacked and scattered about, but neither made a move to unpack them. Regardless of anyone's manicuring, it would never truly be Emily's room. No, Emily would share her room, along with her life, with Kate. She hated that she would be forced constantly to keep up the appearance of separation, even though she was once again grateful for Mia's acceptance. But she didn't want to think of all that in that moment. So she stepped forward and wrapped her arms around Emily's waist and rested her chin on her shoulder.

"Hi, love," she whispered.

"Hello, darling." Emily turned in her arms and immediately pressed the softest kiss to her lips. She let herself get lost in the kiss, tasting the woman she'd longed to be with and now was hers alone.

"So you're going to let your mother rearrange all my hard work?" Kate was teasing.

"Oh, sweetie, there's no stopping her. You might as well embrace that now." Emily stroked her cheek as she laughed.

"Well. She isn't going to organize my room—our room." Kate pulled her across the hall, grinning mischievously. "So perhaps we can make it nice and messy."

"Challenge accepted," Emily murmured as they tumbled together onto their bed.

EPILOGUE

Twenty-three years later, July 1969

"Emily, sweetheart, did you see this?" Kate asked as she walked into the kitchen where Emily was scrambling to get breakfast together. Kate held out the newspaper and pointed to a tiny article deep in the paper.

Sheridan Square Mob Dispersed, the headline read.

Emily skimmed across the article quickly. "Another raid?"

"No." Kate leaned against the counter. "They're still rioting from the raid on Saturday."

Emily stopped. "They're *still* rioting?"

"God, the language they use…" Kate's brow furrowed as she read. "'Police dispersed a hostile group of bra-clad rioters last night after shutting down a notorious gay nightclub, the Stonewall Inn, just this weekend. After the shutdown and following rebellion on Saturday evening, drag queens and flamboyant ne'er-do-wells stood against a helmeted Tactical Patrol in the streets of the West Village in a homosexual display unlike any seen to date.'"

They looked at each other, and Kate slid closer to Emily, placing her hand on the small of Emily's back, a touch of comfort and assurance. It could be a turning point, they realized without speaking. A turn toward a time in which perhaps those like them, those who were forced out and marginalized, criminalized, could use their voices, be who they truly were.

"One of my photog buddies, Larry, mentioned he got a few

shots the other night. No photos with this one, though." Kate still perused the small article, contemplating the situation.

Emily leaned further into Kate, needing contact with her lover. "We deserve to have our story told."

Kate nodded and looked into her eyes. After all their years together, their wonderful life moments were all hidden in shadow, masked. She would never regret the life she'd shared with Kate, but she wanted others after them to never have to hide that love. It would risk their delicately structured world, but she couldn't sit back and do nothing.

"There will be a rally soon, I'm sure," Kate said. Emily watched as her mind went to work. "I have a few folks who will know what's happening."

"I'll call some of the girls, see if they're helping out with the arrests," Emily said.

She watched the determination settle into Kate's eyes, and while she might have feared it, feared for their safety, their way of life, she was excited to take on the next challenge they would face. Together.

About the Author

Jeanette Bears is a queer, non-binary New York City–based writer, filmmaker, and editor. They have directed and shot several short film projects and love the art of storytelling and consuming all things queer (and romantic) in media. While being an avid reader and filmmaker for over a decade, *Late City Summer* is their debut novel.

Jeanette works at a film school in NYC by day, and in their spare time is a freelancer on film projects, along with being a cross-training coach at their local gym. They consume and write copious amounts of fan fiction and love nothing more than being with their wife and two pups in the great outdoors, making adventures of their own.

Find out more about them at jeanettebears.com.

Books Available From Bold Strokes Books

All That Remains by Sheri Lewis Wohl. Johnnie and Shantel might have to risk their lives—and their love—to stop a werewolf intent on killing. (978-1-63555-949-1)

Beginner's Bet by Fiona Riley. Phenom luxury Realtor Ellison Gamble has everything, except a family to share it with, so when a mix-up brings youthful Katie Crawford into her life, she bets the house on love. (978-1-63555-733-6)

Dangerous Without You by Lexus Grey. Throughout their senior year in high school, Aspen, Remington, Denna, and Raleigh face challenges in life and romance that they never expect. (978-1-63555-947-7)

Desiring More by Raven Sky. In this collection of steamy stories, a rich variety of lovers find themselves desiring more: more from a lover, more from themselves, and more from life. (978-1-63679-037-4)

Jordan's Kiss by Nanisi Barrett D'Arnuck. After losing everything in a fire, Jordan Phelps joins a small lounge band and meets pianist Morgan Sparks, who lights another blaze—this time in Jordan's heart. (978-1-63555-980-4)

Late City Summer by Jeanette Bears. Forced together for her wedding, Emily Stanton and Kate Alessi navigate their lingering passion for one another against the backdrop of New York City and World War II, and a summer romance they left behind. (978-1-63555-968-2)

Love and Lotus Blossoms by Anne Shade. On her path to self-acceptance and true passion, Janesse will risk everything—and possibly everyone—she loves. (978-1-63555-985-9)

Love in the Limelight by Ashley Moore. Marion Hargreaves, the finest actress of her generation, and Jessica Carmichael, the world's biggest pop star, rediscover each other twenty years after an ill-fated affair. (978-1-63679-051-0)

Suspecting Her by Mary P. Burns. Complications ensue when Erin O'Connor falls for top real estate saleswoman Catherine Williams while investigating racism in the real estate industry; the fallout could end their chance at happiness. (978-1-63555-960-6)

Two Winters by Lauren Emily Whalen. A modern YA retelling of Shakespeare's *The Winter's Tale* about birth, death, Catholic school, improv comedy, and the healing nature of time. (978-1-63679-019-0)

Calumet by Ali Vali. Jaxon Lavigne and Iris Long had a forbidden small-town romance that didn't last, and the consequences of that love will be uncovered fifteen years later at their high school reunion. (978-1-63555-900-2)

Her Countess to Cherish by Jane Walsh. London Society's material girl realizes there is more to life than diamonds when she falls in love with a non-binary bluestocking. (978-1-63555-902-6)

Hot Days, Heated Nights by Renee Roman. When Cole and Lee meet, instant attraction quickly flares into uncontrollable passion, but their connection might be short-lived as Lee's identity is tied to her life in the city. (978-1-63555-888-3)

Never Be the Same by MA Binfield. Casey meets Olivia, and sparks fly in this opposites attract romance that proves love can be found in the unlikeliest places. (978-1-63555-938-5)

Quiet Village by Eden Darry. Something not quite human is stalking Collie and her niece, and she'll be forced to work with undercover reporter Emily Lassiter if they want to get out of Hyam alive. (978-1-63555-898-2)

Shaken or Stirred by Georgia Beers. Bar owner Julia Martini and home health aide Savannah McNally attempt to weather the storms brought on by a mysterious blogger trashing the bar, family feuds they knew nothing about, and way too much advice from way too many relatives. (978-1-63555-928-6)

The Fiend in the Fog by Jess Faraday. Can four people on different trajectories work together to save the vulnerable residents of East London from the terrifying fiend in the fog before it's too late? (978-1-63555-514-1)

The Marriage Masquerade by Toni Logan. A no-strings-attached marriage scheme to inherit a Maui B&B uncovers unexpected attractions and a dark family secret. (978-1-63555-914-9)

Flight SQA016 by Amanda Radley. Fastidious airline passenger Olivia Lewis is used to things being a certain way. When her routine is changed by a new, attractive member of the staff, sparks fly. (978-1-63679-045-9)

Home Is Where The Heart Is by Jenny Frame. Can Archie make the countryside her home and give Ash the fairytale romance she desires? Or will the countryside and small village life all be too much for her? (978-1-63555-922-4)

Moving Forward by PJ Trebelhorn. The last person Shelby Ryan expects to be attracted to is Iris Calhoun, the sister of the man who killed her wife four years and three thousand miles ago. (978-1-63555-953-8)

Poison Pen by Jean Copeland. Debut author Kendra Blake is finally living her best life until a nasty book review and exposed secrets threaten her promising new romance with aspiring journalist Alison Chatterley. (978-1-63555-849-4)

Seasons for Change by KC Richardson. Love, laughter, and trust develop for Shawn and Morgan throughout the changing seasons of Lake Tahoe. (978-1-63555-882-1)

Summer Lovin' by Julie Cannon. Three different women, three exotic locations, one unforgettable summer. What do you think will happen? (978-1-63555-920-0)

Unbridled by D. Jackson Leigh. A visit to a local stable turns into more than riding lessons between a novel writer and an equestrian with a taste for power play. (978-1-63555-847-0)

VIP by Jackie D. In a town where relationships are forged and shattered by perception, sometimes even love can't change who you really are. (978-1-63555-908-8)

Yearning by Gun Brooke. The sleepy town of Dennamore has an irresistible pull on those who've moved away. The mystery Darian Benson and Samantha Pike uncover will change them forever, but the love they find along the way just might be the key to saving themselves. (978-1-63555-757-2)

A Turn of Fate by Ronica Black. Will Nev and Kinsley finally face their painful past and relent to their powerful, forbidden attraction? Or will facing their past be too much to fight through? (978-1-63555-930-9)

Desires After Dark by MJ Williamz. When her human lover falls deathly ill, Alex, a vampire, must decide which is worse, letting her go or condemning her to everlasting life. (978-1-63555-940-8)

Her Consigliere by Carsen Taite. FBI agent Royal Scott swore an oath to uphold the law, and criminal defense attorney Siobhan Collins pledged her loyalty to the only family she's ever known, but will their love be stronger than the bonds they've vowed to others, or will their competing allegiances tear them apart? (978-1-63555-924-8)

In Our Words: Queer Stories from Black, Indigenous, and People of Color Writers. Stories Selected by Anne Shade and Edited by Victoria Villaseñor. Comprising both the renowned and emerging voices of Black, Indigenous, and People of Color authors, this thoughtfully curated collection of short stories explores the intersection of racial and queer identity. (978-1-63555-936-1)

Measure of Devotion by CF Frizzell. Disguised as her late twin brother, Catherine Samson enters the Civil War to defend the Constitution as a Union soldier, never expecting her life to be altered by a Gettysburg farmer's daughter. (978-1-63555-951-4)

Not Guilty by Brit Ryder. Claire Weaver and Emery Pearson's day jobs clash, even as their desire for each other burns, and a discreet sex-only arrangement is the only option. (978-1-63555-896-8)

Opposites Attract: Butch/Femme Romances by Meghan O'Brien, Aurora Rey & Angie Williams. Sometimes opposites really do attract. Fall in love with these butch/femme romance novellas. (978-1-63555-784-8)

Under Her Influence by Amanda Radley. On their path to #truelove, will Beth and Jemma discover that reality is even better than illusion? (978-1-63555-963-7)